MURDER FOR THE HALIBUT

Liz Lipperman

BERKLEY PRIME CRIME, NEW YORK

THE BERKLEY PUBLISHING GROUP
Published by the Penguin Group
Penguin Group (USA) Inc.
375 Hudson Street, New York, New York 10014, USA

Penguin Group (Canada), 90 Eglinton Avenue East, Suite 700, Toronto, Ontario M4P 2Y3, Canada (a division of Pearson Penguin Canada Inc.) • Penguin Books Ltd., 80 Strand, London WC2R 0RL, England • Penguin Ireland, 25 St. Stephen's Green, Dublin 2, Ireland (a division of Penguin Books Ltd.) • Penguin Group (Australia), 707 Collins Street, Melbourne, Victoria 3008, Australia (a division of Pearson Australia Group Pty. Ltd.) • Penguin Books India Pvt. Ltd., 11 Community Centre, Panchsheel Park, New Delhi—110 017, India • Penguin Group (NZ), 67 Apollo Drive, Rosedale, Auckland 0632, New Zealand (a division of Pearson New Zealand Ltd.) • Penguin Books, Rosebank Office Park, 181 Jan Smuts Avenue, Parktown North 2193, South Africa • Penguin China, B7 Jaiming Center, 27 East Third Ring Road North, Chaoyang District, Beijing 100020, China

Penguin Books Ltd., Registered Offices: 80 Strand, London WC2R 0RL, England

This is a work of fiction. Names, characters, places, and incidents either are the product of the author's imagination or are used fictitiously, and any resemblance to actual persons, living or dead, business establishments, events, or locales is entirely coincidental. The publisher does not have any control over and does not assume any responsibility for author or third-party websites or their content.

PUBLISHER'S NOTE: The recipes contained in this book are to be followed exactly as written. The publisher is not responsible for your specific health or allergy needs that may require medical supervision. The publisher is not responsible for any adverse reactions to the recipes contained in this book.

MURDER FOR THE HALIBUT

A Berkley Prime Crime Book / published by arrangement with the author

PUBLISHING HISTORY
Berkley Prime Crime mass-market edition / January 2013

Copyright © 2012 by Elizabeth R. Lipperman.
Cover illustration by Ben Perini.
Cover design by Sarah Oberrender.
Interior text design by Laura K. Corless.

ISBN: 978-0-425-25182-9

BERKLEY®PRIME CRIME
Berkley Prime Crime Books are published by The Berkley Publishing Group, a division of Penguin Group (USA) Inc., 375 Hudson Street, New York, New York 10014.
BERKLEY® PRIME CRIME and the PRIME CRIME logo are trademarks of Penguin Group (USA) Inc.

PRINTED IN THE UNITED STATES OF AMERICA

10 9 8 7 6 5 4 3 2 1

ALWAYS LEARNING   PEARSON

To my mother, Annie Roth,
who taught me how to love and laugh
and not take myself too seriously.
This one goes out to her and anyone else
who has suffered through or watched a loved one
slip away every day from Alzheimer's.
I'm praying for a cure.

ACKNOWLEDGMENTS

As always, there are many people to thank. First and foremost is my tireless agent, Christine Witthohn, whose friendship and guidance I truly cherish. There is no way I could do this without her.

And then there is my editor, Faith Black, who never fails to encourage me even when I sometimes get off track. I love her sense of humor and her enthusiasm for my stories.

And I can't forget the talented people behind the scenes at Berkley Prime Crime, especially Sarah Oberrender who designed my awesome cover, Ben Perini who illustrated it, and Caroline Duffy, copyeditor extraordinaire who always manages to amaze me.

I've said it before that although writing is a solitary process, it can't be done without a huge support system, and I have been blessed with a good one. First, there are my siblings, Jack, Don, Mary Ann, Dorothy, and Lilly as well as my Bunko pals, Tami, Judy, Marilyn, Nancy, Linda, Jane, Anna, Barbara, and Vaneesa. Kudos to my writing friends, some I've know for a very long time, in RWA MWA, DARA, SinC, and the Book Cents gang, and the GIAMers. Special thanks to my fellow Plotting

Princesses who helped me weave this mystery and are some of my biggest cheerleaders.

I couldn't end this without thanking the four wonderful Celebrity Cruise chefs who sat around a table at the coffee shop onboard one day in full chef gear, white hat and all, and helped me plot this murder. Can you imagine the looks on the other passengers' faces that day as they listened to us discuss how to kill someone with food? Mega thanks to Chef Maciek Kucha-rewic who actually came up with the halibut recipe using the killer ingredient.

Lastly, I can't even come close to expressing my gratitude to my wonderful husband and my kids and grandkids who gave up time with me so that I could follow my dream. I love you all.

CHAPTER 1

Whose harebrained idea was this, anyway?

Feeling her stomach lurch when the deepwater charter boat hit a strong wave, Jordan McAllister prayed the patch behind her ear was all it was cracked up to be. Inhaling those two ham and cheese croissants about an hour before had been a big mistake. Things would get ugly in a hurry if the meal decided to suddenly reappear.

"You doing okay, Jordan?" Michael Cafferty slid in beside her at the railing. "You're looking a little green."

She swallowed hard and pointed to the patch. "Rosie insisted I get a prescription for these suckers before I left for Miami." She swallowed again when the boat slammed into another huge wave. "I'm waiting for the magic drug to kick in."

"Speaking of Rosie, did she and the others get on the

flight okay? I've been so busy overseeing this fishing trip I forgot to call Victor. He's going to pitch a fit."

"I talked to her before we left the hotel this morning for Key West. They were at DFW Airport ready to board their flight. If all goes well, they'll be waiting for us in Miami when we get back to shore. You can make nice to Victor over drinks tonight." She grinned. It had only been a day since she'd seen her friends, and she already missed them, especially her next-door-neighbor Victor Rodriguez, Michael's significant other.

Jordan took a deep breath as the battle raged between her stomach and the motion of the boat. "I should've never let you talk me into this, Michael. What was I thinking?"

"What? The fishing trip or the whole contest-judging thing?"

"Both." Jordan's hand covered her mouth as a wave of nausea pulsed through her. When it finally passed, she continued. "First of all, I'll probably be hanging over this rail all day long. As for the judging, everyone knows I hate fancy food. What made me think I could pull off a gig judging a bunch of gourmet chefs? Geez, Michael, if I make it past the whole tasting thing without gagging, it will be a miracle. They'll laugh me right off the freakin' cruise ship."

When Michael had first suggested she sign on as the culinary expert for the first ever Caribbean Cook-Off, she should have run away as fast as she could. KTLK, the local radio station in Ranchero where he had his own talk show, was the primary sponsor of the contest. Six hand-picked chefs from all over Texas would be showing off their cooking skills as they competed for the grand prize: a contract with one of the biggest talent agencies in New

York to star in a national ad campaign for a giant food conglomerate. They'd be making original concoctions using only specified ingredients. The trouble was, to judge the finished product, Jordan would have to eat it— and she hated gourmet food.

She shook her head. "My newfound fame as culinary reporter for the *Globe* will go right out the window, and I'll be back to writing the personals again."

"Quit worrying. You'll do fine," Michael said before another wave hit, shoving them both into the corner. He turned and hollered to the crusty-looking man at the controls, "How much longer before we actually get to fish?"

"Another ten minutes and we'll throw out the anchor," the old man hollered back. "Why? We got a puker?"

"No," Jordan said, a little too quickly, resisting the urge to put her hand over her mouth again. *Like that's gonna keep me from hurling.* "A tad queasy, that's all."

"Have a cold one, lady." The captain grinned, showing off his gold front tooth. "You'd be surprised at how much that helps."

She'd be surprised, all right. Bending farther over the railing just in case her worst nightmare came true, Jordan took two quick breaths. She'd grown up fishing with her dad and four brothers, but that had been Lake Amarillo and not the Gulf of Mexico. The only big waves there had come from the wake of some smart-ass kid on a Jet Ski brave enough to endure the wrath of the McAllister clan. Usually, a ceremonial display of six extended middle fingers would offer a "salute" as the offending watercraft passed.

"Michael, come here," a voice commanded from the other end of the boat.

"Oops. That's my boss calling. Hang in there, Jordan. I'll check back in a bit to make sure you're okay."

Since the cooking competition was the brainchild of his boss, Michael had put in many hours organizing it. He'd even stayed overnight at the radio station on several occasions after hosting his show. This was too important to let a little thing like her queasy stomach sidetrack him.

She gave him a gentle nudge. "Go. This is your baby. I'm already starting to feel a little better."

Watching him walk away, Jordan blew out another slow breath before focusing on the water and the disappearing speck, aka Key West, behind them. What *was* she thinking taking on this assignment as if she had a clue what she was doing? If her boss at the newspaper knew her tastes leaned toward takeout and fried bologna, she was pretty sure she'd no longer be the *Globe*'s culinary expert with her own byline.

And she was positive he wouldn't have agreed to send her on this cruise to judge food prepared with God-only-knew-what ingredients. Unless her seafood was battered and came with fries, she wanted nothing to do with it.

Feeling like a fraud, she tried to convince herself she wouldn't be a complete ditz, and then decided, so what if she was? Tomorrow, she and her friends would board the *Carnation Queen* and cruise for seven days around the Caribbean. A week of fun in the sun, island tours, and frozen margaritas.

And everything was gratis. All she had to do was judge one stupid cooking competition. How hard could that be?

She gulped, remembering again how totally unqualified she was for the culinary gig. On her first assignment at the *Globe*, she'd critiqued a fancy steak restaurant and ended up shoving foie gras into her purse. Unable to make herself take one bite, she'd filled up on sourdough bread and Chocolate Decadence Cake instead.

So how did a tomboy from West Texas who talked sports better than most men end up as a celebrity judge for six up-and-coming chefs on a cruise ship? She couldn't even cook macaroni and cheese from a box—at least not an edible version.

Asking her to judge fancy food was like soliciting a nun's advice on the best sexual positions.

Sheesh!

A hand touched her shoulder, and she nearly jumped overboard. Turning, she came nose to nose with one of the contestants she'd noticed when they'd boarded the *Sea Shark* in Key West. Even in his playing-on-the-water clothes, Stefano Mancini had been hard to miss, looking more like an Italian playboy than a guy ready to spend all day fishing under the hot Florida sun. She remembered the frowning faces of a few of the other contestants when Stefano had walked aboard the *Sea Shark*. She wondered what that was about. Jealousy, maybe?

With a smile that could only be interpreted as a come-on, the budding chef slipped both arms around her from behind and grabbed on to the railing, basically imprisoning her.

And she'd thought being seasick was the worst thing that would happen to her today.

Close enough to give her a whiff of his citrusy cologne, he reached into his shirt pocket and pulled out a reefer. Arching one eyebrow and grinning like a cat that'd cornered a mouse, he showed her the rolled cigarette. After he dropped it back into his pocket, he slid his hand slowly down her arm with a feathery touch. Totally involuntarily, the fine hairs below her elbow stood at attention.

When he latched on to the railing again, he whispered into her ear, causing another flurry of goose bumps. "Let's you and me go hide out and have a few puffs. I guarantee that will settle your stomach."

Tilting her head to the left so his warm hot breath would quit causing tingles, she declined. "No, thanks. I'll take my chances with the Gulf." She twisted to get out of his clutches, but he was too strong.

Her eyes darted to the front of the boat, searching for Michael, but he was busy chatting with three other contestants and hadn't seen her distress signals.

"Don't say I didn't try."

She fell backward as the boat hit another rough spot, sending salty seawater splashing up at her over the railing. Instantly, she knew it was a bad move, and Stefano's lower body pressing into her backside verified it. Wiggling, she tried to get out of the embrace, which seemed to only add to his enjoyment.

It's official. I'm a bona fide perv magnet.

"Sorry about that last big one," the captain apologized. "Get your gear ready. We're almost to the spot I like to call 'Come to Mama.'"

This time Jordan pushed back hard enough to break Stefano's hold on the railing and darted out of his reach.

"A feisty one. I like that."

"You do know I'm a judge, right?"

He tilted his head and grinned, giving her another dazzling show of perfect white teeth. "All the better."

The whole idea behind this fishing trip was so the contestants could get to know each other. As a bonus, anyone who caught enough fish to feed the three judges and twenty-five lucky tasters would automatically receive an extra ten points. Since one of the chefs would be eliminated after the first round, the extra points could prove invaluable.

"Shouldn't you be getting your pole ready so the others don't get a leg up on you?"

Stefano laughed out loud. "Darling, do you seriously think I need the points?" He winked.

Geez! Who is this guy? "How would I know what you need? I only met you three hours ago."

She moved away when he inched closer to whisper in her ear.

"Trust me. I don't need the points. Not for the elimination round tomorrow or any other time." He pointed toward the others. "Some of those losers couldn't beat me with a hundred-point advantage."

"Pretty cocky, don't you think?"

Jordan took a moment to study him. She was five eight, and Stefano towered over her, looking more like an athletic trainer than a man who spent hours in the kitchen creating five-star meals. In cargo shorts and a green and blue muscle shirt, he was what Jordan classified as serious eye candy. Curly dark hair that fell to his shoulders accentuated his smoky brown eyes and angled cheekbones. He probably used the playful matching dimples on either side of his generous mouth as a beacon to lure unsuspecting females.

Quickly, she looked away, reminding herself she

already had a drop-dead gorgeous Italian Stallion who could lure her in anytime he wanted. Unfortunately, he was deep undercover fighting drug dealers in El Paso.

Her overt attempt to put distance between her and Stefano didn't seem to bother the guy. He arched an eyebrow, as if reminding her he always got what he wanted.

"I'm cooking my signature halibut dish tomorrow, and I guarantee you won't have to think twice about who's the best chef here."

"If you're as good as you think you are, why not throw out a line and get fresh halibut? You never know when those points might come in handy."

A how-stupid-are-you look crossed his face. "Halibut like cold water. They're fished in places like Alaska, not in the Gulf. I made sure everything I needed was sent via overnight delivery when I heard about tomorrow's little show." He straightened two fingers to give her another peek at the cigarette back in his hand. "Until then, I have some free time, and the concierge is hooking me up with the good stuff. Tonight could be the night you and I really get to know each other."

"Hey, Stefano."

Both Jordan and Stefano turned to see a much smaller man approach, sporting a gray fisherman's vest and a Yankees ball cap. About five seven, the newcomer had jet-black hair with matching eyes.

"I snagged the best rod for you. Come on."

"No can do, Phillip. I'm gonna hang out with—" He turned toward Jordan. "What did you say your name was?"

"Jordan McAllister," Phillip answered, sending daggers her way before turning his attention back to Stefano.

"You don't have to fish, but let's grab a couple of beers while you watch me reel them in." He moved closer to whisper, "Beating you tomorrow will require all the extra points I can get."

Before Stefano could open his mouth to reply, Phillip tugged on his arm, but he couldn't budge the bigger man. "I told everyone you'd tell us a few of your funny stories about working with Dean Sterling at the Palace Hotel."

Being the center of attention must have appealed to Stefano because he shrugged and allowed Phillip to drag him over to where the others were getting ready to throw out their lines.

"I'm looking forward to seeing you later, Jordan," he said over his shoulder.

Like that's ever gonna happen in this lifetime.

Finally alone, Jordan discovered that while she'd been bantering with Stefano, the nausea had disappeared, and she was beginning to feel a little mellow. Rosie had warned her that the patch contained a drug that made you feel like you were floating in the clouds.

Truth be told, it wasn't an entirely bad feeling. Without her precious Ho Hos, she needed all the help she could get today. The chocolate treat from Hostess was the only thing that calmed her down when she was stressed. She'd read that chocolate elevated endorphin levels, but she didn't need some scientist sitting in a lab somewhere to convince her of that. Usually, all it took was one chocolate "Prozac" to talk herself off the ledge—two to guarantee it.

Staring out at the water, she watched the blue waves ripple and gleam, and her eyelids suddenly felt heavy, as if a great weight were pulling them shut. She'd kill for a comfy recliner right now. Smiling to herself, she was even starting to think judging the cooking contest wouldn't be so bad.

"Jordan, I want to introduce you to the contestants," Michael called out, splattering her bubble of self-confidence like a water balloon thrown from a second-story window.

She put on her game face and headed in his direction, certain the chefs would sniff out a fast-food queen from a mile away.

"You feeling better?"

"Much."

"Good." Michael slipped his arm in hers and dragged her over to a fortyish-looking man dressed in yellow Nike shorts and a matching shirt. A second look verified his baseball cap, shoes, and watch were all color coordinated—bright lemon.

Who wears a matching watch?

"Jordan, this is my boss, Wayne Francis. He's the one who organized this entire trip and chose you as one of the judges."

The station manager extended his hand. "Nice meeting you. Dwayne Egan speaks highly of you."

She nearly swallowed her tongue at the mention of her boss at the newspaper. Egan spoke highly of her? Never once in the six months since he'd handed over the reins to her column, the Kitchen Kupboard, had he even hinted she might be doing a bang-up job. Even though Jordan's trick of slapping a fancy Spanish or French name on Rosie's casserole recipes and passing them off as gourmet specialties had doubled the newspaper's sales, the old cheapskate was probably afraid she might ask for a raise if he commended her in any way.

So the bugger talked nice about her behind her back. She filed that little tidbit on her mental laptop to use when it was to her advantage.

"Michael has only nice things to say about you, too, Mr. Francis."

"Call me Wayne."

"Best boss I've ever had," Michael chimed in before introducing the only other women on the small fishing trawler. "Jordan, this is Casey Washington. She's one of the sous chefs at Hirasoto's Steak House in Fort Worth," he said of the first one. Then he pulled the smaller woman forward. "And this is Marsha Davenport, who interns at the steak house. It's unusual to have two chefs who work together end up competing against one another, but they were both chosen in our statewide search."

Jordan shook hands with both women, noticing how much firmer Marsha's grip was, despite the fact she looked to be ten years younger and fifty pounds lighter than Casey.

Dressed in cutoffs and a T-shirt that allowed a peak at a perfectly flat abdomen, Marsha could have passed for a Dallas Cowboys cheerleader. Sun-streaked hair cut in a stylish bob framed her delicate face, bringing out the green-blue of her eyes.

Casey, on the other hand, looked to be in her early thirties with mousy brown hair and equally dull hazel eyes, heavily made up in a multitude of various tones of blue eye shadow. Wearing a pair of frumpy black capris that begged for an iron, and an oversized green T-shirt that read NEVER TRUST A SKINNY CHEF, Casey swiped a pudgy hand across her brow to mop up the sweat threatening to drip into her eyes.

"You might as well meet them all," Michael said, waving over the other three contestants.

"I met Phillip and Stefano earlier," Jordan said, not looking forward to another go-around with the flirty Italian chef, who winked at her when he walked up with the other two.

Michael pointed to a tall Hispanic man, who extended his hand. "Meet Luis Herrera. He hails from San Antonio where he oversees all the food at La Cantina on the Riverwalk."

"Nice to meet you, Luis."

"The pleasure is all mine," he said in heavily accented English. Bending forward, he brought her hand to his lips.

Every part of Luis's six-foot-plus frame not covered by clothing was decorated with tattoos, most of them dragons. From the way he narrowed his eyes Stefano's way, Jordan detected some seriously bad blood there, although Stefano didn't seem the least bit rattled.

First chance she got, she'd get Rosie to check into that. Her friend had a knack for finding out intimate details from perfect strangers. Something about her made people blurt out the most outrageous stuff. Like the time a man she'd met in the produce section of the Piggly Wiggly told her his pipe hadn't worked since his prostate was removed, and he hadn't had sex in over a year.

Like she was a plumber and could do something about it.

"There's one more contestant, but he'll join us on the ship tomorrow," Michael continued. "His wife delivered their first child yesterday, and he stayed in Dallas an extra day to help out until her mother arrives later today."

"So is everyone ready to fish?" The captain moved away from the wheel. "I'm Johnny, and my first mate is Mo. We're going to show you how to catch enough fish to feed the entire cruise ship tomorrow. You're looking at some of the bluest water on this planet." He chuckled. "Okay, I may be exaggerating a little, but you will catch some pretty big fish out here."

"Like what kind?" Marsha asked, straightening her back to give everyone an up-close-and-personal look at her assets through the thin T-shirt.

"Groupers. Snappers. You name it. Mo and I will be available to help reel in the big ones. And they can get really big."

He pointed to three large coolers under the covered section in the middle of the boat. "There's beer, wine coolers, water, and sandwiches if you get hungry. We'll fish for two hours or so and then head back to Key West." He turned and reached for the bottle of sunscreen Mo was holding out. "Cover yourselves with this, or I guarantee you'll be sleeping standing up tonight."

After Casey got a wine cooler and a sandwich from the front cooler, she and Marsha set up in one corner while Luis and Phillip staked out the other. Grabbing two beers, Stefano made a beeline for the covered area and flopped down on a wooden bench.

Although sitting in the shade appealed to Jordan, there was no way she'd deliberately position herself to be alone with Stefano again. Instead, she reached for the sunscreen and decided when in Rome . . .

Selecting a pole, she hoped fishing was like riding a bike and she still knew how to do it. Soon, she and Michael were fishing alongside the others and having a blast. Thanks to the patch, she'd downed two cold ones and another sandwich without paying a gastrointestinal price.

A little over an hour later, the guys had caught five decent-size fish each, and the girls were sneaking up on them with three and four respectively. Secretly, Jordan was pulling for her fellow females—even had a dollar bet riding on it with Michael.

She was about to anchor her rod and get another beer when her line jerked, nearly pulling her over the railing.

She screamed for help and held on with everything she had as Mo ran over with a gaff.

Jordan laughed when Johnny appeared with a big net. "That's a little ambitious, don't ya think?"

"You never know, missy."

He handed Mo the net and stood behind Jordan, putting all of his two hundred fifty or so pounds into reeling in the catch. When the fish broke through the surface of the water, fighting like a wildcat, Johnny jerked the rod just enough to lift it completely out. Mo put down the gaff and stretched his body over to capture the large fish in the net.

"Whoa! That's a mutton snapper, and if my eyes are as good as they used to be, this baby's over twenty pounds," Johnny said as Mo hauled it aboard.

Johnny took the large hook out of the fish's mouth with pliers from the tackle box and put Jordan's catch in the holding tank. The commotion of landing the fish and the cheers that followed had enticed Stefano out of his shady hiding place, and even he congratulated Jordan.

"Too bad you don't get points for that," Luis commented from behind her.

"It would be a sin to let a good-looking fish like that go to waste," Michael's boss commented. "Whoever cooks snapper tomorrow in the flash-cooking elimination round can use it but can't count it toward their own stash. If more than one of you wants it, we'll have to draw straws."

Feeling giddy at having caught the biggest fish so far, Jordan reveled in the backslapping and the praises. She'd forgotten how much fun this sport was but was thankful she wouldn't have to clean or cook the fish. Closing her eyes, she could almost taste her mother's beer-battered fried fish and hush puppies.

To this day that was the only way she could stomach fish.

She opened her eyes in time to see Stefano choose a fishing pole and head toward the other two women, making no bones about his obvious interest in Marsha. With a little luck, Jordan thought, the tiny bombshell might just be the perfect solution to keeping the Italian Romeo occupied.

Seizing the opportunity, she claimed his vacant bench in the shade and quickly felt the tension of the day slip away. The swaying of the boat as the waves lapped against the side lulled her eyes closed, and soon she was asleep. Something about the salty air and the hot sun got to her every time.

Not to mention the three Bud Lights.

She jerked awake when she heard what sounded like the scream of a wounded animal. Johnny and Mo ran past her to the front of the boat, and she jumped up and followed.

On the deck, writhing in pain, Stefano swore like a true sailor. By now, everyone had surrounded him. With his back facing Jordan, she couldn't see what was going on.

Glancing at Casey, she mouthed, *What happened?* The unmistakable glint of pleasure in the woman's eyes flashed only momentarily before she shrugged.

"It was an accident. My line crossed over Marsha's when he was helping her get the hook out of the fish she'd caught. When I jerked my pole to pull in my own catch, somehow it happened," she said.

Just then Stefano rolled over, still shouting obscenities, and Jordan got her first look at what was causing him so much pain.

Protruding out of both sides of his right thumb was a large saltwater fishing hook.

CHAPTER 2

"Oh, hell no," Stefano cried when he saw Captain Johnny donning rubber gloves and coming at him with a first aid kit and a pair of metal cutters. "At least not until I get some liquor into me."

"That's not a good idea," Johnny explained. "Not to mention that it's against my policy for treating an injured client."

"I don't care anything about your stupid policies," Stefano yelled. "You're not coming anywhere near me with that big metal thing until I get a couple of shots into me."

The captain looked up at Michael's boss to see how he wanted to proceed. Clearly, Stefano was not about to let him take out the hook until he got alcohol.

"Get him a drink," Wayne said to Johnny before turning back to the captain. "It's on me if anything goes wrong."

When Mo returned with a bottle of whiskey, Johnny poured a double shot and handed it to Stefano. "Drink this and then hold your breath while I get it out."

He waited for the injured man to gulp down the drink. When the last drop was gone, Stefano shut his eyes, took a deep breath, and held it. Johnny cut the line right below where it protruded from Stefano's hand and then grasped the hook. Using the pair of metal cutters Mo handed him, he cut off the barb. With one big pull, he removed the remaining hook from Stefano's thumb, and a fountain of blood spurted. Quickly, Johnny reached for a clean rag from Mo and pressed it against the puncture wound.

"Damn it to hell," Stefano shouted. "That hurt worse coming out than it did going in. I need another shot of that cheap whiskey."

After getting a nod from Johnny, Mo went to the back of the boat and opened a locked compartment on the side. He pulled out a half-empty bottle of Johnnie Walker Red and refilled the shot glass before hurrying back to Stefano, whose vocabulary was now laced with every kind of obscenity known to mankind.

"I knew you were hiding the good stuff." Stefano threw his head back and chugged the liquor.

The movement was just enough to knock Johnny's hand off the wound, and the blood again spurted. Getting a first look at the wound and his own blood, the injured chef moaned softly before his eyes rolled back into his head. He fell back on the deck, thumping his head in the process.

"Get the smelling salts," Johnny shouted.

The others stood over Stefano while Johnny replaced the old rag with a clean dressing to stop the bleeding. Mo passed the ammonia stick under Stefano's nose, and after a few seconds, Stefano gasped, his eyes fluttering open.

"Lie still, matey, unless you want to pass out again," Mo warned.

Stefano looked around, his eyes honing in on Casey. "You'll pay for this, slut."

"It was an accident, you jerk." Even as the words left Casey's mouth, her eyes sent an entirely different message. "If I wanted to hurt you, I would have used something a whole lot better than a hook." She held up a filet knife from the tackle box. "Like this."

"Relax, man. It's not too bad," Johnny reassured him after pulling the dressing back and inspecting the wound closely. "You're gonna need a tetanus shot when we get back to Key West. A round of antibiotics, too. There's always the danger of flesh-eating bacteria from saltwater fish."

Stefano's eyes were still closed, so Jordan assumed he hadn't heard that last part, especially since he didn't resume his tirade at Casey.

"Okay," he mumbled.

Who wouldn't be okay after four straight shots of Scotch? Jordan thought, eyeing Casey, who was getting her line ready to recast as if nothing had happened. She decided the jury was still out on whether or not this really was an accident.

A sneak peek at the rest of the group still congregating around Stefano verified Casey wasn't the only one who didn't seem all that broken up about the injury. Luis Herrera wasn't even trying to hide his grin. Jordan made a mental note to sic Rosie on him as soon as she could. She'd find out what was up with his attitude.

Mo and Johnny helped Stefano to his feet and led him to the shaded area where he slumped on the bench, obviously feeling no pain at the moment. After Johnny pulled the anchor, he revved up the *Sea Shark*'s engine and headed back to port.

Casey made her way over to Michael and Jordan, a half grin still on her face. "And then there were five," she snickered. "Guess you won't need to eliminate one of us tomorrow at the Greased Lightning Elimination Round."

The gang was already at the hotel waiting in Jordan's room when she and Michael returned.

"Catch any fish?" asked Ray Varga, the oldest among her fellow residents at Empire Apartments, when he saw her.

"She snared the biggest snapper I've ever seen," Michael answered for her. "You should have seen her reel that sucker in."

Ray gave her a squeeze that made her wince. In his sixties and retired for several years from the police force, Ray still worked out daily and had the body of a much younger man.

"Sorry, sweetie. Sometimes I squeeze too hard."

"Tell me about it," Lola Van Horn said, stealing Jordan from him to embrace her. "The man hasn't learned that sometimes less is more."

In her early seventies, Lola lived next door to Ray and shared more than cups of coffee with him.

"You didn't say that last night, shortcake," Ray replied, unable to conceal the mischief in his voice.

"Criminy!" Rosie LaRue said from the bed she'd share

with Jordan later. "Do you really think we want to hear about what you and Lola do behind closed doors, Ray? Some of us aren't so lucky, you know." She fist-bumped with Jordan, then patted the bed. "Power to the sisters. Now sit and tell me how you outfished all the men, Jordan. Then let's talk about tomorrow. I'm so excited, I probably won't be able to sleep tonight."

Jordan sat on the edge of the bed and scrunched her mouth in a pout. "I wish I could eat your food tomorrow instead of the fishy stuff the chefs will be cooking."

"Oh, pooh! Just take one small taste and spread the rest around on your plate," Victor Rodriguez said from the other side of the room. "I used to do that when the nuns tried to make me eat crap I didn't like."

"She can't play with her food, Victor. Everyone will be watching her. However, as a judge, she only has to take a few sample bites of each dish, anyway," Michael said.

"Oh, so now you talk to me?"

Michael lowered his eyes, like a preteen kid who knew he was in trouble. "I couldn't find a minute to myself before the fishing trip, Victor, and there were no bars on my cell phone out at sea. I'll make it up to you."

Victor's eyes lit up. "How?"

"With a nice dinner tonight along with your favorite drink, a chocolate martini."

"You're going to do that, anyway." Victor narrowed his eyes. "Take me on the booze cruise when we get to Saint Kitts."

"You know I'm not supposed . . ." Michael threw up his hands in surrender. "Ah, what the heck. Agreed. Now quit pouting."

"You love it when I pout."

"Geez! What part of 'no sex talk' did you not get? Without mentioning any names"—she poked Jordan—"some of us are flying solo on that mission."

"Yes, dear." Victor plopped on the bed beside Rosie and Jordan. "We are *so* going to have a blast. Now that we're all finally together in one spot, you have our undivided attention, Michael. Tell us again how you managed to get all of us involved in this shindig."

Michael sat in the chair by the window. "Jordan and I are working on the cooking competition. Ray is private security for Beau and—"

"Who?" Rosie interrupted.

"Beaumont P. Lincoln, Beau for short. He's the founder and CEO of Sinfully Sweet."

"I love those," Lola chimed in, giving her almost-maroon dyed hair a flip. "I gave this one guy a tarot reading a few months back and told him his luck would change. When he won a couple of grand on a scratch-off, he came back with a box of Baileys Irish Cream Fudge from Sinfully Sweet. He said they make goodies from all kinds of liquor. My mouth is watering right now just thinking about it."

"Cheapskate. He wins a potload of money, and all you get is candy," Rosie said, clucking her tongue.

"Oh, but not just candy, Rosie. A person can get a real buzz by eating an entire box like I did." She giggled. "I may have forgotten to mention the C-note he slipped me. It does pay to give good readings." She tapped her puffy lips, compliments of a plastic surgeon she counseled once or twice a week.

"Anyway," Michael continued, "Beau's security guy left for Costa Rica to help his parents fight the local government and keep their property. He has no idea when he'll be able to return, if ever. Beau didn't think he could properly train another person in that time frame, so he talked about backing out as a judge. When I told him about Ray, he met him and was impressed. He agreed to hire him for the cruise."

Jordan glanced at the retired cop, now grinning almost comically. She loved this man. When she'd arrived in Ranchero alone and frightened, the gods must have been watching over her, guiding her to Empire Apartments. Since it was the least shabby of the apartment complexes she could afford without searching for a roommate, she'd jumped on it.

Her salary, first for writing the personals and more recently as the culinary reporter at the *Ranchero Globe*, would never make her rich—in fact, it barely paid her bills—but at the time it was the only job she could find that would actually allow her to use her journalism degree from the University of Texas.

After following her boyfriend all over Texas and ending up in Dallas where he got a great job as a sports reporter for a TV station, she'd promptly been dumped for the petite weather girl who sported a humongous store-bought chest. Ironically, her ex was living *her* dream life (exclusive of the big-busted girlfriend, of course), which made his success even harder to stomach.

Vowing never to return home to Amarillo with her tail between her legs, Jordan had snapped up the *Ranchero Globe* offer and moved to the small town fifty miles northeast of the Dallas metroplex. The last thing she needed on top of her broken heart was to listen to her parents and four older brothers say "I told you so." They'd never liked Brett in the first place and had warned her about putting her own career on the back burner while she moved all over Texas with him.

Rosie, who was like a big sister to her, lived in the apartment next door. She'd introduced herself before Jordan even had a chance to unpack her four suitcases and her goldfish, Maggie. Along with Victor and Michael, who jointly owned the building, the rest of the first-floor gang had adopted her and quickly became her second family.

Although she still dreamed about sitting in the press box at athletic events, she couldn't complain about her job at the newspaper. When the culinary reporter broke her hip in a water-skiing accident two months after Jordan was hired, the editor had offered her the job.

There had been only one huge problem. Dwayne Egan wanted her to post gourmet food recipes twice a week in her new column. Since her skills in the kitchen were limited to frying bologna and making Pop-Tarts, she'd almost turned down the offer.

That was before Victor had come up with the brilliant idea of making up foreign names for Rosie's recipes. Her famous pork chop casserole was now Côte de Porc á la Cocotte. Even Egan had been amazed at the response from the local community. The recipes had quickly become the talk of the town, and she was now a household name—at least to the twenty-two thousand or so residents of Ranchero who had no idea she was clueless in the kitchen.

"Jordan?"

Victor's voice snapped Jordan back to the present. "What?"

"You were miles away. We're talking about our jobs."

He turned to Lola. "So what are you doing?" Victor asked.

"Reading tarot cards for the guests and teaching a class on séances."

"Ha!" Victor blurted. "The last séance you performed nearly ended in disaster. Remember, sweetie?"

"That's because you and Jordan's brother popped in uninvited," Lola fired back. "And don't 'sweetie' me. I was ready to kill you that night."

Jordan smiled at her friend who had become a second mother to her. Lola owned Lola's Spiritual Readings in downtown Ranchero where she read tarot cards, among other psychic services, for some of the wealthiest people in the county. Standing barely five three, if that, and wearing caftans over her adorably pudgy figure, Lola loved to eat, especially the mouthwatering desserts Ray cooked up.

"I know I'm going to help with the entertainment, but what's she doing?" Victor scooted over and put his head on Rosie's shoulder.

"What do I do best?"

He pursed his lips in deep thought. "Make jewelry and sell it on eBay?"

Rosie laughed. "You're right. And I'm darn good at that, too, but I'm talking about something else. What do I do every Friday night when you guys all come over to play cards?"

"Cook?" When she nodded, he shrugged. "Cruises are famous for their great abundance of good food. Plus, there will be six chefs vying for the title of Caribbean Cook-Off Champion. No offense, darling, but why would they want you to cook?"

Rosie punched him in the arm playfully. "You have

such a way with words, you clod." She turned to Michael. "Tell your little friend what you worked out for me before I smack him upside the head."

Michael shook his head. "That's my baby. He opens his mouth, and his foot pops right into it." He walked closer to the bed. "Just so you know, my boss and Dwayne Egan, Jordan's boss, thought it would add a nice touch if they made some of Jordan's recipes available for people to sample. Since Jordan will be busy with the contest— not to mention no one in their right mind would eat anything she cooks—my boss insisted I hire Rosie after I gave him a taste of one of her casseroles. They turned one of the smaller restaurants on board into what they're calling *Ranchero Globe*'s Kitchen Kupboard. It will be open only for lunch and only to the people who are part of the KTLK group, the twenty-five tasters chosen from a lottery, and, of course, the judges and all of us."

"So, I guess since most of the recipes Jordan prints are right out of Rosie's cookbook, our own Friday-night chef will be running the restaurant?" Victor asked.

"You got it," Michael said "Now Rosie is a head chef for a week."

Jordan reached over and high-fived her friend. "At least I'll eat well at lunch."

"Dinner won't be so bad, Jordan. I'll sneak some leftovers to our room if you absolutely hate what the chefs cook," Rosie said.

"Oh, I'll hate the food, for sure, especially the first night." Jordan shook her head. "Any fish that doesn't include beer, batter, and frying is not my idea of tasty."

Michael laughed. "Tomorrow's Greased Lightning Elimination Round may not be that bad, Jordan. The chefs will only have thirty minutes to prepare their dish, and like I said earlier, you only have to take one or two bites of each. We can sneak up to the poolside grill later on for chili dogs and fries."

"Why do they even need to cook tomorrow? I thought you said one of them was already knocked out of the competition today. Wasn't that the whole purpose of the elimination round?" Ray asked.

"Eliminating one wasn't the only reason for the first leg of the competition. The five remaining contestants will still be graded on this round, with that score added to their final tally." Michael tsked. "The injured guy was the frontrunner. Too bad he got hurt."

"Don't you mean skewered?" Jordan asked. "I wouldn't be a bit surprised to find out it wasn't an accident."

"I know," Michael agreed. "Casey and Stefano clearly have a history, and not in a good way."

"Okay, then," Victor said, apparently bored with the conversation. "I'm ready for that chocolate martini."

"Me, too," Rosie said, jumping up from the bed. "But make mine and Jordan's an appletini."

"Not for me. I'm strictly a margarita girl, Rosie. An appletini would probably send me to the hospital with a massive migraine."

As she said it, Jordan couldn't help thinking about Stefano and wondering if he was still in the emergency room. Despite his cockiness, in both the culinary and the womanizing departments, he would've added a certain element of entertainment to the competition. After her encounter with him on the boat, she'd even imagined him including "special" brownies on his menu.

Now, he'd have to stand on the sidelines and watch,

assuming he even came on the cruise. And all because of a careless accident.

Careless accident or carefully planned sabotage?

Jordan sighed. She'd probably never really know.

"Holy crap! Look at the size of that thing," Victor exclaimed. "Hope everyone brought their cell phones, or we're gonna spend half the time looking for each other on that monster ship."

Rosie cocked an eyebrow. "Do you really think you're going to get a signal out in the middle of the ocean?"

Victor slapped his head. "Oh, yeah! What was I thinking?"

"Actually, my little honey is right. You can get a signal out at sea, but the roaming charges are astronomical and aren't included in the deal we got," Michael explained before pointing to a door marked EMPLOYEES ONLY. "Come on, guys. We're boarding over there ahead of the rest of the guests." He led the way in that direction.

After boarding, they walked down a long hallway to a room filled with all the people Jordan had met on the fishing boat and several others she didn't recognize. There they began the tedious paperwork required for check-in.

"Here's the girl who caught the biggest fish yesterday."

Jordan recognized Wayne Francis walking toward her.

"Too bad you aren't competing, Jordan," Michael's boss continued. "That snapper would have given you an automatic ten-point advantage today."

"I'm cooking it, instead," Casey said. "You're going to love my Snapper à la Caribbean."

"Love to hate it, you mean."

They all turned to see Stefano saunter in, his right thumb heavily bandaged.

"Bet you thought you'd seen the last of me, huh, Casey?"

"One could only hope, Stefano," she responded, not even trying to hide the venom in her voice. "Now I can beat you fair and square."

Stefano's grin didn't come close to buffering the threat in his voice. "Over my dead body."

CHAPTER 3

"Now, now, folks. Save the aggression for those great seafood dishes you'll be cooking tonight." Wayne turned to Stefano. "The hospital cleared you for kitchen duty?"

Stefano huffed and held up his bandaged hand. "It'll take more than a lame attempt like this to stop me from winning that half-a-million-dollar contract."

"Bring it on," Casey fired back before walking away, leaving Stefano to fume alone.

Jordan made eye contact with Rosie and hitched her brows before mouthing, *My money's on the girl.*

Rosie mouthed back, *You're on.*

"Hey, Jordan, they need you over here," Michael called from the other side of the room.

She picked up her tote bag and headed that way. Half-way there, she stopped suddenly, her attention diverted to the woman standing in the doorway. At about five-foot-eight, she had the most gorgeous spiked, chestnut-colored hair Jordan had ever seen. And it definitely wasn't the end result of a Supercuts visit. The newcomer walked over to Wayne and shook his hand.

By this time, everyone in the room had stopped to stare. Mindlessly, Jordan touched the unmanageable, curly red locks she'd been gifted with at birth—according to her mother—and was so caught up in hair envy, she didn't realize Michael was speaking to her until he poked her in the side.

"Did you hear me, Jordan?"

She pulled her eyes away from the woman, aware that her mouth was still hanging open. "Who is that?"

"Emily Thorpe. She's the one who put this entire competition together and worked it out with my boss to be a sponsor. She's easy on the eyes, all right."

"Easy on the eyes is not the way I'd describe her," Lola said, moving next to them with Rosie, Ray, and Victor a step behind. "Ray would call her a stunner."

"I'll say," Ray chimed in before Lola playfully slapped his head.

"I get to call her that. You don't."

"You have to admit, dear, she could stop a train at a hundred yards," he added, further tempting disapproval from his lady. "I can't wait to see her in a bikini."

"You old codger. You can't even keep up with Lola," Rosie deadpanned.

Ray laughed. "No, but it's fun trying." He grabbed both Lola's and Rosie's arms and entwined them with his. "Come on, gals, let's finish the paperwork so we can get a look at the upper decks. They tell me there are four pools and six different Jacuzzi tubs."

"Seven," Victor said, following the others.

The group stopped to stare at him.

"What? My back's been giving me problems, so I checked."

"You guys go on. I need to steal Jordan for a minute." Michael nudged her toward the new arrival.

The woman smiled as they approached. "Hello, Michael. It's good to see you again." She turned to Jordan. "And who is your lady friend?"

"Emily, this is Jordan McAllister from the *Ranchero Globe*. She'll be judging the competition along with Beau."

Emily studied Jordan for a few seconds before commenting, "I'd pay a lot of money to have hair like yours, but I'm afraid it wouldn't look nearly as good on me as it does on you."

Jordan felt the color creep up her cheeks. *Seriously? This woman wants to trade hair? How fast can you say 'abracadabra'?*

"I have to trick my beautician into working on this mop."

Emily chuckled. "I like your style, Jordan. I think you and I will be great friends before the week is out." She turned when Michael's boss called her name. "Gotta run, but I'm sure I'll catch up with you later."

Even from the back, the woman was stunning, Jordan thought as she watched her walk away. "Wow!"

"I know. She's a knockout," Michael said. "And she seems to have taken a liking to you."

"Is she a chef?"

Michael looked at her in disbelief. "You don't know who she is?"

"Should I? Is she famous?"

"Ah, yeah. She owns ETI in New York City, and from what I understand, she's rolling in dough."

"I've never heard of ETI."

"That's because you've never wanted to be a model or an actress. Entertainment and Talent Incorporated. She's a lawyer and has a client list that would make the Academy Awards seem like a party with her peeps."

Jordan took her eyes off Michael long enough to glance over at Emily Thorpe, who was now chatting with Casey and Marsha. Next to her, even Marsha looked mediocre.

"How'd she get involved in this competition, Michael? No offense, but it sounds like small potatoes next to her day-to-day life, if what you say is true."

"Oh, it's true. Wayne was over the moon when she called out of the blue and suggested this whole contest thing. Seems one of her clients is from Ranchero and talks about the town all the time. Wayne saw it as a way to drum up listeners for the station." He nodded. "It was a brilliant idea. People had to tune in to the station all day every day for the opportunity to call in at special times and win a chance for a free cruise as a taster. Our ratings shot up thirty points."

"I see why Wayne wanted her, but why would she want to do it? It doesn't sound like she's hurting for money or clients." Jordan paused before adding, "Again, no offense, but these chefs aren't exactly celebrities."

"I hear you, Jordan. I can only tell you that she worked it out to sign on the winning chef as a client and already has a TV campaign set up that will make both of them rich—or in her case, richer."

Jordan clucked her tongue. "Why didn't I learn how to cook instead of playing flag football every day with my brothers?"

Just then, Rosie rushed over and pulled Jordan away.

"Come on. Let's get you signed in so we can take a look at our room and get this party started," she said, the excitement in her voice contagious.

Jordan followed her to the counter, peeking over her shoulder one last time to see Emily throw back her head in laughter at something Casey said. If Jordan hadn't already known Emily was rich and famous, she never would have guessed. She seemed so down-to-earth.

So far Jordan liked most of the people she'd met, leading her to believe this might not be so bad after all. And watching the fireworks between Casey and Stefano could prove to be more fun than the time she and the gang went to a bar in McKinley to watch Rosie mud wrestle.

If she could just squeak by without having to eat too much of the fancy food, she would pull off the con of the century. Dwayne Egan was counting on her to do the newspaper proud—and it would definitely take a well-executed con to do that.

When the paperwork was finished, they went to find their rooms, which, thanks to Michael, were all together in the same corridor, perfect for late-night powwows or card games.

The rooms were small but comfortable, and Jordan and Rosie quickly unpacked before meeting up with the others for lunch on the eleventh deck. Never had Jordan seen so much food in one place. Nor had she seen so many people filling their plates with more than they could possibly eat in a week.

Spying a row with nothing but desserts, Jordan felt their sugary pull. She started that way before Rosie held her back.

"Oh, no you don't. It's going to be several hours before you eat again. We have to get some real food into you before you go after all that chocolate."

Jordan snickered. "You know me so well. Okay, lead me to the fried chicken."

She was pleasantly surprised at how good everything tasted. Since the only chicken available was swimming in some kind of white sauce, she chose spaghetti and meatballs with lots of fresh-baked bread.

Two chocolate mousses later, she was ready to take on the seafood at the competition, which was scheduled for seven that night. She'd already figured out how she could come out of this without totally embarrassing herself. Her plan was to take one small bite and then pretend to be a little nauseous. A little seasickness would be believable. Might even garner her sympathy.

With their stomachs filled, the gang decided it was time for a tour of the ship. One look at the main pool with its huge waterslide and a Jacuzzi in every corner, and the miniature golf course on the upper level, and Jordan couldn't help getting excited. This would be a fun week for all of them. She finally began to relax, mentally promising to make a genuine effort to befriend all the contestants, including Stefano.

Nothing was going to ruin this trip, not even the Casanova chef.

She gulped. Then why did she suddenly feel like something was not quite right?

Carnation Theater was huge, and there was already a standing-room-only crowd. The twenty-five people who had been selected as tasters were seated in the first three rows when Michael led Jordan to the steps at the side of the stage.

"Why can't I sit with you and Wayne?"

"Because we're going to be emceeing the whole thing. Besides, they want you over there with Beau and George Christakis."

"Who?"

"George Christakis. You don't remember?" When she shook her head, he shrugged. "I can't believe you forgot that the fabulous world-renowned chef from the Cooking Channel was going to be a judge with you and—"

"I love his show," Rosie interrupted. "How in tarnation did you manage to talk him into this?" She did a one-eighty, squealing when she saw him on the stage. "Ohmygod! He's even more handsome in person than he is on television. Wonder if he's married."

Victor playfully punched her arm. "He bats for the other team, dear. Sorry." When Michael sent a look his way, Victor added, "Not that I noticed him or anything."

Michael turned back to Rosie. "Apparently, he and Emily are good friends, and she talked him into coming as a favor to her. Because of him the cruise sold out in less than a week." He took a hold of Jordan's elbow and led her to the steps. "Come on. I'll introduce you. I got to spend a few minutes with him earlier, and he's a great guy—nothing like the other judge, Mr. Beau 'I'm rich and important' Lincoln."

"Where is Beau, by the way?" Jordan asked, scanning the stage.

Michael shook his head. "He's already acting like a spoiled celebrity and barely made it to the ship before we set sail. Wayne sent one of the workers to his suite to escort him and his wife to the theater." He led Jordan to the right side of the stage.

When they were in front of the judges' table, Christakis looked up and a smile tipped the corners of his mouth. "You must be the lovely food critic I've heard so much about." He stood and extended his hand. "George Christakis. I've been told I should consult you for a few new recipes. I spent a little time talking with the crowd from Texas before I came on stage. They tell me your Budin de Papitas con Pollo would be a big hit with the New York crowd."

Jordan laughed out loud as she shook his hand. She couldn't tell whether he was being serious or teasing her. Had he figured out that the recipe was really Potato Chip Chicken (Rosie's, of course)? She decided to play innocent until she knew for sure.

"Remind me to kiss whoever has been lying to you, Mr. Christakis, but I—"

"Call me George."

"Okay, George. I'm sure my friend Rosie will be serving it this week, and you can try it, although I have to tell you it's nothing like you're used to."

He ignored that remark. "Your friend is serving it on this ship?"

"Yes. She's running a small diner on the upper deck called Ranchero Globe Kitchen Kupboard. It will be open for lunch only to the judges and the people involved in this competition. It's my editor's idea. He thought it would be nice if she served some of the recipes I've published in my column." She stopped short of blurting that they were straight out of Rosie's recipe files in the first place.

He nodded. "That sounds like something I definitely don't want to miss."

She decided even if he knew about the ruse, she couldn't let him go to the restaurant thinking he was getting fancy food. "It's not really gourmet food," she confessed. "More like gourmet casseroles."

Okay, maybe "gourmet casseroles" was stretching it a bit, but the man should be forewarned.

"All the more intriguing. I hope you'll join me one day for lunch there."

Grinning, she pulled her hand out of his clasp. "It would be my pleasure."

When she was sure it was safe, she did a hasty onceover of the middle-aged gentleman with the warmest brown eyes she'd ever seen. With his salt-and-pepper hair and the adorable dimple in his chin, he definitely was as handsome as Rosie's first impression. Even though Jordan had never actually watched the Cooking Channel and had no idea how George Christakis stacked up against his fellow TV chefs, she gave the guy serious hottie points.

She moved around the table to take the center chair, but before she even sat down, she heard a commotion on the opposite side of the stage. When she looked up, she got her first peek at the multimillionaire who had made his fortune selling alcoholic desserts. About six two, Beau

Lincoln had slicked-back dark hair with equally dark eyes and a body that screamed daily workout. When he smiled, he resembled a young George Clooney.

Dressed in navy slacks and a navy and gray polo shirt, he looked to be in his midthirties. It was only after he stopped to talk to Wayne Francis that Jordan noticed the petite blonde behind him. Five one or two at the most, the woman wore a red sundress that left nothing to the imagination and made one wonder if she had just left the Playboy Mansion.

Wayne led the couple over to the table. "Jordan and George, meet the other third of the judging lineup, Beau Lincoln."

Shamelessly, the new arrival let his wandering eyes explore every inch of Jordan, his hand clinging to hers all the while and for far longer than she was comfortable with.

Sheesh! Doesn't the idiot know his wife is right behind him?

"My job just got a little more pleasant," he said when he finally released her hand.

After his wife cleared her throat, he must have remembered he wasn't alone and pulled her in front of him. "And this is my lovely wife, Charlese."

Jordan reached for her hand, noticing how clammy it was. "Nice to meet you."

Wayne reached for Charlese's arm and pointed to where Rosie and the gang sat about four rows back. "We're getting ready to start. Luca will take you to your seat now." He handed her off to a steward dressed in a perfectly starched white uniform.

"So, Jordan, tell me about yourself. How long have

you been the culinary reporter at the *Globe*?" Beau asked
after settling in beside her.

When Beau inched closer, she moved slightly to her
left, toward Christakis. "Just a few months."

"Michael said you were a chocoholic. Ever had one of
my Sinfully Sweet desserts?" When she shook her head,
his eyes lit up. "Then you must let me come to your room
after the competition. I have a box of freshly baked
Kahlúa brownies that has your name on it."

Don't hold your breath. She wrinkled her brow. *Wait!
Did he just say Kahlúa brownies?*

Her attention was diverted when Marsha Davenport
strolled up to the judges' table.

"I couldn't wait to meet you, Mr. Lincoln. I've heard
so many good things about you."

Jordan couldn't miss the way the lady chef stretched
across the table to shake Beau's hand, giving both her and
the entrepreneur a straight-to-the-belly-button view down
her blouse. Even the chef's apron didn't hide the attri-
butes she'd no doubt paid a chunk of change to enhance.

Beau moved away from Jordan and settled back in his
chair to take advantage of the peep show. Jordan imagined him salivating at the tasty morsel in front of him, but
at this point, she was just grateful for the diversion.

"Call me Beau. And who might you be?"

Marsha pretended to be shy and fluttered her eyelashes.
"Marsha Davenport. I intern in Hirasoto's in Fort Worth."

"I know that restaurant well," Beau said. "Like chocolate, Marsha?" When she nodded, he gave her hand a
squeeze. "I'll bring some of my delicacies to your room
later so you can sample them."

Hey, those are my brownies!

Jordan wondered what the jerk planned on doing with his little Hugh-Heffner-castoff wife while he plied Marsha with God only knew what kind of "delicacies."

"I'd like that. If you'll excuse me, I have to get to my station, Beau. Hope you like my salmon." She stood and walked to where the other chefs were getting ready, making sure her backside wiggled just enough to cause him to drool a bit more.

Suddenly thinking about Stefano, Jordan giggled to herself. The playing field had narrowed, and the arrogant chef now had his work cut out for him tonight. Instead of bragging about how he wouldn't need the bonus ten points from the fishing trip, he should've been worrying about Marsha and her sexy little body that was already scoring points with Beau.

"I'm glad to see all of you," Emily said as she walked up the steps and over to them. Leaning down, she kissed Christakis on the forehead. "George, I'm so glad you made it. I owe you."

"Nonsense, my dear. I wouldn't have missed this for the world. It gets so stuffy in New York sometimes. It's good to get out of the city and see how the real people live." He pointed to Beau. "Like my fellow judges. I think I will be highly entertained this week."

Emily turned to Jordan. "And I'm delighted to have you as well, Jordan." She stepped closer to stand directly in front of Beau. "Thank you for agreeing to be a judge also, Mr. Lincoln."

Jordan almost felt sorry for Beau, whose tongue was nearly hanging out of his mouth after his first glimpse of the entertainment lawyer. He must have thought he had died and gone to Hooter Heaven.

"Jesus!" Jordan heard him say under his breath.

"Are we ready to get this show on the road?" Emily asked without offering her hand.

"Yes," Jordan replied.

Beau could only nod. Jordan couldn't help thinking Marsha had just lost out on the Kahlúa brownies, too.

Emily moved to the middle of the stage and took the mic from Michael's boss. "Good evening, ladies and gentlemen, and welcome to what we hope will be the first of many annual Lone Star Caribbean Cook-Offs. I'm Emily Thorpe, and along with Wayne Francis and KTLK in Ranchero, Texas, I have the privilege of being a sponsor for this wonderful event. First off, I want to thank the good people at Carnation Queen Cruise Lines for their help in putting this together, as well as the talented staff at KTLK for making it happen. Of course, we wouldn't be here if it weren't for all of you wonderful listeners who chose to be a part of this fun cruise with us. So, are you all ready to see the chefs cook?"

The crowd went wild, all except Beau's wife, who definitely was not a happy camper and was sending daggers in Emily's direction. Had she seen her husband's reaction to the dazzling lawyer? And if so, why was she giving Emily the evil eye? Her only fault was looking gorgeous. She couldn't help it if Beau was as sleazy as they come and just as horny.

"Let's start by introducing the talented chefs who came from all over the Dallas–Fort Worth area to show off their talents." The crowd cheered after each name, rocking the house when Stefano was introduced. "The competition will take place only on the days we're at sea so that y'all can enjoy the wonderful islands we'll visit. Tomorrow night we'll begin with appetizers, and then on Thursday when we're on our way back to Miami, the chefs will give us their best dessert recipes. We've saved the most challenging part, main entrees, for Friday night, after which the points will be tallied and a winner crowned.

"Tonight's Greased Lightning Elimination Round will start us off. Our chefs have each chosen their own favorite fish to cook, but they'll have to incorporate every ingredient from the baskets at their stations in their recipes."

She reached for an opened basket from one of her assistants and held it up. "Each basket has identical ingredients chosen by the executive chef on the ship. There are mangoes, pineapples, crab meat, a few exotic seasonings, and even guava berry liqueur. The chefs will have thirty minutes to prepare enough for the three judges and the twenty-five tasters." She paused to allow the crowd to show their approval before she continued. "Now it's time to meet the three people who hold the fate of our chefs in their hands."

Emily turned toward Jordan and Beau. "The pretty lady with the great hair is Jordan McAllister from the *Ranchero Globe*. She writes the popular Kitchen Kupboard column, so we know she's highly qualified to pick out great-tasting food."

Jordan nearly choked on the sip of water she'd just taken.

"Sitting on her right is Beau Lincoln, owner and CEO of Sinfully Sweet, a Fortune 500 company that sells the most delicious cocktail desserts I've ever tasted.

"And I don't think I need to tell any of you who the distinguished gentleman to Jordan's left is. Please help me welcome world-renowned chef and owner of the fabulous Chez Lui restaurant in New York City, George Christakis."

The man seemed almost embarrassed by all the hoopla. The crowd's appreciation and subsequent standing ovation brought a half smile to his face. He stood and waved, causing another storm of applause.

When the crowd finally quieted down, Emily continued. "So without further ado, let's get started. Remember, chefs, one of you will be eliminated tonight, but you'll still get to hang out and enjoy a great cruise. The final winner will receive a hundred thousand dollars, courtesy of Gourmet Kitchens, along with the opportunity to do a national ad campaign with me for Classic Cuisine." Her assistant handed her a remote control. "You're on the clock," she said as a huge digital timer appeared over the chef stations and began the thirty-minute countdown.

The chefs immediately opened the baskets and got down to business. Soon the smell of cooking fish filled the air as the chefs frantically chopped and mixed, poached and sautéed—and intermittently sprinted to the back of the stage to grab additional ingredients from a table laden with fruits and vegetables.

With only five minutes to go, the atmosphere on the stage was near chaos; Jordan watched the contestants scurrying to and from their stations, as if the clock were a time bomb. Except for Stefano. In contrast to the other chefs, the cocky Casanova was jovial as he tasted his dish, added more seasoning, and nonchalantly tasted again.

Maybe this guy was as good as he said, Jordan thought,

watching him take one more bite before setting down his fork.

In a flash, the smile on his face disappeared and his eyes bulged open. Doubling over the table as though in severe pain, he grabbed his throat and terror flashed across his face. It took a few seconds for Jordan's brain to register that he might be in serious trouble, but then she jumped up and ran toward him.

Before she could reach him, Stefano's eyes rolled back in his head, and he fell face-first into his signature halibut dish.

CHAPTER 4

"Get the doctor!" Jordan screamed. Running behind the table, she reached Stefano at the same time as Michael. After lifting the chef's face out of the plate and gently lowering him to the floor, Michael checked his neck for a pulse.

"Nothing." On his knees beside Stefano, he began giving him chest compressions.

The nearly two thousand people in the audience were eerily silent, watching as Michael attempted to revive the fallen chef. The other contestants quietly huddled in a corner, the meals they'd been preparing still cooking at their stations.

Jordan watched Beau Lincoln meander over to where Marsha stood silently with her competitors. Apparently, the dramatic attempt to save a man's life playing out in front of him was the last thing on his mind. Talking

Marsha into a cozy, after-dinner chocolate fest in his room was probably right up there at the top, though.

Disgusted, Jordan's attention reverted back to Stefano just as the ship's doctor rushed onto the stage, medical bag in hand and stethoscope around his neck. He bent down and motioned for Michael to stop CPR while he checked to see if the heartbeat had returned.

"Continue," he commanded before reaching into his black bag for a prefilled syringe. Quickly, he tied a tourniquet around Stefano's arm, found a vein, and injected the medicine directly into it.

A steward appeared with a defibrillator, and after charging it, the doctor administered the first shock to Stefano's chest. His lifeless body briefly jumped off the floor with the jolt, then stilled. When the steward knelt down on the other side of the dying chef and took over the chest compressions, Michael rose and joined Jordan on the sidelines.

The look in his eyes told her all she needed to know.

"He's not going to make it, is he?" she asked.

"Don't know," Michael responded, clearly shaken. "It doesn't look too good for him right now."

A vivid image from a few months back flashed across her mind. The night of the Cattleman's Ball in Fort Worth when her date died in her arms wasn't something she would soon forget. Though Stefano wasn't her date tonight, Jordan didn't like the way she was beginning to feel. Was it possible she was turning into a female version of the Grim Reaper?

Quickly chasing that thought out of her head, she concentrated on what was going on with Stefano. After two more injections and another hit with the defibrillator, the doctor reached over and covered the steward's hand with his own, stopping CPR. A few seconds later, he stood and stepped toward Emily. Jordan noticed for the first time that the highly successful businesswoman appeared to be close to losing it. The apprehension in her eyes was hard to miss.

"He's dead." Although the doctor spoke softly, his voice echoed across the stage, causing a collective gasp from the other contestants.

Finally finding her composure, Emily took a deep breath and nodded. "Was it a heart attack?"

The doctor shrugged. "That would be my best guess, but we'll have to wait on an autopsy to know for sure."

Emily looked defeated, realizing she had lost control of the situation. "Now what?"

"We'll keep him in the morgue until we reach San Juan the day after tomorrow. From there, they'll fly the body back to Miami for an autopsy." Shaking his head, the doctor motioned to his two assistants, who were waiting on stage with a gurney.

The chilling silence that had overtaken the room for the last ten minutes gave way to a low rumbling that quickly increased to a crescendo. By the time Stefano's body was loaded onto the stretcher and wheeled off the stage through the back door of the theater, the smell of burning fish permeated the massive room. But nobody seemed to care.

After a hushed discussion at the back of the stage with Michael's boss, Emily came forward and was handed a mic to address the crowd once again. "We are deeply saddened by the death of Stefano Mancini. Because of this unthinkable tragedy, we are cancelling tonight's Greased

Lightning Elimination Round. After consulting with the doctor, Wayne Francis and I will make a final decision on whether or not to cancel the entire competition."

When the crowd didn't react, she continued. "We'll let you know as soon as we can. Whatever the decision, if any of you feel you can no longer participate in this event, we will attempt to refund your money, although ultimately, that will be decided by the people at Carnation Queen. If they agree, you can return to Miami on the first available flight after we dock in Puerto Rico."

She was interrupted when Phillip walked up from his station in the back, his face as white as the table linen.

"Stefano is really dead?"

Emily nodded. "Like the doctor said, only an autopsy can tell us why but it could have been a heart attack, perhaps brought on by some underlying heart arrhythmia. It's possible that the intensity of the competition and the rushing to finish may have brought on a sudden reaction that stopped his heart."

"Stefano didn't have heart problems," Phillip said, his voice cracking. "I would've known about it. It has to be something else."

"Stefano probably didn't know about it himself." Emily put her arm around the chef, who was at least two inches shorter than her. "What else could it have been, Phillip? We've all heard about athletes who drop dead on the football field for no apparent reason, and it isn't until they do an autopsy that they discover there was an undetected genetic problem. Or maybe it had something to do with his injury yesterday."

With tears running freely down his face, Phillip turned to Casey. "You did this to him. Everyone knows how much you hated him. Does winning this competition mean so much to you that you'd kill for it?"

Without changing her expression, Casey said, "Yes, I hated Stefano and don't care who knows it. The man was a slimy little weasel, and if everyone here is being honest, they'll agree. But I can assure you that as much as I'd like to take the credit, I had nothing to do with Stefano's death."

Before Phillip could respond, Michael approached and put his hand on the distraught man's shoulder. "I know you and Stefano were good friends, Phillip. I can only imagine how much you'll miss him, but blaming someone isn't going to help. We'll have to wait a few days to find out the actual cause of death. In the meantime, let's try to remember all the good things about Stefano."

"He was allergic to nuts."

Everyone turned in the direction of the voice. Although Jordan hadn't been formally introduced to him, she knew the man was Thomas Collingsworth. He was the contestant who had stayed in Texas an extra day to make sure his wife and firstborn child were settled in on their first day home from the hospital.

About five ten, Thomas looked as if he'd just crawled out of bed, slapped on an old shirt, and wandered onto the stage. Even the newly starched chef's apron didn't hide the wrinkled pants he wore beneath.

Emily was the first to react. "How do you know Stefano was allergic to nuts, Thomas?"

The man stared at her before blowing out a noisy breath. "He had a reaction at my apartment about eight or nine months ago."

Suddenly, Phillip raced to Stefano's workstation and

held up the bottle with exotic spices. It was one of the mandatory ingredients for the elimination round. After twisting off the top, he dipped his finger in and then popped it into his mouth.

"Oh my God! Someone call the doctor and tell him Stefano is having an allergic reaction." When no one moved, he screamed, "Dammit. Someone call the doctor."

Marsha rushed over and wrapped her arms around him. "It's too late. He's gone, Phillip."

"No," Phillip shouted, wrestling out of her embrace. "If Stefano's allergic to peanuts, the doctor can fix it with a shot or something."

"He's been without oxygen too long," Marsha said in a soothing voice. "I'm so sorry."

At the mention of peanuts, the executive chef made eye contact with Emily. "I thought you said none of the tasters for this competition had any food allergies." His English was heavily laced with a Brazilian dialect.

Suddenly back in the spotlight, Emily answered with renewed confidence. "That was one of the questions on the forms I sent to all the contestants as well as the twenty-five tasters. I made sure we specifically asked about food allergies." She paused for a moment. "I can't remember for sure without consulting the consent forms, but I know I went over every one of them with my assistant. Stefano had to have checked the no-allergy box, or we would have spotted it."

"Why didn't you tell us this before?" Wayne asked Thomas, more than a little annoyed. "We might have been able to save him if we'd known."

Displeased at Wayne's accusatory tone, Thomas nailed him with a glare. "Stefano swore my wife and me to secrecy—thought it might cost him a chance to work at certain high-level jobs if word got out. It happened so long ago, I'd totally forgotten about it. Besides, he never ate anything he didn't cook himself or hadn't watched while it was being prepared."

He moved closer to Wayne, obviously still angry over the last remark. "I didn't even think about his problem with peanuts until just now. I have a good nose for spices, and I'm pretty sure there were no nuts of any kind in my bottle."

Emily stepped between the two men, who were dangerously close to swinging fists. "I gave specific instructions that although no one listed food allergies of any type, there would be no nuts of any kind in the baskets." She turned to the head chef. "Antonio?"

The head chef, in turn, glared at his assistant, whose high white baker's hat resembled a big white cupcake, making Jordan wish she was off somewhere eating one right now instead of watching this scene unfold in front of her. It was hard to wrap her head around the fact that Stefano was actually dead. She'd never been able to come up with the right thing to say in a situation like this, and today was no different.

The assistant threw both hands in the air, causing his hat to bobble precariously on his head. "I prepared the spices myself. There are no peanuts in there. It's simply a mixture of fresh cinnamon, sugar, and cloves, with a little orange and lemon zest."

Phillip once again unscrewed the bottle and dipped his finger into the jar. After popping his finger into his mouth, he shoved the opened container toward the chef. "Taste this, and then tell me there are no nuts in it."

The chef did exactly as Phillip had only moments before. After a few seconds, he licked his lips and looked up, bewildered. "I'm absolutely positive I didn't put ground nuts in any of these spice bottles." He made eye contact with his boss, silently pleading with the executive chef to believe him. "But there definitely are ground nuts in this one."

After a moment's hesitation, the head chef went to Casey's station where he picked up her spice bottle and tasted the contents. Without speaking, he moved from table to table, repeating the process. When he'd sampled all of them, he came back to Emily.

"I swear I don't know how the nuts got in the dead man's bottle."

"Was it in any of the others?"

He hung his head. "No."

CHAPTER 5

"For God's sake, how could you let something like this happen?" Beau bellowed, standing now with angry eyes leveled on Wayne Francis. "There are over three million people in the United States who are allergic to nuts, and a lot more who don't have a clue a peanut could kill them. Any one of us could be affected by it. Why in the hell would you even take a chance with it here?"

He started toward Michael's boss before George Christakis interceded with a hand to the angry man's chest. The famous chef was a good two inches taller than Beau and looked like he worked out regularly, too.

"Calm down, Lincoln," George warned. "Let's not start blaming anyone before we even find out what killed the man. It could have been something as unrelated as a brain aneurysm or something."

Beau's face was now bright red, and his breath came in

loud short bursts as he continued his tirade against Wayne. "You're still the same dumb-ass you always were, even in high school, Francis. I worked hard to get where I am today, and in one short day, you may have screwed up everything if the dead guy's family decides to sue."

At that moment, Wayne Francis looked about ready to kill Beau with his bare hands, but to his credit, he took a deep breath and said, "Everyone signed a waiver, Lincoln. There will be no lawsuits over this, I guarantee. At least not one naming you. So why don't you calm down and quit thinking only about yourself."

The two men glared at each other for a few more seconds before Beau looked away. "Good to know." He turned slightly and whispered into Marsha's ear.

As if on cue, Emily reached for the mic and stepped to the center of the stage to address the crowd once again. "Let's not jump to any conclusions until we get an official cause of death from the medical examiner in Miami. For now, all we can do is wait. An announcement about whether or not we go forward with the competition will come as early as tomorrow morning over the intercom."

With shaking hands she handed the mic to the young steward and ambled toward Jordan and Michael, who were standing in the back with Wayne. When she reached them, she closed her eyes and blew out a long breath. Although her voice just moments before had seemed calm and in control, her eyes told a different tale.

By the time the crowd finally began to disperse, a few of the other contestants had joined them.

"I don't know about you, but I could really use a drink right now," Emily finally said. "I'd love some company at the Starlight Lounge. It's quiet there, and we can decide how to proceed with the contest—if we do decide to proceed."

Everyone nodded. A drink after what had just happened seemed appropriate. Maybe even two or three.

Emily checked her watch. "Let's meet in twenty minutes. That'll give all of us time to go back to our rooms and freshen up."

"Sounds good," Jordan said. "Whoever gets there first can get a table big enough for all of—"

"Where are we going?" Beau interrupted.

The look that passed between Jordan and Emily confirmed they were in agreement. Neither wanted to spend any more time than they absolutely had to with the obnoxious entrepreneur, but there was no way they could say that without causing a scene.

"The Starlight Lounge on deck ten," Wayne finally admitted, probably thinking it might be a good idea to diffuse the guy after his earlier blowup. "We're meeting there in twenty minutes."

Beau turned ninety degrees and looked directly at Marsha. "You going?"

When she nodded, he flashed a grin. "Okay, then, count me in. Tossing back a drink or two with y'all is the perfect way for us to get acquainted."

Yeah, right. The only one he wanted to get acquainted with was the one who had given him a peek down her blouse earlier. How blatant could the man get?

"Isn't it awful the way that poor man died?"

They all turned to see Beau's wife wobble up the steps and sashay across the stage in ridiculously high spiky heels.

Beau had the decency to take his eyes off Marsha's

chest, although he did look a little annoyed at having his
wife interrupt the fantasy that must've been playing out
in his head.

"Honey, some of us are meeting to discuss what's
going to happen next. Why don't you go back to the room
and get into your comfy clothes? I'll have the concierge
send up a bottle of their finest champagne."

Charlese Lincoln narrowed her eyes as if she could see
directly into her husband's mind. In all probability, this
wasn't her first rodeo with the man and his roving ways.
Chances were pretty good she'd been a player in his womanizing game before. Jordan's money was on Charlese
having once been the one waiting to get cozy with Beau
while wife number one got sent to the room with booze.

After a moment, Charlese shrugged. "Okay. I'll see
you later. Don't stay up too late, darling. You promised to
get up early and lay by the pool with me."

She stood on tiptoes to kiss him, then turned and
walked off the stage. It was almost comical the way every
man present ogled her backside and perfectly shaped,
seemingly endless legs as she and her jersey mini dress
headed toward the exit.

Even Michael.

Emily was the first to react. "After you guys pull your
tongues back into your mouths, I'll see you all at the Starlight Lounge."

Jordan stepped off the stage and found Rosie. Together
they made their way out of the empty theater.

"Did you see the way Beau came on to Marsha right in
front of his wife? No way I'd let my husband go drinking
alone with a sex kitten like that."

Rosie laughed. "Sweetie, think about it. Charlese put up with Beau's crap the entire time she was chasing him. Now it's obvious she doesn't give a rat's patootie. More likely, the man had his last around-the-world ride with her the night before she walked down the aisle. My guess is that Mrs. Beau Lincoln is in love with his money, and she's just biding her time until she and her lawyer can sit across the table from the man and negotiate a seven-figure alimony settlement."

Jordan made a face. "Yuck. But when you put it that way, I'd say Charlese has earned every penny she'll get. Just imagining him in the bedroom is enough to nauseate me."

"Ha! Maybe it's time you changed that patch behind your ear." Rosie opened the door to the room and allowed Jordan to enter.

"Or maybe I should just be thankful the slimeball has decided to shower all his attention on Marsha instead of me and leave it at that."

"It's what I'd do. There isn't enough money in the world to convince me to do the horizontal boogie with that jerk."

Jordan giggled. "Oh, I don't know about that. I've already checked, and there are no Ho Hos on this ship. I can't stop thinking about those Kahlúa brownies he offered me."

By the time Jordan and Rosie arrived at the Starlight Lounge, Victor and Michael and the five contestants were already there and had commandeered two large booths in the corner. Most of the chefs were sitting at the one closest to the bar and already had a round of drinks in front of them as they chatted with Wayne. Victor waved Jordan and Rosie over to the other booth.

"There you are," Emily said from the bar. "What are you two drinking?"

"Margaritas," Rosie hollered before plopping down beside Michael. "Are you okay?" she asked him. "I know how hard you and Wayne worked putting this together. Were you and Stefano friends?"

He shook his head. "I met him for the first time on the fishing boat yesterday, and personally, I thought he was a world-class jerk. So, no tears lost there. But I do feel for Wayne and Emily, who invested a lot of time and money getting this contest together, expecting to make a profit. As the owner of KTLK Wayne socked a lot of his own personal savings into this venture."

"How badly will this affect them?" Rosie asked.

"If enough people leave the ship in Puerto Rico, both of them will be out a huge chunk of change."

"Emily can afford it, but Wayne can't," Victor chimed in.

"No talking about unpleasant stuff," Emily said as she lowered the tray she'd carried from the bar onto the table. "Drinks first, and then we'll discuss business."

"Thanks, Ms. Thorpe." Jordan reached for a margarita, which just happened to be her all-time favorite adult drink.

"Call me Emily. Like I said before, I think you and I are going to be great friends."

Jordan smiled back at her. Something about the woman made Jordan feel that, even though she was rolling in dough and living the high life in New York, Emily was just another small-town girl. And one Jordan was looking forward to getting to know better.

She raised her glass to clink with Emily's. "Here's to new friendships."

"And finding a way to get past tonight," Michael added as they all toasted.

"I'll make sure that happens," Beau said, appearing out of nowhere, two drinks in hand. "A couple bourbons on the rocks and a checkbook can make even the worst problem go away." He scanned both tables, then slid in beside Marsha.

Jordan got Rosie's attention and rolled her eyes. She looked toward the table of chefs to see if any of them had the same reaction as she did, but nobody seemed to notice the clod had joined them.

Phillip and Luis were having an animated discussion across the table from Beau and Marsha, and Thomas was busy showing Wayne something on his cell phone. From the way Wayne was grinning, Jordan guessed it was pictures of Thomas's newborn son. Casey sat slumped, staring at the bar, trying to get the waitress's attention to order another round. She'd chugged her first drink while Beau and Marsha played touchy-feely, totally ignoring her.

"So, what do y'all think about going ahead with the competition?" Wayne addressed the entire group when everyone was on their second cocktail.

Well, not everyone. Beau was on his third double.

When no one commented, Wayne continued. "None of us could have predicted this would happen, but we have to look at it as an unfortunate accident. I'm sorry Stefano's dead, but I say we let the show go on. A lot of people paid good money for a chance to see the cook-off." He raised his hand to acknowledge the cheers from the contestants.

"I agree, Wayne," Emily said. "As of right now, the cause of Stefano's death, according to the doctor's best guess, was a heart attack. But even if it isn't, we shouldn't allow it to change our plans. The cruise will continue, so why not the competition?"

"What about the fact that Stefano's spice bottle was laced with ground nuts and the other bottles weren't?" asked Ray, who'd just walked up with Lola. The two squeezed in between Michael and Rosie before Ray went on. "Don't you think it's a little fishy—pun intended—that the dead man was the only one allergic to nuts?"

"That's true, Ray, but there's no proof that was anything other than a weird coincidence—an unfortunate mistake that was made in the kitchen preparing the baskets," Victor said.

"I don't believe in coincidences," Ray shot back. "Matter of fact, neither does the head of security on this ship. He contacted me about an hour ago and asked for my help with the investigation."

"Investigation?" Wayne put his drink down with a thud. "They're actually treating this like it wasn't accidental?"

"Standard operating procedure when someone dies on the ship," Ray explained. "I'm meeting him tomorrow to look over the security tapes from the main kitchen."

"So, are you saying, in light of this, we should cancel the cook-off?" Emily asked.

"Definitely not," Ray replied. "If foul play was involved, the last thing we'd want to do is change the normal routine. We need to see how this thing plays out."

"Then I think we have our answer," Wayne said, smiling as though he'd just won the cook-off himself.

"Although I'm saddened that Stefano is dead, there's really nothing more we can do. Let's at least say good-bye with a toast." Victor lifted his glass, and everyone except Casey and Thomas raised theirs in agreement.

"On that note, I'm going to head back to my room and catch some z's. The baby woke up three times before my alarm went off at six this morning." Thomas stood and said good night.

Jordan watched him walk out of the bar thinking she wouldn't be far behind. Even though she didn't have a newborn to blame, she hadn't slept well at the hotel the night before. She'd use the restroom, then head to her room. She stood up, intending to head that way.

"I think Lola and I are going to call it a night, too," Ray said, helping his lady out of the booth. "We'll catch you in the morning."

To Jordan's surprise, the bathroom was huge compared to the small one in her and Rosie's stateroom where she could barely turn around without opening the door. She chose a stall in the far corner and went in, suddenly realizing she was even more tired than she'd previously thought. She had just taken a few deep breaths to keep from falling asleep when she heard the bathroom door open and familiar voices talking in hushed tones.

"We can't let anyone know about Stefano. Because of your little trick on the boat yesterday, everyone will automatically assume we had something to do with his death."

"I couldn't help myself. The jackass had his hand right over the hook trying to impress you after you reeled in that striper."

Jordan's hand flew to her mouth to cover a gasp: it was Marsha and Casey talking about what they'd done to Stefano. She blew out a silent breath, hoping they wouldn't discover she was in the back stall. Slowly moving closer to the door, she opened it just a tad to hear more clearly.

"I know, but we have to be smart. I'm going to take Beau back to the room and start working on him." Marsha cleared her throat. "Can you stay away from the room for a little while after we leave? Maybe have another drink or two? My guess is the man is probably as much of a dud in the dark as he is in broad daylight. I'm pretty confident this won't take long."

"Don't forget, he's a rich dud that we need right now if we're going to pull this off. One of us needs to win so we can split the cash."

"I know. Come on. Let's get back before he misses me. I swear, the man has three arms, and they're all over me."

Jordan stood behind the slightly opened door a few more minutes after she heard them leave. When she was sure she was alone, she exited the stall and washed her hands before sneaking out the door and walking over to the bar for a drink, just in case the two women saw her coming back to the table.

She couldn't wait to tell the gang what she'd heard.

"You sure you can handle one more drink, sugar?" Rosie asked.

Jordan nodded. "Where is everyone?"

"They all wimped out on us," Rosie said before yawning. "Actually, the idea of climbing into my soft bed is sounding better by the minute. Drink up and take me home, child. I'm too old for this crap."

Ordinarily Jordan laughed at just about everything

Rosie said, but this time she wasn't paying attention. She couldn't stop thinking about the conversation she'd overheard in the bathroom and what it could mean. Had Casey and Marsha teamed up to kill Stefano?

She glanced over at the table, noticing the two women and Beau were the only ones left. They'd just ordered another round of drinks, and a steward had arrived with a basket of fries and another of onion rings. As Jordan lifted her margarita for a sip, an idea popped into her head.

After setting her nearly full drink on the table, she grabbed Rosie's sleeve. "Come with me," she said before turning to the three remaining guests. "Well, we're off to bed, too. See you in the morning."

Casey gave them a nod as she stuffed an onion ring into her mouth. The other two didn't even bother to look up.

As soon as she and Rosie were outside the bar, Jordan repeated what she'd heard in the bathroom.

"Holy crap," Rosie said. "Those two conniving be-otches. We need to tell Ray what you heard."

"No. He's probably already sleeping, and we don't know for sure what they really meant about Stefano. It could be something insignificant."

"Like what?"

"No clue, but maybe it was just Casey taking advantage of the opportunity to get Stefano out of the competition." Jordan stopped suddenly, and Rosie followed suit. "Um!"

"Uh-oh," Rosie said suspiciously. "I know that look. Do I really want to know what's in that pretty little head of yours?"

Jordan narrowed her eyes. "I think we need to have a

peek in their room before we take this to Ray." She checked her watch. "Come on. Their room is right down the hall from ours. We've probably got a half hour before they finish with all that food and head this way."

"Brilliant idea, Einstein, but there's one major problem. How are we going to get in?"

Jordan grabbed Rosie's arm and made a 180-degree turn. "Somehow, we have to get the key."

CHAPTER 6

As soon as Jordan and Rosie reentered the bar, the waitress approached them to say the lounge would be closing in fifteen minutes and they'd already missed last call. After assuring her they would only be a few minutes, Jordan made eye contact with Rosie and cocked her head in the direction of the far corner.

Rosie started that way, and Jordan followed. Beau and Marsha were so caught up in an animated conversation, they didn't even look up until the two had plopped down in the empty chairs across from them. Casey was asleep with her head on the table and a half-empty drink in front of her. An earth-shattering snore caused her to jerk awake, but she quickly returned to whatever dream she was having.

Rosie reached for a cold French fry from the nearly empty basket. "So, it looks like you two are gonna be here for a while, right?" She pointed to the four full drinks in front of them.

Marsha laughed. "We've been talking about the cooking industry, and we lost track of time. Beau thought we needed reinforcements before they cut us off."

Cooking industry, my butt! "It looks like you need black coffee more than reinforcements," Jordan said, scanning the table for Marsha's or Casey's purse.

Initially disappointed when she didn't see one, she decided the women either hadn't brought their purses with them or had them on their laps. Either scenario was a dead end for her plan to learn more about the conversation she'd overheard in the restroom earlier. Then Jordan noticed Casey was using her black clutch as a pillow. Blowing out a frustrated breath, she scolded herself for thinking the hunt for clues would be easy.

"What brought you two back?" asked Beau, his words slurring and his glassy eyes obviously struggling to focus.

"No reason. We—"

"We wanted one last drink," Rosie interrupted. "Unfortunately, we're a little too late."

"Here," Beau said, sliding Casey's drink toward Rosie. "I don't think she'll miss it, do you?"

Casey chose that moment to lift her head and give them a drunken grin. It gave Jordan just enough time to edge the clutch out and shove a few wadded-up linen napkins in its place before the inebriated woman dropped her head back to the table.

"I was afraid the clasp might hurt her face," she explained when both Beau and Marsha shot her a questioning look.

Beau grinned before chugging the rest of his drink. "She wouldn't even notice. She's not feeling any pain right now. Probably won't until morning when that headache hits like a mother."

Nothing like the proverbial pot calling the kettle black.

Rosie cleared her throat, and Jordan looked up in time to see her point to Casey's purse. *Get the key,* she mouthed.

"So, Beau, tell me about your chocolate treats. I sure would kill to have one right now," Rosie said, in an obvious effort to distract the couple.

"Did you know Sinfully Sweet hit the international market this year?" He stretched across the table and slid one of Marsha's full drinks toward Rosie, even though she hadn't yet touched the cocktail he'd offered just a moment ago.

"Thank you. And yes, I did know the company was doing great. It was a brilliant move, but then again, I'm not surprised a smart, savvy guy like you pulled it off." She gave him one of her sultry looks, designed to bedazzle an unsuspecting male, while she lied through her teeth.

Sheesh! Rosie didn't have to lay it on that thick, Jordan thought as she maneuvered Casey's purse off the table and into her lap without detection. She unclasped the small black clutch and immediately found the keycard in a side pocket, along with a wrapped condom.

Pulling her hand out of the purse as if she had touched a lit match, Jordan wrinkled her nose. A condom? Casey had obviously started out the evening with big plans before drinking herself into a stupor.

But big plans with whom? Or maybe it was only a case

of the frumpy chef dipping into her old Girl Scout training and showing up prepared just in case she got lucky.

Jordan cleared her throat, and Rosie glanced her way. When Jordan nodded, the older woman shoved the drink back toward Marsha. "As much as I love talking to you two, I'd better mosey on up to my room and hit the sack. I just remembered I have to get up really early to cook tomorrow. Thanks, anyway." She motioned to Jordan. "Ready?"

They said their good-byes and headed out the door. Once they were in the hallway, they quickened their pace, nearly sprinting by the time they approached the elevator. Neither spoke during the ride down three levels to the deck where Marsha and Casey shared a room. Only after she'd pushed the stolen key into the lock and they'd entered did Jordan finally feel safe enough to breathe normally.

She'd never done anything like this before—unless you counted the time when she and her best girlfriend snuck into the nun's private kitchen back at Saint Anthony's and raided the refrigerator. Although she and her partner in crime hadn't been caught and had ended up with a fantastic plate of snickerdoodles, she knew in her heart she'd have to pay the price at the pearly gates over those cookies. Unfortunately, just like so many years before, Jordan's inner voice was screaming at her to get out before it was too late.

She wondered if the Gatekeeper was watching now.

"We've only got about ten minutes," Rosie said, bringing her back to the task at hand.

"Okay. Okay. I'll look through all the stuff on the table, and you rummage through the drawers."

Rosie nodded in agreement and moved directly to the

dresser. She sat on the bed and opened the first drawer. Before Jordan even made it to the table, she spied the box labeled with the Sinfully Sweet logo. Unable to resist, she took off the lid and let out a squeal at the site of huge chocolate brownies, each individually wrapped.

"Shh," Rosie cautioned.

"Sorry. Chocolate messes with my brain." She turned her attention back to the goodies. "So, Little Miss Hope-you-like-my-salmon Marsha did get the Kahlúa brownies, after all," she said, more to herself than to Rosie. "Wonder what she had to promise to get them."

"We don't have time for that, Jordan. Hurry," Rosie admonished.

Who doesn't have time for chocolate? Jordan thought as she unwrapped one of the brownies and shoved half of it into her mouth. The sensation she got from the Kahlúa and chocolate flavors was enough to send her over the edge.

"Jordan, hurry up."

Rosie's impatient voice caused her to jump, and she quickly popped the other half of the brownie into her mouth before opening the top file on the table. The file contained a lot of recipes but nothing that would implicate either Marsha or Casey in any wrongdoing in Stefano's death—assuming there even was a wrongdoing.

"Sweet Jesus!"

Jordan stopped chewing and spun toward Rosie, who was now holding up a small bottle and grinning like she'd just opened the right door on *Let's Make a Deal.*

"What is that?"

"You're not going to believe it, but I think it might be the smoking gun."

Jordan jumped up and ran over, reaching for the bottle. It was a small jar of cocktail peanuts. Before she had a chance to comment, she heard the unmistakable sound of voices trickling in from the hallway. It took only a second to recognize Marsha's sexy giggle. Jordan would bet money there was a follow-up hair flip and decided she could probably learn a thing or two about flirting from the petite chef.

The voices stopped momentarily, and Jordan stood perfectly still, holding her breath. Until she heard the click of the door as it opened.

Crap!

Her head snapped up at the same time as Rosie's, and she saw that the older woman looked as panicked as she herself felt.

"In there," she whispered, grabbing two more brownies before following Rosie into the small closet to the left of the two twin beds.

She pushed the sliding door almost shut at the exact moment that Marsha and Beau walked into view— "walked" being the disputable word in Beau's case. She wondered how a little thing like Marsha could hold up the entrepreneur's drunken six-foot frame.

"Come here, baby," he slurred.

Jordan swiveled toward Rosie and mouthed, *Sex alert*, before Rosie rolled her eyes.

"In time, love. Make yourself comfortable while I freshen up a bit," Marsha said in a deep, throaty voice. Her words were followed by a sound that Jordan could only assume came from a wet sloppy kiss.

"Don't take too long, you sexy thing. Big Beau is missing you already."

No, he did not just refer to himself as Big Beau.

Jordan clucked her tongue before Rosie shot her a disapproving glare and put her finger to her lips to shush her. For a few seconds the only other sound in the room was the faucet running in the bathroom—until Beau began to snore.

"The man is such a lover," Jordan whispered, handing Rosie one of the brownies before opening the other and taking a huge bite. She stopped chewing when she heard Marsha open the bathroom door.

For a few seconds, she held her breath, thinking Marsha might open the closet for a robe or something. Instead, she turned her back on Beau and stepped away from the bed. With her cell phone to her ear, she began to talk in a hushed tone and asked to speak to Casey. Jordan assumed the chef was still passed out at the lounge.

Like Beau could hear!

His obnoxious snoring shook the walls, reminding Jordan of the time she'd gone to a monster truck rally with Victor. The entire crowd had worn earplugs that night.

"I need you to get down here as fast as you can," Marsha said into the phone. "We have a problem. Beau's passed out on my bed, and we have to get him sobered up and back in his room before his wife misses him."

There was a pause before Marsha continued. "I told you not to worry about that. Nobody has any idea we were anywhere near the kitchen this afternoon, and unless you open your big mouth, no one will ever know. I made sure of it. Just get down here, so I don't have to explain this in the morning. That would totally blow our chances of splitting that prize money."

For several minutes after Marsha hung up, Jordan and Rosie stood in silence, afraid to move with Marsha so close. As Jordan tried to figure out how they could get out of the closet, she racked her brain for possible excuses why they would be in the closet in the first place. No matter how this night ended, the fact that she'd just over-heard Marsha admitting she and Casey had done some-thing in the kitchen before the competition was worth getting caught.

Deciding to face the consequences and then run straight to Ray to tell him what they'd heard, Jordan pushed the sliding door back and was surprised to find only Beau in the room. He was sprawled sideways across the bed and still snoring like a chainsaw. He could have passed for one of those big trucks himself, maybe even the brother of the famous Grave Digger, one of the more popular trucks on the circuit. She peeked around the corner and realized Marsha had gone back into the bathroom. After racing to the table for one last brownie, she tiptoed past the bath-room door with Rosie following close behind.

Quickly, she opened the door, and the two of them bolted down the corridor, passing a steward along the way who was carrying a tray with a pot of coffee and several cups. Beau's wake-up call, no doubt. By the time they made it to their own room, they were laughing out loud, celebrating their good fortune over not being caught by sharing the stolen brownie.

"Mmm. These could be my new solution to not having a boyfriend right now." Rosie licked her lips. "I guarantee I'll have this recipe figured out before we dock in Miami."

Jordan high-fived her friend. "And we didn't even have to entertain Big Beau like Marsha did."

That brought on another round of giggling as the two women got ready for bed.

"Rosie, are you thinking the same thing I am about what we heard Marsha say on the phone to Casey?"

Rosie climbed under the covers. "I'm trying not to think the worst, but it really did sound like maybe there was something going on before the competition." She sighed. "We need to tell Ray what we overheard."

Jordan shot up in the bed. "Are you crazy? Now that we've escaped that compromising position in the closet, I've reconsidered telling Ray what we just heard. We'd have to admit we stole Casey's key and broke into their room." She shook her head. "No way. Let's just keep our eyes and ears open until we have something more solid to go on before we go running to him with our suspicions."

"What about the peanuts I found in the drawer?"

Jordan thought for a moment. That one was not as easily explained, but she had to convince Rosie not to run to Ray just yet.

"You saw the way Casey can put away food. It's probably just something she brought with her for a late-night hunger attack." She blew out a breath. "Come on, Rosie. You know Ray will freak out when he finds out we've been breaking and entering. Let's wait awhile and see what happens. I promise we'll go to him the minute our own investigation uncovers something worth reporting."

"I hate to admit it, but you're probably right. I'm not in any mood to hear one of Ray's lectures."

"So, we agree? Starting tomorrow, you and I will be on the lookout for any clues that might indicate the women are up to something sinister," Jordan said, satisfied she had convinced her friend not to tell Ray just yet.

"Okay. It's probably just our overactive imaginations, anyway. We'll look like fools if it turns out there isn't anything suspicious to find."

Jordan narrowed her eyes. "Then why were those two sneaking around in the kitchen before the competition?"

CHAPTER 7

"Rosie, you have definitely outdone yourself," Jordan said, popping the last bite of lunch into her mouth before licking her lips. "No wonder so many readers raved about this recipe last week."

"Calling it Pollo de la Hacienda del Rey was genius," Lola commented, pushing her empty plate away. "That gives this mouthwatering Tex-Mex dish a little class. And if you ever decide to open up a real restaurant, it would jack up the price at least five bucks."

Rosie giggled. "When the Latinos realized that Pollo de la Hacienda del Rey was actually my aunt Lolly's famous King Ranch Chicken, they'd probably start another Spanish war." She stood before glancing up at the huge clock on the wall and plopping back down. "I should get back to the kitchen, but I can't resist sitting a little longer with you all. I'm sure the guys can handle it by themselves for another ten minutes or so."

Jordan turned to Victor as the waiter set a second plate with the fabulous casserole in front of him. "That was brilliant, my friend."

His fork stopped abruptly, midway to his opened mouth, and he swiveled to face her. "What was?"

"Your idea to make up fancy names for Rosie's recipes." Jordan checked out the heaping fork he held. There was no way he could get that much food into his mouth at one time. Was there?

Watching him shovel it in and add another forkful to the mix made her smile. The only person who wasn't entertained by his antics was his partner, who was watching with a scowl on his face.

She stole a quick peek at her watch. If this played out the way things normally did when the cute and chubby Victor ate too much, it would be only a matter of minutes before Michael mentioned for the umpteenth time that Victor was supposed to be watching his diet.

A few seconds later, Victor would fire back an expletive along with a thinly veiled sarcastic remark that it was a crying shame he wasn't perfect like Michael. Despite the barbs back and forth, everyone knew the two were devoted to each other.

Victor surprised her by totally ignoring his partner and speaking only to her. "That was rather brilliant, if I do say so myself," he said before wiping his face with the napkin. "Lord knows you would have been demoted back to writing just the personals if your editor knew the real story behind all those 'gourmet' recipes you print every week."

"Dwayne Egan didn't get all the way up the *Globe*'s chain of command by being stupid." Michael shook his head, apparently forgetting about Victor's eating habits for the moment. "He knows exactly what Jordan's doing, and he doesn't care. He sells more newspapers than he can count when Jordan's column hits the newsstands all over the—" He stopped when he noticed Victor eyeing the chocolate cake in the display case on the counter.

Victor waved down the nearest waiter. "Please tell me I'm looking at Rosie's German Chocolate Cake over there," he said when the waiter approached. When the young man nodded, he clapped his hands. "That's my favorite dessert."

"Sweetie, you might want to skip that since you're planning to spend the afternoon by the pool," Michael reminded him.

Unfazed by the remark, Victor smacked his lips. "I'll definitely have a piece of that, please." He surveyed the table. "Anyone else? My treat."

"Oh, you crazy fool. Nobody's buying that load of crap. The last time you sprang for anything was— actually, I don't think you've ever brought out your wallet and yelled 'Surprise!' " Lola teased.

Shrugging, Victor countered, "You have a point, my dear. Good thing all this wonderful food is free." He turned to the waiter patiently waiting. "Don't get stingy on my piece, please," he instructed, earning one of Michael's evil looks.

"Me, too," Jordan said. "And don't give him a bigger piece than me." She winked at the cute waiter, who smiled his appreciation.

After the waiter walked away, Victor whined, "No

fair. He's obviously more impressed by your wild red hair than my brilliant black eyes."

"All's fair . . ."

Chocolate was worth a little flirting, she thought, especially since she'd never been able to resist Rosie's German Chocolate Cake. Besides, tonight was the appetizer round of the cooking competition. Visions of crabmeat and oysters made her stomach turn. Give her a gigantic plate of Southwest egg rolls or ultimate nachos, and she was one happy camper, but she was pretty sure she wouldn't see either tonight. Better to play it smart and fill up on Rosie's food right now, because she'd probably starve later.

"Oh hell. Me, too," Lola said, calling after the waiter, who turned and nodded to acknowledge her order. Straightening her caftan over her stomach, she added, "There's a lot more room left under this thing."

"That a girl," Rosie said before she turned to Michael, a confused look on her face. "What was all that talk between Beau and your boss last night? Are they old friends?"

"Were," Michael said, leaning in to whisper. "Wayne said they were pretty tight in high school where they both played football, but he said Beau was a jerk even before he got so famous."

"That doesn't surprise me," Lola said. "A snake is a snake even after it sheds its skin."

"He's a snake, all right," Michael continued. "Wayne said he severed their friendship when Beau did something so nasty, even his popularity and good looks couldn't save him from public ridicule."

Everyone at the table inched closer.

"Don't stop now, sweetie," urged Victor. "Inquiring minds and all that."

Michael swept the room with his eyes before speaking. "I wouldn't want this to get out since Beau is a judge, but Wayne said he stole the recipe for his Sinfully Sweet goodies from a young girl back in high school."

"That makes him a jerk, but why would that be the talk of the town?" Lola asked, nearly lying across the table to hear better.

"Not that." Michael dropped his voice even lower. "Apparently, the girl was the daughter of a local minister and never dated. She was as homely as she was shy. Somehow, Beau slithered his way into her life and got her pregnant, then dumped her after she gave him her grandmother's recipes."

"Sheesh!" Jordan exclaimed. "Why am I not surprised? The guy's a piece of work."

"It gets worse. Apparently, the girl's father disowned her, and she wrapped her car around a pole one night. Wayne said she never came home from the hospital, and Beau didn't even send a card. Even laughed about it. After that, Wayne said he couldn't stomach the guy anymore."

"Then why did Wayne sign him on for this contest?"

Michael laughed. "It was Emily's idea. Wayne wanted so much for this first cook-off to go over big, he thought he could get past all the old stuff. Apparently, Beau agreed because he thought it might be advantageous to mingle with the A-list people in the food industry—aka, George Christakis. That and the fact he couldn't resist meeting a woman with more money than him."

"So Wayne put aside the fact that this guy is a serious

dirtbag and signed him on, all in the name of promo-
tion?" Rosie asked, shaking her head.

"Pretty much. Personally, I wonder if it was worth it,"
Michael said.

"Here you go." The waiter placed the dessert in front
of Victor, Jordan, and Lola.

And Rosie's cake didn't disappoint. As they dug into
the rich chocolate layers, Ray walked through the door
with a good-looking middle-aged man. When the two
sauntered over to the table, Jordan and her friends could
see the man had two black eyes and a large cut on his
forehead.

"Is that what I think it is?" Ray slid over two chairs
and sat down on one before motioning for the newcomer
to take the other.

"Yes, and it's going fast, so you'd better hurry. You
might even want to start with dessert today since what
you see is almost the last of it." Rosie waved to the waiter,
then took a moment to check out the man with Ray. "Do
you want to try a piece?"

"Absolutely."

His smile was enough to send a warm pink blush
across Rosie's cheeks, but the color deepened even further as he extended his hand across the table to her. "Jerry
Goosman, but all my friends call me Goose."

"Goose is head of security," Ray explained. "He and I
have been poring over yesterday's security tapes from the
kitchen."

Jordan shot a quick look Rosie's way, but the fiftyish
woman was checking out the new arrival, her hand still
in his.

"Where'd you get those shiners, Goose, if you don't mind me asking?" Victor moved in for a better look.

"Not at all. The night before we boarded the ship in Miami I was downtown on business and saw a young man getting roughed up by two hoodlums. This is what I got for stepping in, but at least I chased the thugs away before they could do too much damage to either of us."

Rosie's eyes sparkled. Goose's tale of heroism was like an aphrodisiac to her.

"See anything unusual on those tapes?" Jordan asked, hoping the tapes had captured Casey and Marsha in the kitchen before the contest.

Ray shook his head.

"Nothing?" she asked, remembering the conversation she'd overheard when she and Rosie were hiding in the closet in the lady chefs' room the night before. Marsha had actually admitted doing something sneaky in the kitchen before the competition.

"Nothing out of the ordinary," Goose answered.

"Goose, if Rosie can spare you for a few seconds, I'd like to introduce you to the rest of my friends," Ray said, a hint of irritation in his voice.

It was old news to everyone around the table that Rosie was like a block of metal to a magnet whenever a tall older man was around, especially if said tall older man wore a uniform. Although Goose was dressed in jeans and an orange and blue plaid button-down shirt, the fact he was a security officer put him front and center on Rosie's mental radar screen.

Jordan snuck a peek toward the security chief and noticed his left hand was ringless. With salt-and-pepper hair cut in a short conservative style and green eyes that crinkled when he smiled, Jerry Goosman was just the kind of man Rosie was attracted to.

Jordan smiled to herself, thinking she hadn't yet met a good-looking man her friend wasn't attracted to. Married four times—five if you counted her weekend-long remarriage to husband number three—Rosie knew her way around flirting. With her bleached blond hair pulled back into braids and her tie-dyed T-shirt that showed off a pretty good figure, she could have been a flower child from the seventies—and probably had been.

Jordan almost felt sorry for the security chief, knowing her friend was about to start her mating ritual, which usually began before the unsuspecting man had a chance to catch his breath. She hoped Goose was up for the challenge, because once Rosie had her mind set, nothing stopped her.

After introductions were made and the empty dessert plates cleared, Lola finally asked the question on everybody's mind. "So, Goose, are you married?"

His eyes darkened, and for a minute, Jordan thought he might tear up.

"Technically, I am," he admitted. "But it hasn't been a marriage for a long time now."

The smile on Rosie's face disappeared. "Please don't tell me your wife doesn't understand you."

Jordan made eye contact with Ray and braced herself for what she knew from experience would not be pleasant for the poor guy. Anyone who knew Rosie was aware that her pet peeve was infidelity, having been the victim of two womanizing husbands. Goose had just stepped on a live mine with blond braids and big blue eyes.

"Mary Alice was diagnosed with early onset Alzheimer's five years ago." He pointed to his chest. "After she bought me this God-awful shirt not once but twice in the same week, I knew something was terribly wrong. My wife was a schoolteacher and had the memory of an elephant, plus she hated plaid. I wore it then to please her and now because it reminds me of her." He tilted his head back as if to stop a falling tear. After a moment, he continued. "I took care of her at home for as long as I could, but when she nearly died after setting the house on fire, I knew we needed help."

The silence that followed proved no one had a clue how to respond.

Finally, Lola reached across the table and covered Goose's hand with hers. "I'm so sorry. I took care of my mother while she withered away from Alzheimer's. It's not an easy thing to watch."

Goose cleared his throat, and when he looked up, the heartbreak was all over his face. "It's been a year now since she was able to recognize me. I visit her every Saturday when the ship docks in Miami, but she has no idea who I am." He paused. "Calls me Daddy."

"I'm so sorry," Rosie echoed Lola's sentiments. "Where is your wife?"

Goose sniffed. "At first she was in a nursing home that accepted our insurance, but that was a nightmare. They put her in a ward with several other unfortunate souls who screamed half the night. Mary Alice still had moments of lucidity back then, and she begged me to take her home."

"Oh man, that must've been tough," Michael said.

"It was. I knew it was too dangerous to leave her at

home alone, but there was no way I could keep up the house payments without a job."

"So, what'd you do?" Michael asked.

By now everyone at the table was mesmerized by Jerry Goosman's story. Both Lola and Rosie looked like they were about to cry with him. In a matter of minutes the man had gone from a married man on the prowl to Saint Jerry taking care of his invalid wife.

"I found a great private home on the outskirts of Miami overlooking a man-made lake. It's run by a family whose own mother had Alzheimer's and a staff of seasoned, professional caregivers, so they know how to handle others with the same disease. Unfortunately, my insurance wouldn't pay for it. So, I sold our house and moved into a one-bedroom apartment. It's pretty crappy, but I'm never there anymore, anyway."

"I hate insurance companies," Victor said, shaking his head. "Last year I had to fight like a tiger to get a simple mole removed from the back of my neck. They said it was cosmetic surgery." He huffed. "Cosmetic surgery, my butt. I finally had to have one of my regular customers at the antique store pretend to be a lawyer and send a threatening letter." He touched the back of his neck and grinned. "I do look better without it, don't I?"

Lola shot him an are-you-seriously-comparing-a-mole-to-Alzheimer's look, and he quickly wiped the grin off his face. She might be old and a tad chubby, but the woman had a stare that could put the fear of God in anyone.

The awkward silence that ensued was mercifully interrupted a moment later by Emily's arrival.

"Looks like you're all here," she said when she approached. "Good, because we have to go over the details of tonight's competition. We need to make a decision about the best way to handle Stefano's death without making it the focus of the entire night."

No one responded. The men and women alike were entranced by Emily's striking appearance, the way her sleek sundress accentuated every curve of her chiseled body. There was definitely a personal trainer on her payroll. Even Victor was speechless, which was a miracle in itself.

The woman was a walking goddess, and she didn't even seem to notice that all eyes around the table were focused on her beauty, not her words. Jordan wondered what it would be like to be that gorgeous for just one day.

Ray stood and offered his seat before sliding over next to Lola and plopping down. The man knew his lady better than any of them did and had apparently decided even sitting next to the beautiful New Yorker might prove dangerous to his health.

"I heard the cruise line has decided to refund anyone who wants to leave tomorrow when we dock in Puerto Rico. Has anyone signed up yet?" Michael asked, unable to hide the anxiety in his voice.

Emily opened the file she'd brought with her. "We gave them two hours after we announced that the show would go on. That ended right before lunch with only three couples opting out. One was an older gentleman and his wife who had a bad case of seasickness. The other two didn't give reasons. At any rate, Wayne and I are relieved most of the people decided to stay on." She turned to face Michael. "Lighten up. Your boss and I will make sure this still turns out to be amazing."

"Emily, have you met Jerry Goosman? He's head of security," Ray said.

Goose shook her hand. "I've heard a lot about you. It's good to finally meet you."

Ray continued. "He's spearheading the onboard investigation into Stefano's death."

A look of panic crossed Emily's face. "Wayne told me you two didn't find anything when you checked the tapes from the kitchen."

Goose nodded. "So far we've found no evidence to indicate Stefano's death was anything more than a careless mistake. But as long as the ship is liable and can be slapped with another wrongful death suit, I'm obliged to continue the investigation until I can completely rule out foul play."

CHAPTER 8

Victor gasped. *"Another* wrongful death suit? You mean others have died suspiciously on this ship?"

"Relax," Ray said. "Goose was only referring to the legal issues when someone accidently gets hurt or drinks enough to drown a cow and ends up overboard. He wasn't talking about anything criminal, right, Goose?"

"That's correct, although last year a man was accused of pushing his wife overboard. The Miami cops took him into custody when we docked, but last I heard, they still hadn't found enough evidence to actually charge him with anything."

Victor swiped his hand across his forehead. "Whew! That's a relief. Note to self: don't drink and lean over the railing, especially after ticking off one of these ladies here."

The overacted display was enough to restore everyone's

good mood. For the next thirty minutes, Emily and the group laid out plans both for the evening's events and for addressing the issue of Stefano's death without allowing it to weigh down the spirit of the competition.

Finally, Rosie stood and shoved her chair back. "Oh, Lord. I lost track of the time. I need to get back to the kitchen and make sure things are in order for tomorrow's lunch."

"What will you be cooking?" Victor asked, licking his lips.

"Something new—stuffed cabbage rolls. I got the recipe from Meg, the skinny bartender down at Cowboys. She calls it Pigs in the Blanket."

Lola looked confused. "I thought that was sausage wrapped in a crescent roll."

"In Texas it is, but this gal hails from Pittsburgh and is as Yankee as it gets. Shoot, she even adds sugar to her cornbread. No self-respecting southern girl would ever be caught dead doing that." She huffed. "Anyway, she brought me a 'piggy' to try, and I'm here to tell you, it was the best damn thing I've tasted in a long time. She can call it whatever she wants, for all I care."

"Ooh, I can't wait to try it," Victor said, sending an I-dare-you-to-open-your-mouth look Michael's way. "You coming up to the pool later, Rosie?"

Her eyes twinkled with mischief. "While y'all are lying around in the sun, Luigi, the pastry chef, will be giving me a personal tour of the kitchen." She winked. "Just me, Luigi, and eight hundred sugar-filled treats."

"Ohmygod! You have to bring some back to our room," Jordan said, excited. "I'd give anything to have another one of those Kahlúa . . ."

She slammed her hand over her mouth as Rosie shot her a look, saying a silent prayer that no one had picked up on the slip. Victor, who usually never missed anything, especially if it was about food, tilted his head her way, his eyes questioning. She knew a little help from above wasn't in the cards today.

"Kahlúa what, Jordan?" he asked, his lips curled in a comical pout. "And why didn't I get one?"

Rosie faked a laugh. "Jordan didn't get one, either. Beau Lincoln hit on her last night and offered his famous brownies if she'd let him come to her room."

Jordan blew out a relieved breath. Thank goodness Rosie thought fast on her feet. Jordan herself had never been a good liar and was positive she couldn't have pulled it off. Even though, technically, Rosie hadn't lied.

"Are you serious? The man's loaded," Ray piped in. "If he wants to get friendly with our cute little redhead here, he'd better come up with a lot more than a brownie, especially since Rosie's awesome chocolate cake has set the bar pretty high."

"There isn't enough money in the world to convince me to play nice with that man. Besides, he tossed me aside like a dirty rag when he got a look at Marsha." Jordan scooted her chair back. "Who's going to the pool with me?"

"I am, even though I had that extra plate of food." Victor shot Michael a look, daring him to say something. When it was obvious his partner had no intentions of going down that road again, Victor shrugged. "You coming?"

Michael shook his head. "Can't. I'm having coffee with Wayne to go over tonight's details. Have fun, though, and don't forget to use sunscreen."

"Ray and I will be holed up all afternoon going over the rest of the security tapes," Goose said.

"That means I'm available," Lola chimed in. "Might as well get some use out of that new bathing suit since it cost an arm and a leg and doesn't cover either."

"I'd love to join you," Emily said. "If that's all right with everyone."

Oh, great! A visual of Emily in a drop-dead gorgeous bikini flashed through Jordan's head. But she said, "Of course," hoping the woman didn't pick up on the reluctance in her voice. She was already comparing her own black-and-white suit with a padded top to Emily's imagined skimpy one.

"Terrific. Let's say we meet in twenty minutes?"

"Sounds good." Jordan stood and said good-bye to her friends who were staying behind and then walked to the elevator with the others.

She had just enough time to freshen up before Victor and Lola showed up ready to go. Wondering what to say to a woman like Emily, she was thankful she wouldn't have to be alone with her. Giggling to herself, she imagined Victor talking her head off. He would have no problem making conversation with the rich, insanely gorgeous New York lawyer. Michael always teased he could carry on a conversation with a tree stump.

On the way up to the Lido Deck and the main pool, they chatted about the appetizer round of the cooking contest to be held later that evening. The heat of the sun hit them the moment they stepped out into the open, reminding Jordan once again to smear on the sunscreen. Emily was already at the far end of the pool and waved to them. They walked over to where she'd commandeered four chaise lounges in a coveted spot close to the bar.

"Come on, guys. Last one in has to buy drinks," Victor said, nearly knocking Jordan over to get past her to the pool.

Lola spread her towel on the chair and followed suit. "You two coming?" she asked before jumping in with a big splash.

When Lola resurfaced, Jordan replied, "I'll be in in a minute. I want to get really hot and sweaty first. It makes it so much better when the cold water hits."

"Good idea," Emily said, pulling off her cover-up and stretching out on the lounge chair.

Once again, all eyes were on her. Jordan's earlier thoughts of Emily in a bathing suit hadn't even come close to what she really looked like. In a bright navy and green bikini, Emily could have been one of the models in the annual *Sports Illustrated* Swimsuit Edition—no doubt, the cover. And just as before, the woman didn't seem to notice that everyone had stopped to stare.

Jordan spread her towel and lay down on the chair beside her. For a few minutes neither spoke, both amusing themselves by watching Victor's antics as he tried to do a handstand in the water.

"You are so lucky to have friends like that," Emily finally said, a hint of sadness in her voice. "I love them all already."

"I know," Jordan responded, silently counting her blessings. "What about your friends? Did any of them come with you on the cruise?"

Emily lowered her eyes. "I spend sixteen hours every

day at the office, and I still end up taking work home with me. Since I am OCD about working out at least an hour before I go to bed every night, it doesn't leave a whole lot of time to make friends, let alone keep up with them. I suppose that's why sponsoring this cruise was so appealing to me. At least here I have a few hours to myself, even though I spent all morning on the computer trying to fix a major problem back in New York."

"Are you a native New Yorker?" Jordan asked, feeling sorry for the woman, whose entire life revolved around work. Maybe being rich wasn't all it was cracked up to be.

"I grew up in the South and spent the better part of my young adulthood in Colombia."

"Wow! I'll bet that was fun. Were you an exchange student?"

For a second Jordan thought she saw anger flash in Emily's eyes before she smiled and said, "I was sent there to live with my aunt and her husband after my parents died in a car accident. They were missionaries and ran a local orphanage."

"I'm so sorry," Jordan replied, suddenly thanking her lucky stars that both her parents were not only still alive but also healthy and happy. She didn't know what she'd do if something happened to either of them.

"It wasn't so bad," Emily said, but Jordan couldn't help noticing the sadness in her eyes before she looked away and pointed across the pool. "Isn't that Casey over there?"

Jordan shot up and followed Emily's gaze. Dressed in an oversized man's shirt and the same capris she'd had on at the bar the night before, Casey Washington was holding hands with an equally dumpy-looking man: none other than Thomas Collingsworth. From the way Casey was brushing against him and hanging on his every word, Jordan had no doubt this guy was the reason for the precautions she'd found in Casey's purse the night before.

Hearing Victor call out to them, Thomas turned to face the pool. Dressed in tight-fitting trunks that only emphasized his overlapping belly, the man froze when he recognized Victor and the others.

"What's Casey Washington doing getting up close and personal with Thomas Collingsworth? Isn't he married?" Emily asked.

Not only was Collingsworth married, his wife had just had their first child. He'd even missed the fishing trip so he could stay in Texas to be with her.

How much sleazier could he get?

Guess he'd decided if the cat's away . . .

Jordan continued to stare, her mind racing with the implications. Something was clearly going on between Casey and Thomas Collingsworth, but was it just an affair? Could the cheating jerk also be involved in whatever had triggered Casey and Marsha's trip to the kitchen before the competition?

She gasped, suddenly remembering that Thomas Collingsworth was the only one who had known about Stefano's allergy to peanuts.

Yet he hadn't said a word last night when Stefano was fighting for his life and taking his last breath.

CHAPTER 9

The theater was already near standing-room-only capacity when Jordan and Rosie walked in. There must have been close to three thousand people in attendance, anxiously awaiting the first round of the cook-off competition. On stage, a five-man band had the crowd on its feet and clapping in time to "Margaritaville," sung by a guy Jordan recognized as the cute Croatian waiter from Rosie's restaurant. She thought about what she'd do if her job required multitasking like the ship's crew, but she came up empty. Carrying a tune was not one of her talents and was restricted to the shower and an occasional karaoke bar. And even then only after everyone was well on their way to a good buzz.

Now, if they needed a really good quarterback . . .

"Over here," Victor called from the front row.

Both Jordan and Rosie scrambled over to where Victor

and Lola had saved every seat on the front row of the section to the right of the stage. Ray and his new best friend, Goose, arrived at the same time as the women and settled next to Lola.

"So what are they cooking tonight?" Ray asked.

"Appetizers," Jordan responded, wrinkling her nose. "And I have a pretty good hunch it won't be jalapeño poppers or a bloomin' onion. I hope I can get through tonight without making a complete idiot of myself."

Rosie patted her arm before ungracefully plopping into the seat next to Victor. "Here's what to do, honey. Make sure you keep the napkin on your lap at all times. Take the smallest bite you can get away with and slide it to the side of your mouth by your molars. Then smile sweetly and give it a fake chew. When no one is looking, wipe your mouth and spit it out."

Jordan sighed. "But how can I judge anything if I do that?"

"Oh, please," Victor interjected. "Do you really think anybody's counting on your gourmet critique? Or Beau's, for that matter?" He shook his head. "Seriously? A fudge maker and a clueless cook with her own column?"

Rosie playfully slapped his arm. "You have such a way with words, you moron." She studied Jordan's face, concern in her eyes.

But Jordan was giggling. She loved Victor and his filterless opinions.

"I was only trying to make her feel better," he said defensively. "With the legendary George Christakis up there tasting the food, nobody gives a hoot about anyone else's opinion. If Georgie says it's good, it's good." He pointed at the steps where the world-renowned chef was making his way onto the stage. "He's like the Brett Favre of gourmet cooking—even makes an appearance on *The Biggest Loser* every season."

"I didn't know you watched that show, Victor," Lola said, leaning around him to wave to Jordan and Rosie. "It's one of my favorites."

Victor's eyes lit up. "I love that show, although Michael says everyone could lose weight if the only thing they did all day was exercise and eat ground turkey."

"He's right," Lola replied. "But it's more than that. The contestants work through their self-esteem issues, and they learn how to make healthier choices."

"Jordan!"

Hearing her name, Jordan peered up at the stage and saw Michael peeking out from the edge of the curtain. He motioned for her to come up.

"Gotta go," she said, rising from the seat with a sigh. It would be so much more fun if she could watch the competition with her friends, but this cruise didn't come cheap, and she had to earn her keep.

As she walked up the steps, the band finished up and the crowd roared its approval. She reached for the curtain, which was even more gorgeous up close. The rich, red velvety material with vertical strands of gold thread weaved throughout sparkled under the overhead theatrical lights. She was positive it must have cost a pretty penny, just like everything else on the ship.

It wasn't called the *Carnation Queen* for nothing and sported some of the most gorgeous furnishings she'd ever seen. And even though she was hired help, so far, she'd been treated like royalty by every one of the crew members, who hailed from countries all over the world.

"Hurry up," Michael called out when she squeezed behind the curtain.

Catching her breath after her first glimpse of the stage, she took a moment to study it further. Just like the night of the elimination round, it had been transformed into a gigantic kitchen for the competition. Eight coolers surrounded a huge table overflowing with vegetables and fruits. Another table was lined with spices, liquors, and eight bags of marshmallows. Visions of gourmet s'mores popped into her head, which immediately lifted her spirits. Maybe she could get through this, after all.

"What's with the grin?" Michael asked, taking hold of her arm and leading her over to the judges' table where George Christakis and Beau were already seated.

"I'm thinking this could turn out to be fun," she admitted, now picturing herself dipping a hunk of banana into Rosie's Amaretto Fruit Dip with the creamy marshmallows.

When they approached, Christakis gave her a tiny salute. Beau, who looked like he could have passed as the poster child for the popular Texas saying "Rode hard and put away wet," didn't even bother to glance up.

I've been crossed off his hanky-panky list, Jordan thought. *What a shame.*

Taking her seat between the two men, she wondered if the sweets maker felt as bad as he looked. She seriously hoped he did. She'd never liked cheating men, no matter how much chocolate came with the deal. When Beau raised his head and a soft groan escaped his lips, she smiled to herself, confident he had a huge headache to go with the rest of his hangover.

The five chefs were walking onto the stage and making

their way to their cooking stations, which consisted of a double electric stovetop. Overhead mirrors above each station would allow the audience to watch every step of the food preparation. On the way to his station in the back, Thomas lightly touched Casey's shoulder and was rewarded with a half smile. If Jordan hadn't already suspected something was going on between the two of them, she would have dismissed it as an innocent exchange between competitors.

But Jordan knew it was more than that and squinted across the stage to roll her eyes at Michael, who had heard the story of the two chefs walking hand in hand around the pool from Victor and responded with a nod. Her attention was quickly diverted when Emily walked onto the stage, dressed in a bright yellow sleeveless dress that showed off every curve to perfection.

And she had a lot of them.

"Get ready, folks. The curtain's going up in five minutes." She waved to Jordan and mouthed, *See you later?*

Jordan nodded. As much as she wanted to hate the woman for looking the way she did, she couldn't. Poolside, Emily had confided she didn't make friends easily— had blamed it on working too many hours. Jordan had been flattered when Emily made it clear she'd like to get to know her better. Although Jordan loved the Empire Apartments gang like her own family, it would be nice to have a girlfriend her own age aboard.

Microphone in hand, Michael walked to the center of the stage to address the crowd. "Ladies and gentlemen, it's time to begin the appetizer round of the Caribbean Cook-Off. At the end of the cruise, one of these five chefs will walk away with a contract worth a half million dollars as the spokesperson for Classic Cuisine, Inc. Join me in welcoming our sponsors, Emily Thorpe, owner and CEO of Entertainment and Talent Incorporated in New York, and Wayne Francis, owner and manager of KTLK, the best talk radio station south of the Red River."

The crowd went crazy as the curtain was raised, and for a moment, Jordan imagined herself at Cowboys Stadium right after the national anthem. She let her anxieties slip away with the excitement, deciding to go with the flow. But just in case things got dicey, she reached for her napkin and placed it in her lap per Rosie's instructions. A girl had to be prepared for the worst.

"Welcome, everyone," Emily began when the crowd finally quieted down. "With tonight's competition the hunt is officially on for the best chef among these five worthy competitors who were handpicked from all over the state of Texas. We're so glad you chose to stay with us after the unfortunate incident last night. We promise you won't be sorry you did. Now, let's get on with tonight's competition featuring appetizers." She paused, turning slightly as the crowd acknowledged the chefs with another rousing round of applause.

"Before we get started, I'd like to introduce you again to our chefs and give you a little background on each," she said when the noise died down.

For the next ten minutes Emily reintroduced the competitors to the crowd; then she waved her arm toward the judges' table. "Now, let's meet the three people with the difficult job of picking the best chef. Please give a warm *Carnation Queen* welcome to my friend and celebrity chef, George Christakis."

For what seemed like a good five minutes, the

audience showed their appreciation. Beau and Jordan were introduced to a shorter but no less enthusiastic welcome.

Moving back to the front, Emily walked over to Casey's station. "Tonight, our chefs will be preparing an appetizer of their choice within a thirty-minute time limit. Along with their favorite main ingredients, each will be provided with a basket with four ingredients that they must include in their dish." She opened the basket and pulled out a jalapeño pepper and a bottle of cayenne pepper. "Being from Texas, you all know, the spicier the better," she explained.

Reaching in again, she came out with a small bottle of honey and a huge mango. "As I mentioned, every one of these four items must be included in the dish. So, without further ado, let's get started." She raised her arm in the air and brought it down as a signal to the person operating the overhead countdown clock. "Chefs, get ready. Start cooking now."

The stage erupted in activity as the contestants ran back and forth between the tables in the back and their workstations, gathering their ingredients. For the next half hour, the aroma of cooking food permeated the entire theater. Jordan took the time to chat with George Christakis, deciding she liked the man, who seemed utterly indifferent to his own celebrity status. She discovered he had a partner and a school-age son back in New York and was a huge Giants fan. Despite that last fact— the Giants were one of the biggest competitors of her beloved Cowboys—she greatly enjoyed the chat.

Finally, the overhead clock signaled time was up, and the chefs stepped away from their stations, hands in the air to show they had stopped cooking, finished or not. Emily had been moving from station to station and chatting with the contestants about their dishes the entire time. Now she announced that each chef would explain their entry to the judges and then wait for the critique and the score.

Jordan swallowed hard and looked out to her friends for courage. Seeing Rosie giving her a thumbs-up helped a little. She took a deep breath and let it out slowly. She was about to find out what kind of acting skills she possessed.

She said a quick prayer to Saint Jude, the patron saint of hopeless cases, just in case she came up short.

CHAPTER 10

Casey was first to approach the table carrying three small plates, which she set in front of Jordan and the other judges. Four stewards dressed in freshly starched white uniforms passed out her plated appetizer to the tasters in the front row of the middle section of the theater. A quick glance at Casey's entry told Jordan all she needed to know. This one would end up in her napkin. She fought to keep the plastic smile on her face.

Mentally high-fiving herself for pretending to look excited about the small brownish blob on her plate, Jordan was soon brought back to reality as the smell wafted up. Quickly, she placed her napkin over her mouth and nose. She didn't need to hear Casey's description of her entry to know she'd never be sharing this concoction over margaritas with friends. All the same, she nearly gagged when Casey described her Chicken Liver Pâté, Southwest Style.

No way 'chicken liver' and 'Southwest' should ever be uttered in the same sentence, Jordan thought.

No God-fearing Texas cowboy would even consider putting this stuff anywhere near his mouth. It ranked right up there with cow patties, in Jordan's book, and it was a certainty this one would end up in her napkin. She snuck a peek Beau's way and eyed his napkin in case she needed a clean one for her nose when the others presented their dishes. He was so intent on eyeing up Marsha, he didn't even notice when she discreetly slid his over and onto her lap in one swift movement.

When she saw George tasting the pâté, she took a deep breath before sectioning off a tiny portion with her fork. Then she shoved it into her mouth, sliding it over to the corner just as Rosie had instructed and holding her breath at the same time so the smell didn't do her in. After pretending to chew for a moment, she touched the napkin to her lips as daintily as she could and spit out the liver.

Yuck! She reached for her water glass and took a big drink to wash any residual liver gunk out of her mouth.

"Okay, judges," Emily said, moving swiftly to the table. "Tell us what you thought about our first entry. You have five cards in front of you with each contestant's name. Please rate the dish on a scale of one to five, using creativity, presentation, and taste as the criteria."

Jordan reached for the card with Casey's name and quickly scrawled a 3 on it. She figured going the middle of the road would neither hurt nor help Casey. The only real score would come from Christakis, as Victor had so delicately put it.

"George, what did you think about Casey's dish?" Emily asked, moving first to her friend.

Christakis held up his card, showing a large 3. "As much as I adore chicken livers, they should never be used with peppers and honey."

My thoughts exactly! Jordan bit her lip to hide her glee. Maybe she didn't suck as a judge, after all.

"In my opinion, Casey would have been better served using a chicken wing or even a thigh to go with her required ingredients. That said, it didn't taste bad, but it did taste like she simply threw the ingredients together without blending the flavors."

Jordan cast a glance at Casey and noticed the anger radiating from her eyes and her pursed lips. She was glad the woman didn't have a sharp fishing hook in her hand right now.

"Jordan, what did you think?"

She swallowed the lump in her throat. This was make-or-break time for her.

"I actually thought exactly the same thing as George. Although it had a good flavor, I can't imagine any of my cowboy friends trying this one, nor can I picture gourmet cooks out there preparing it. It's too fancy for one and not fancy enough for the other."

She deliberately avoided eye contact with Casey as she held up her card, again giving thanks that the chef didn't have a sharp instrument in her hands. Something about this woman scared her. Maybe because Jordan had seen her in action on the fishing boat and then overheard her self-incriminating conversations with Marsha.

When it was Beau's turn to evaluate Casey, he gave her a 4.5 and mumbled something about liver with a spicy flavor starting a new trend.

Yeah, a trend with you buttering up Marsha's friend

so you can play house with Marsha right under your wife's nose.

As Emily once again strolled over to center stage, Casey walked back to her station with a half smile on her face. She probably thought the decent score from Beau would keep her in the game.

Next, Luis brought his dish to the judges, and Jordan sighed in relief. Warm Mushroom Salad with poached egg and spicy mango vinaigrette. Although the name brought up images of food she'd never order anywhere, Jordan was able to swallow the bite she took, thinking it wasn't half bad.

George Christakis gave the dish high praise and rated it a 4, as did Jordan, leaving Luis poised to walk away with high marks.

Until Beau gave it a 2.5, complaining that the lettuce was soggy. Jordan couldn't help wonder what was up with that, especially when she saw the look that crossed between the two men before Luis turned and walked back to his station.

Phillip's entry was Seared Scallops with Mango Salsa, which Jordan was also able to get down. She'd never had scallops before and probably would never order them from a menu, but at least they didn't end up in her napkin. With George's 4, her own 4, and Beau's 3, Phillip had the winning entry so far. Jordan relaxed in her chair, thinking this was way easier than she'd expected.

Until Thomas set his entry in front of her.

"Pan-Seared Sweet and Spicy Salmon Bites with a Diced Jalapeño and Mango Salsa," he announced, obviously proud of his creation.

Once again, Jordan was pretty sure this one would

never find its way to her stomach since she preferred her fish with a heavy cornbread batter, but she was willing to give it a try. "Pan seared" meant not totally cooked, in her book. She convinced herself that if she stared really hard at it, the fish would jump off the plate. She prepared her palate for the worst as she placed a small portion in her mouth. All her good intentions to at least give it a chance went out the window, and she couldn't even pretend to chew before she dabbed her mouth with her napkin and spit it out.

Unable to stop the shudder that followed, she hoped no one had seen it or, God forbid, that Casey's pâté didn't fall from the napkin and expose her for the fraud that she was.

After George's 4.5 and her 2.5, it was Beau's turn to evaluate the dish. Before he flashed his card, he narrowed his eyes and smirked.

"Salmon done right is my favorite fish. This one, however, was done so totally wrong, it was barely palatable." He held up the sign with a 2.

Anger flashed across Thomas's face before he inhaled noisily and turned on his heel without a word. Apparently he thought killing Beau on the spot would not be his smartest move. Jordan almost felt the need to warn Beau to be on the lookout for some sort of retaliation. She'd seen the same look on her brothers' faces when they'd been dissed, and each time someone had paid a price when they least expected it.

As Thomas made his way back to his station, Emily stepped up to the mic. "As you can see, this contest is far from being over. So far, we have Phillip at the top with an 11, followed by Luis and Casey with 10.5 each, and Thomas close behind with 9. It's anybody's guess who will walk away a winner and who will walk away period. Remember the contestant with the lowest score is eliminated. So, let's see what our final contestant has to offer." She pointed to Marsha. "Show us what you've created."

Marsha picked up the three plates and brought them over to the judges' table, walking first to Beau. As she set the plate in front of him, she licked her lips seductively.

Give me a break! That ought to get her a penalty for unsportsmanlike conduct, Jordan thought.

"Hope you like this. I made it special just for you tonight. It's sweetbread with a dipping sauce made from pureed jalapeños, honey, and mangoes." She placed the other two dishes in front of Jordan and Christakis.

Jordan almost felt sorry for Beau when Marsha turned again and zeroed in on him. She hoped his wife was far enough away that she couldn't see the silent conversation between the two of them or the way Marsha made sure her leg made contact with his before she turned back to position herself in front of all the judges. Trophy wife or not, no red-blooded female would be able to tolerate being humiliated in front of the huge crowd by the obvious mating ritual going on between those two.

Thomas's wrath would be child's play compared to the rage of a scorned diva.

Glancing down at the appetizer, Jordan was surprised to see that it resembled a chicken nugget. So far she'd made it through four of the appetizers without making a complete fool of herself. She was pleased to see that the last entry might be something she actually enjoyed.

Reaching for one of the chunks, she dipped it into the sauce. As soon as she popped the morsel into her mouth, she let out a relieved breath. Although it didn't taste exactly like a chicken nugget, it was close enough that she was ready to declare Marsha and her sweetbread the over-all winner.

She ate the other two chunks, pleased with herself for having survived the evening. With her lips still burning from the jalapeño dip, she wiped her mouth with the clean napkin, then pushed the plate to the side. Choosing the scorecard with Marsha's name, she scribbled a big 4.5, taking off half a point for the sauce. If it had been served with a nice avocado ranch or a creamy honey mustard dip on the side, she would have given it a perfect score.

"It looks like we're ready to hear the judges' decision," Emily said, moving to stand beside Marsha. "This is the all-important vote where we find out who is eliminated tonight and who wins and gets an advantage in tomorrow night's competition. Judges?"

Somehow Marsha had managed to open the top button of her purple sweater. Even though most of her chest was covered by the apron, a tiny bit of her ample cleavage peeked through. A visual designed to get the judges' attention, which it definitely had. Poor Beau was nearly foaming at the mouth.

What was it about men and boobs?

"George, what did you think of Marsha's sweetbread?" Emily asked.

Christakis eyed her for a moment, glancing once toward Beau, making Jordan wonder if he knew some-thing was going on between him and Marsha. Then he held up the card with a large 3 scribbled on it. For a min-ute, Jordan thought the audible gasp had come from her, but then she realized it had actually been Marsha, who was now staring at Christakis in disbelief.

"Although I love sweetbread and I appreciate the rich white sauce you made, I found the glands to be over-cooked and gristly. It would have worked so much better if you had spent a little more time sautéing them rather than frying them in the oil."

Glands? Jordan squeezed her eyes closed, grabbed the napkin, and spit into it, but the morsels were long gone. Catching her breath, she looked up to see that everyone was staring, and she felt heat crawl up her cheeks.

"You cooked glands?" Her eyes begged Marsha to deny it.

"Yes. It's one of my favorite appetizers."

Jordan took several deep breaths in a row, hoping to push back the lump in her throat threatening to ruin her debut as a cooking judge. "What kind of glands?" she whispered, so low that only those close to her could hear.

Christakis twisted in his chair to face her, laughter in his eyes. "The thymus gland. What did you think sweet-bread was?"

There was no way she'd admit she thought she had eaten chunks of fried chicken. "I figured it was glands, but I wasn't sure what kind," she lied.

Mentally, she slapped her head for the lame response. She knew it was glands but didn't know what kind?

Crap!

This time Christakis couldn't hide his glee and bit his lips in a futile attempt to keep from showing it.

And what in God's name was a thymus gland, anyway?

"The gland is located in the neck vertebrae area of a young calf," Christakis said, as if he had just read her mind.

"Don't keep us waiting, Jordan," Emily interrupted. "How did you rate Marsha's sweetbread?"

Jordan searched the audience, trying to figure out some way to telepathically change her card. Victor was laughing so hard, he was doubled over. Even Lola, who was the most empathetic of the group, was smiling. There was nothing to do but show her score. The audience went wild when she held up the card.

"I gave her a 4.5. Congratulations, Marsha. I really liked your dish." She reached for her water glass and chugged it, hoping to drown the little thymus glands floating in her stomach. She was positive they were down there plotting revenge on her for having eaten them. But this time even the water didn't take the taste out of her mouth, and she swallowed several times to keep from gagging.

Feeling a tap on her pants leg under the table, she reached down and made contact with Christakis's hand. Discreetly, he passed something to her. When she realized it was a mint, she glanced up at him to see him wink.

"I threw up all over myself the first time I ate sweetbread," he whispered, before turning back to Emily as if nothing had happened.

"So, Beau, right now Phillip is in the lead with eleven points. With George's and Jordan's score, Marsha has 7.5. If you give her higher than 3.5, she'll win tonight's competition. Show us your card."

Beau did a complete scan of Marsha's body before finally settling on her face. Jordan could feel the sexual tension from where she sat and wondered if the intense stage lights had anything to do with the heat between the two of them.

Beau cleared his throat. "I found her sweetbread to be cooked just the way I like it, and I thought the mango dip added a distinct Caribbean flavor along with the wonderful Southwest touch to cut the sweetness. For that reason, I gave her a 5." He held up the card, and the crowd erupted in applause.

"Congratulations, Marsha. Besides winning five thousand dollars tonight, you've also earned an added advantage. In the next round of the competition you'll all be cooking scrumptious desserts, and Marsha, you'll get to specify first the dessert you'd like to prepare. That main ingredient in your selection will no longer be available to any of the other contestants. If you know that one of your competitors has a specialty using a certain ingredient— say, chocolate—it could really be to your advantage to take that choice away from them. Think about it, and then give us your decision tomorrow night." She turned to Thomas. "Unfortunately, with the lowest score, Thomas, you are eliminated from the competition."

Emily turned back to the crowd. "That concludes tonight's competition. Tomorrow morning we dock in Puerto Rico for ten hours. There are still several openings available for the land excursions, but if you prefer to tour the island on your own, have a great time. We'll see you back here on Thursday at eight p.m. for the next leg of the contest."

Beau stood and walked over to Marsha's station to congratulate her.

"The man is so transparent," George observed, almost in a whisper.

"I know," Jordan replied, wondering if that's why he'd given Marsha a low score himself. Was it because he knew in all likelihood that Beau would give her a high score? Or was it simply because he didn't particularly like the way she'd cooked the sweetbread, as he'd mentioned?

"Thanks for the mint," she said, deciding she definitely liked this man, no matter the reason he'd given Marsha the low score.

"Jordan, I nearly wet my pants when I saw the look on your face when you found out you had just eaten calf glands."

She was never so glad to see Victor and the gang running toward her, along with the twenty-five tasters now flooding the stage to talk to the contestants. It meant they could say their good nights and head up to the Lido Deck grill for a nice big chili dog, overflowing with mustard and onions.

"What can I say? They tasted like Chicken McNuggets," she said, giggling. But chicken nuggets or not, she was looking forward to taking the taste out of her mouth permanently. The sooner they got to the Lido Deck grill, the better.

"Jordan, are you going to introduce us to your friend?" Lola asked, coming up behind Victor. She shoved her hand toward George Christakis, obviously deciding not to wait on formalities. "I'm Lola Van Horn, Mr. Christakis, and I'm a huge fan of yours."

George reached for her hand and brought it to his lips. "And I've been told I can't leave the ship without one of your fabulous tarot card readings, Ms. Van Horn."

"Call me Lola, and I'm absolutely looking forward to finding out what my cards say about you. I'm giving a class on Friday when we're at sea, but I'd be happy to come to your room and do a private reading for you anytime."

Ray squeezed between Lola and George. "Ray Varga," he said, extending his hand. "I'll be coming with her for that private room thing."

George threw back his head and laughed. "As adorable as your lady is, Mr. Varga, I can assure you she will be safe with me."

"It's Ray," he advised, then winked. "I'm still coming with her, just the same."

Before George could respond, Jordan heard Victor exclaim, "Sweet Jesus." She turned toward the middle of the stage just in time to see Charlese Lincoln, all decked out in diamonds and emeralds as if she were at a gala instead of a cooking competition, hotfooting it directly toward her husband as fast as her high heels would allow. Beau, who was falling all over Marsha, had no clue his wife was now standing behind him taking it all in.

Marsha's eyes widened in surprise as she tried to warn him, but he was so busy flirting that he either chose to ignore his wife or he didn't realize how angry she could get.

Until it was too late.

He jerked around when Charlese cleared her throat, his flirty grin quickly changing to sheer panic.

"Lambkins," he cooed. "Have you met—"

"Don't Lambkins me, you horse's ass. Did you think I couldn't see you making all over this slut on stage?"

She turned her angry eyes on Marsha, her hateful expression reminding Jordan of the possessed girl in *The Exorcist*. She half expected the woman's head to spin around like Linda Blair's.

In a singular motion, Charlese reared back her hand and slapped Marsha across the face, causing an ugly red mark to sprout on the surprised chef's cheek.

"Next time you decide to sleep with someone else's husband, you'd better make damn sure it's not mine, or I'll kill you myself with my bare hands, you skank," she slurred.

Marsha, who had now recovered nicely from the assault, narrowed her eyes. "Bring it on."

Even from far away, Jordan knew Charlese's breath probably reeked of liquor, and she imagined the woman would put up a pretty good fight if it came down to it. But she'd lay odds Marsha Davenport would come out the winner if that scuffle ever materialized.

Little Miss Token Wife had no idea the woman she had just called a skank might very well be a killer.

CHAPTER 11

Beau pulled on his wife's arm and dragged her away from Marsha's station, just as Casey appeared beside her friend, arms on her hips and, apparently, ready to jump into the middle of the squabble, if necessary.

"Nothing like a good catfight to make me ravenous," Victor whispered. "Come on. I'm starving. Let's get out of here before they kill each other."

Jordan could have kissed him right there on the spot. At that moment, she wanted nothing more than to be taken away from all the drama. "Let me find Emily and tell her we'll meet up with her at the grill."

"She's coming again?" Victor scrunched up his nose as if he had just gotten a whiff of something rotten, like a bad egg.

Surprised by his comment, Jordan narrowed her eyes in question. "I thought you liked her."

He shook his head. "She's okay, I guess. It's just that she's always with us. I haven't had two minutes alone with you to talk bad about everybody on the ship. You know how much I love to do that."

Jordan patted his shoulder. "Ah, how sweet. You miss me." She stole a look toward Emily, who was in an animated conversation with her friend George. "Let me tell her we're going, and then we'll sneak out of here before the rest of the gang. I'll even let you buy me a margarita."

"Ha! I knew there was a catch." He winked. "You have no idea how much I hate it that Emily's prettier than me. That's the real issue here."

Jordan laughed out loud. "Join the club. She's prettier than all of us, but she'll never be the friend that you are to me."

His eyes lit up. "Hurry up and tell her we're leaving. I have a million things to talk about." He did a three-sixty. "And what's up with that ugly rug on that obnoxious chunky dude over there?"

Jordan's eyes followed his and settled on one of the tasters who had flocked to the stage. The overweight middle-aged man was so busy sneaking tastes of all the leftover food that he was unaware his toupee had shifted.

"Oh, yeah," Jordan said, winking. "It gives a whole new meaning to getting your head on straight." She kissed Victor on the forehead. "I've missed you, too, my friend, and I'm looking forward to hearing your snide remarks about everyone on board. Just give me a minute to say my good-byes."

She turned and headed back toward Michael to make sure he didn't need her for anything else. Next, she told Emily they'd meet her on the Lido Deck, and then she and Victor quietly exited the stage. They walked to the elevator, giggling like two schoolkids who had just gotten away with playing hooky.

Two chili dogs later, Victor was back to his old self again. By the time the rest of the gang showed up, they were on their second margarita, and the bad taste in Jordan's mouth from the sweetbreads had finally disappeared.

Settling back in her chair, Jordan watched her friends chow down. She didn't need Emily—who still had not arrived—to tell her how lucky she was to have them in her life.

Thinking about Emily, she stole a glimpse at the elevator in the middle of the ship, wondering what had happened to her. She'd said she wanted to chat a little longer with George before joining them, but it had been a good thirty minutes since the competition ended and Beau and his wife had stomped off to their room. Jordan figured she must have lost track of time talking with her old friend and secretly hoped he'd be with her when she finally did show up. George Christakis was someone she'd like to get to know better, especially after the mint thing.

Out of the corner of her eye, she spied Thomas Collingsworth alone at the bar.

"Be back in a sec," she said, getting up and strolling that way.

It seemed like the perfect opportunity to do a little snooping. She hadn't pegged Thomas as the brightest bulb on the tree, and she hoped that maybe without Marsha and Casey around, she could get him to slip up and say something he shouldn't.

After sliding onto the bar stool beside him, she motioned

to the waiter. Thomas finally looked up when he heard her order a margarita, his face showing his surprise at seeing her there.

"Hey there, sorry about tonight," she began, hoping to break the ice. The man looked like he'd just been told his dog died.

"Thanks," he mumbled before holding his empty glass up to signal for a refill.

Okay, this was not going to be easy. Obviously, he wasn't the most social butterfly on the ship, either, keeping to himself most of the time. That was why his cavorting with Casey when his wife had just given birth to their newborn son seemed so out of character for him. Maybe if she got him talking about food, he'd loosen up.

"Is salmon one of your favorite appetizers?"

"Not really."

Help me out here, Tommy boy. This is like pulling teeth. She decided to go straight to the heart of the matter.

"So, have you and Casey been friends long?"

If she'd wanted a reaction, she definitely got one. His head shot up and he glared at her.

"Don't go judging me when you don't know the whole story." He slurred the words, challenging her with his eyes.

That was more like it. "Who said I was judging you, Thomas? Far be it for me to throw the first stone. I was only asking because you two seem so . . . chummy."

"My relationship with Casey, or anyone else for that matter, is none of your business. Until you've walked in my shoes, you can't know how I feel." He turned back to his drink, effectively ending any further conversation.

But Jordan hadn't graduated at the top of her journalism class for nothing. Her ex had always said she could sweet-talk the best of them while going straight for the jugular.

"Seems funny that you only remembered your friend Stefano had an allergy to nuts when he was on his way to the morgue. You'd think that little piece of information would have come to you long before it was too late."

Jordan knew that was unfair, but she hoped to get a reaction. When she didn't, she decided to take her drink and go back to her friends, who knew how to keep a conversation going. Let Thomas wallow in misery all by himself. She stood up and was surprised when he held out his hand to stop her.

"Wait." He threw back his drink and gulped down the nearly full glass of liquor before turning to her, the anger fading from his eyes somewhat.

"You think Stefano was my friend?" He huffed. "A real friend doesn't sleep with your wife."

Jordan nearly spit out a mouthful of margarita as she settled back down on the bar stool. She had anticipated him admitting to being jealous because Stefano was a better cook. Or maybe even that he despised the Italian chef for his arrogance. But never in her wildest dreams had she been expecting that the anger was caused by his wife's infidelity with Stefano.

"Stefano slept with your wife?" She couldn't keep the disbelief out of her voice.

He nodded, reaching for another drink from the bartender. "How do you think I knew about his allergy in the first place?"

Out of her peripheral vision, Jordan spied Victor

standing up and waving for her to come back to the group, but there was no way she was leaving Thomas now. Not when the conversation was just getting juicy.

She turned back to the chef. "I don't know. I assumed because you were friends—"

"I've already told you that we weren't friends," he interrupted. "Stefano didn't care about anyone except himself."

"So how did you know he was allergic to peanuts? Did he tell you?"

Thomas snarled. "Didn't have to. Sarah called me one day and told me she was at the hospital with Stefano after he'd nearly died in our bedroom. She knew I'd find out the details and put two and two together, so she confessed she'd been having an ongoing affair with him for the past three months." He lowered his head. "All that time I thought he was coming around the house so much to see me."

"When did that happen?" Jordan asked, knowing she was crossing dangerously into mind-your-own-business territory. "Was it the first time he'd ever had a reaction?"

Thomas's expression never changed. It was as if he were confessing to a priest and wanted if off his chest. "Nine months ago." He turned and nailed her with a glare. "And no, he knew he was allergic to nuts—carried an epinephrine injector with him at all times. Usually, he managed to inject himself before his throat swelled so badly it cut off his breathing and—"

"Why didn't he have the injector with him last night?" she interrupted.

"I have no clue. I do know he hated anyone knowing he had a weakness, as he called it. Maybe he didn't bring it because he knew he would only be eating what he cooked. For whatever reason, his stupid pride cost him his life." He stopped to take a swig before continuing, "Are you getting the picture here? Is it so hard to understand why Casey and I want to spend time together? She understands me and hated Stefano even more than I did."

"What was *her* beef with him?"

He shrugged. "He screwed her over big time when she applied for a job where he worked. The head chef had been really impressed with her credentials when he'd set up the interview. But somewhere between that phone conversation and her actual face-to-face, things changed. She found out too late that Stefano had hinted to his boss that she was lazy and took shortcuts. Apparently, she was blackballed with all the good restaurants in Dallas and ended up at the Japanese steak house in Fort Worth— which she hates, by the way. She swore she'd get even." He tried to laugh, but it came out as a snicker. "Looks like the bastard got what he deserved, wouldn't you say?"

He turned back to his drink, allowing her a moment to collect her thoughts. *Holy crap!* Was it possible Thomas's newborn son was really Stefano's? As much as she wanted to ask, she couldn't make herself say the words. Even she wasn't that heartless. But if what she suspected was true, Thomas Collingsworth had just confessed to having a gigantic reason for wanting to see Stefano dead.

And he had admitted his connection with Casey might be more than just a sexual fantasy thing. Could they really be co-conspirators in all of this, as she'd speculated earlier? That wasn't something he would just blurt out and incriminate himself, even if he was drunk. But if Casey and Thomas were in cahoots, what was Marsha's reason for being in the mix?

Whatever the case, she couldn't help but feel sympathetic toward Thomas, and even Casey.

"I'm sorry," she said finally, softly. What do you say to someone who had just admitted being betrayed not only by his wife but also by a man he'd considered a good friend. It put his dalliance with Casey in perspective.

And yes, she had been judging before.

She stood. "I have to go, Thomas. I'll see you tomorrow when we dock in Puerto Rico."

She couldn't get away fast enough, deciding it was time for her and Rosie to have a little chat with Ray. Given the new information, she concluded it was highly possible that Thomas and the two lady chefs had conspired to harm Stefano. Regardless of Stefano's gross failings as a friend, he didn't deserve what happened to him. Maybe they'd only intended to take him out of the competition, but the fact remained he'd died in the process—and Jordan needed to tell someone who was qualified to investigate and would find out the truth.

When she reached the others, she did a quick scan. "Where's Ray?"

Lola glanced up, clearly irritated that her conversation with George Christakis had been interrupted. "Beau asked him to help get his drunken wife back to the room. I think he was afraid the woman would kill him in the elevator or something. And Emily went to her room. Said she was exhausted and would see us all tomorrow." Without waiting for Jordan's response, she turned back to the chef.

"Jordan, what's wrong?" Rosie was beside her in a flash, apparently noticing the intense frown on her face.

She could almost hear her mother's voice warning her about girls who frowned all the time getting crow's feet in their thirties. She forced her face muscles to relax, making a split-second decision not to tell her friend in front of the others.

"I'm fine. Just tired."

If the whole gang heard the story, she and Rosie would have to admit to breaking into Marsha and Casey's room, and she wasn't ready to do that yet. Confessing to Ray would be bad enough. She'd fill Rosie in when they got back to their room, and together, they'd go to Ray in the morning with the new information. She prayed he wouldn't blow a gasket.

As hard as she tried to join in the fun with her friends, Jordan couldn't get her mind off what Thomas had just told her. Finally, a little after midnight, the party broke up, and everyone wandered back to their rooms. Since they had only ten hours on shore in Puerto Rico, no one wanted to miss out by oversleeping the next morning.

In the room, as she and Rosie settled into bed, Jordan recounted her conversation with Thomas.

"Holy cat lover!" the older woman exclaimed. "We have to go to Ray with this, Jordan. It's gotten too big for us."

"I know," Jordan agreed. "I wanted to tell him tonight, but he never made it back." She shook her head. "For the life of me, I still can't figure out why Ray had to go with Goose in the first place. I thought he'd only signed on as head of security for Beau, not for the whole ship."

"True," Rosie said. "But when Goose asked him to go along, Ray jumped at the opportunity. Guess he misses actual police work more than we realized. That and he's taken a shine to Goose." She sighed. "Too bad the man's married."

"I'm sorry. I can see how attracted you are to him. I

also know you would never knowingly go after another woman's husband, even if the woman will probably never recognize him again." She bent over and kissed her friend on the cheek. "Okay, let's get on with the plan. The first opportunity we get to speak to Ray alone, let's do it. The sooner he knows about this, the better, although I'm pretty sure both he and Goose are convinced this whole Stefano thing is only an unfortunate accident."

"And they're probably right," Rosie insisted.

"I agree, but Ray still needs to hear about it. He's a cop, and cops are naturally suspicious. He'll know how to handle it. I don't understand, though, why the security tapes from the kitchen didn't show Casey and Marsha nosing around." She yawned. "I wish Alex was here. He'd know what to do."

Rosie crinkled her eyes mischievously. "Is that the only reason you wish he was here?"

"That and the fact that I miss him like crazy. It seems like he left Ranchero for El Paso so long ago." She sighed. "Oh well, our sleuth days are over once we tell Ray. It will be up to him and Goose to figure it all out. Our only job tomorrow is to have as much fun as we can in Puerto Rico."

"Victor said Goose arranged a private tour at the Bacardi factory for all of us. Apparently he knows the owner and worked it out so we'll be treated like VIPs."

"Cool. I've been dying to try a real mojito ever since we came on the ship. 'Night, Rosie."

She turned off the light and pulled up the covers, but she couldn't quit thinking about how Ray would react when they told him what she'd discovered earlier. Knowing him, he'd probably pooh-pooh her conversation with Thomas, seeing him as some unfortunate soul with a sob story. She wasn't so sure.

What if that unfortunate soul had just managed to get away with extracting a deadly dose of revenge?

CHAPTER 12

Jordan and Rosie met up with Lola, Victor, and Michael on the third deck before going through security to exit the ship and begin their adventure in Puerto Rico.

"Where's Ray?" Jordan asked, realizing he wasn't with Lola.

Dressed in a flowing bright yellow caftan that Jordan had never seen before, Lola shrugged. "I was asleep when he got back last night, and he was already gone when I got up this morning. He left a note saying he and Goose needed to make sure nothing went wrong when they transferred Stefano's body to the proper authorities and that Beau requested he stay on board for some reason. Said he'd catch up with us around three at Señor Frog's in the main—"

"Oh great," Victor blurted, a frown spreading across

his face. "Goose was supposed to pull some strings and get us special treatment at the Bacardi distillery today. I was really looking forward to it."

Lola cupped his face in her hand. "You didn't let me finish, my impatient friend. Ray also said Goose had arranged a tour of the island followed by a visit to the distillery. The driver should be waiting for us on shore."

"Hot damn!" Victor said, now all grins. "He's my new favorite gringo."

"I thought I was your favorite gringo," Jordan said, pretending to pout. "You are such a pushover for freebies."

"You, my dear, are my favorite *chica*. Get used to speaking Spanish here. We're in beautiful Puerto Rico."

"So, where's Emily?" Rosie interrupted.

"Apparently, she's with Ray and Goose," Lola answered. "The note said she'd also see us at the bar later."

"By the time they get there, I hope we're well on our way to a good buzz," Victor said. "I talked to a guy last night who's been on the tour before, and he mentioned free drinks." He kissed his fingers. "Mojito, here I come."

"Strawberry daiquiri for me," Rosie said, pushing him toward the doorway.

As soon as everyone had cleared security, they walked off the ship and through a building that opened up onto a blue cobblestone street laced with shops and stucco houses in various shades of brown and yellow, with teal and butterscotch thrown into the mix.

"Over there," Lola shouted. "That guy's holding a sign that says 'MICHAEL CAFFERTY.'"

"Pinch me," Rosie said. "Is that a black Hummer limo behind him?"

"It sure is," Victor said, nearly knocking her down to get there first.

The others were right behind him, and after verifying the limo was for them, they piled in. All talking at once, they got their first look at the luxurious white leather seats and the minibar to the side. When Goose had talked about making sure they had a great time ashore, Jordan had assumed he was merely trying to impress them. She'd expected a bus, maybe even a van, to take them to the distillery, but never in her wildest dreams had she pictured them in their own limo. The man obviously delivered.

The driver closed the back door and walked around to the other side and slid in. After starting the engine, he eased into traffic. "I'm Fernando," he said, glancing over his shoulder. "Goose wanted me to remind you about the stocked bar back there. It also has some munchies, so feel free to indulge while I take you on a quick tour of this wonderful island. We'll make a few stops to see some of the sites up close. I'll explain everything as I drive, but be sure to stop me and ask questions when you have them. Are we ready?"

"Yes sir. *Muchas gracias*," Victor said, already pulling out a beer. After unscrewing the cap, he took a long swig. "Icy cold. Just the way I like it."

He quickly found the pretzels and salted peanuts, breaking them open and settling back in the seat while Fernando related the history of the island and its rich Hispanic culture, and they were treated to the beautiful sights of both old and new San Juan.

As Fernando drove he explained Puerto Rico's relationship to the United States. "Although we're not actually considered a state, we've been United States citizens since 1970."

"And as such, you vote in our elections, right?" Rosie asked when they'd stopped to get a better look at a beautiful cemetery filled with amazing headstones, most topped with elaborate crosses or statues of saints

"We do now, but it wasn't always that way," he replied. "Puerto Rico was given to the United States in the Paris Treaty that ended the Spanish-American War in 1918. Initially, we were ruled by military governments and then a civilian government appointed by the president of the United States. It wasn't until 1952 that we finally were able to hold our first democratic elections."

"Wasn't there a vote for independence a few years back?" Lola asked.

"That's a good question," Fernando said after they had all climbed back into the limo and were on the road again. "There was an election to let the people decide. You have to understand that forty-five percent of the population here are for statehood, while another forty-five percent prefer that we stay the way we are. The other ten percent are either for total independence or they just don't care one way or the other. Anyway, the measure failed to get a majority, and for the time being Puerto Rico will remain a commonwealth of the United States."

"Look at that huge—what is that anyway?" Victor asked, already bored with the conversation about Puerto Rican politics.

"Castillo de San Cristóbal, otherwise known as Saint Christopher's Castle," Fernando answered. "It's the largest military fortification ever built by the Spanish and has been here since the seventh century. The first shot fired in the Spanish-American War was from here. It sits on twenty-seven acres of land and is one of our most popular tourist attractions."

"Can we stop and look around?" Rosie asked, sipping her second wine cooler.

"Not if you want to grab a quick bite before we go to the Bacardi distillery. It's after noon, and I'm supposed to have you back at Señor Frog's by three o'clock."

Victor snorted, juggling his hands up and down. "Let's see—old Spanish fort or free rum. No contest, my man. Drive on. I can look this place up on the Internet and see the inside when I get back to Ranchero." He clicked a picture of it with his cell phone. "Now where's that food you promised?"

Fernando drove them to a small, out-of-the-way restaurant where they were treated like celebrities the minute they walked through the door.

"This is my wife, Carmen," Fernando confessed when a pretty young Puerto Rican woman appeared. He bent down to kiss her on the forehead. "And they make the best *lengua rellena* on the island."

Jordan narrowed her eyes. "Please tell me *lengua rellena* means a burrito with a lot of cheese."

"It's stuffed beef tongue, a delicacy on the island," Fernando's wife explained in broken English.

"Oh God! Even I won't eat that," Victor said. "Isn't there a taco joint around here?"

"Lucky for you they also make the best *carne guisada puertoriqueña* in the area." After Jordan scrunched her nose up, he added, "Puerto Rican beef stew with the best

pan de agua swimming in melted butter," he explained.
"That's just about the most delicious bread you'll ever
taste."

"Stew and bread sounds great. I'm starving, too," Jordan said, following Fernando and his wife to the table.

After they finished lunch, which was every bit as delicious as Fernando had promised, they piled back into the
limo and soon were on their way to the Casa Bacardi
Visitor Center. With her stomach full, Jordan leaned back
into the soft white leather and thought about sneaking a
power nap, but before she could even close her eyes, they
hit a bump in the road, and Victor squealed.

"There's the famous bat."

"What famous bat?" she asked, craning her neck to
see the huge white sculpture that showcased the entrance
to the visitor center.

"It's Bacardi's logo," Fernando explained. "As far back
as the original rum-making days in Cuba, the old dark
distilleries had hundreds of fruit bats hanging from the
ceiling. They'd come out at night and feast on the discarded fruits and sugarcane. Because the company did so
well, the bats were held in the highest regard and soon
were looked on as bringing good luck. Even after Castro
took over as dictator and Bacardi moved his operation to
Puerto Rico, he kept the bat as the company logo. It's
become so well known that anyone who sees it automatically thinks 'Bacardi rum.'"

"We won't see any real bats, will we?" Rosie asked,
touching her blondish hair, which was pulled into one
long braid down her back. "Me and bats don't get along."

Fernando laughed. "No bats. In fact, the tour doesn't

even include the actual distillery. Something about security. Where you're going is bright and cheery with lots of flavored rum for you to taste."

"Now that's what I like to hear," Victor said.

"I wish Ray could've come with us," Lola said, a touch of sadness in her voice. "He loves rum."

"I hope everything went okay today," Michael replied, unable to hide his concern.

"What could possibly go wrong? Aren't they just making sure the body gets to the right place?" Victor asked.

Michael nodded, but the worry on his face remained. "Yeah, but I'm wondering why he and Emily had to be there with Goose. Do you think something's up?"

"Quit worrying, Michael," Victor said, reaching over to pat his partner's back. "What could possibly happen to a dead guy that's any worse than what's already happened to him?"

It was a little after three when Fernando pulled up to a large white building with a huge upright frog in front. After piling out of the car, the group said good-bye to the driver and raced toward the door and the enticing sound of reggae music coming from inside the restaurant. Jordan was surprised when she peeked inside. The place was packed, and from the looks of it, most of the patrons were already feeling no pain. One girl was even dancing on the table to the lively music that was ten times louder once they were inside the building.

Hearing her name, Jordan spotted Ray and Goose at a large circular table in the corner. "There they are."

She pointed before heading in their direction. The others followed, and before she could ask why Emily wasn't with them, she appeared with a waiter at her side.

"Meet Carlos," she announced. "If you want anything to drink other than margaritas, you need to tell him now. I doubt we'll see much of him after that with this crowd." She smiled up at the scrawny waiter, and his adoring face left no doubt he would never be too busy to wait on her. Like all the other men in the room, he couldn't keep his eyes off her.

"How about some chips and salsa, Carlos?" Goose asked. "And maybe queso."

Carlos nodded. "Any other drinks?"

After everyone agreed that the margaritas were more than enough, he turned and left to get the appetizers.

"How was your tour?" Goose asked when they were all seated around the table. "Fernando is amazing, isn't he?"

"I don't know how you pulled that off, my friend, but it was fantastic," Michael said, reaching for a pitcher and pouring drinks for everyone.

"Fernando and I go back a long way. I met him on one of my first trips here, and we've been friends ever since."

"Fernando wouldn't even let us tip him," Rosie said. "It must've cost you a pretty penny."

His eyes twinkled when he looked at her, obviously a little smitten. "You're all worth it," he said. "Actually, it didn't cost a dime. Fernando and I have an arrangement. I recommend his limo tours to the passengers, and he helps me out every now and then. The man's made a fortune off me."

"All the more reason to celebrate." Victor held up his

glass. "Here's to old friends, meeting new ones, and the best cruise ever."

Everyone toasted. Jordan looked around the table, thinking she was the luckiest girl alive. She was in Puerto Rico with all her wonderful friends as well as a couple of new ones—Goose and Emily. How much better could it get than that? She was about to add to Victor's toast when Carlos appeared with the food.

"Thought you'd like to try our specialty—The Frog's famous nachos." He set the huge platter in the center of the table before turning to Emily. "It's on the house."

She rewarded him with a smile that would probably liven his dreams for a while.

For the next twenty minutes, they filled up on the snacks and emptied the pitchers. Waiting for Carlos to bring two more, Michael turned to Goose.

"I hope everything went well today."

Goose eyeballed Ray before nodding. "The body is now on its way to Miami where it will be taken to the Dade County Morgue for an autopsy."

For some odd reason Jordan felt a twinge of sadness at the finality of it all. Even an arrogant jerk like Stefano didn't deserve to die so young.

"What are they expecting to find?" she asked.

Goose shrugged. "Maybe evidence of a heart attack or stroke, but my guess is, given what Thomas said about Stefano's peanut allergy, they won't find anything other than an elevated histamine level and a swollen throat. Those are the classic symptoms of anaphylactic shock."

"Really. How do you know so much about it?" Lola asked.

Goose looked puzzled by the question. "Doesn't everyone who's ever taken penicillin know about anaphylactic shock?" He turned to Ray for help.

"He's right. Anaphylactic shock happens a lot to people who are allergic to penicillin. The throat enlarges and cuts off the air supply in a severe reaction," Ray explained.

"So, if someone knew Stefano was allergic, they could have exchanged the spice bottle with one that had ground nuts, right?" Lola said. When no one responded, she continued. "Who had a good reason to kill Stefano?"

Rosie laughed. "Who didn't? The man was an ass."

"Ass or not, most people wouldn't kill him for that reason alone." Lola turned to Ray. "Besides, didn't you say that since the security tapes didn't show anything unusual, you assumed no one had tampered with the food baskets they used in the competition that night?"

Ray bit his lip, glancing up for a second to again make eye contact with Goose. When he nodded, Ray continued. "There might be a little problem with that assumption."

Jordan stretched across the table, nearly putting her sleeve into what was left of the queso. "What do you mean, 'a little problem'?" she asked, remembering that Marsha and Casey had discussed being in the kitchen the day of Stefano's death, yet they hadn't appeared on any of the security tapes.

She and Rosie hadn't yet had the opportunity to talk to Ray about their suspicions, and now this. More than ever, they needed to get him alone to tell him what they'd learned. And the sooner the better.

Goose cleared his throat. "When Ray and I were going back over the tapes from last night, we decided to recheck the ones from the galley on the first day."

"And?" This time Jordan leaned so far across the table, she tipped over the salsa. After quickly mopping it up with napkins, she turned her attention back to Goose, dying to know if he'd seen the two women in the kitchen. "Well?"

"After taking another hard look at the tape, Ray noticed a discrepancy in the time stamp."

Hearing that, everyone turned to Ray for an explanation, including Emily.

"It looks like there's a ten-minute interval where the camera either malfunctioned or else someone cut the tape and then spliced it back together."

"Holy cow! Does that mean Stefano really was murdered?" Lola asked.

"No, darling," Ray continued. "It only means we have to find out what happened to the tape. Goose thinks the equipment simply malfunctioned for that short time, but it seems too coincidental to me. And you all know how I feel about coincidence."

Emily squealed and jumped up when a middle-aged man with a recessive hairline bumped into the table, splashing her drink onto her lap. Obviously two sheets and counting on the way to the proverbial three sheets to the wind, the man straightened up.

"Sorry," he mumbled, after a noisy hiccup. "I'm looking for the bath . . ." His eyes honed in on Emily, now frantically swiping at her slacks with the napkin. "Anna? Is that you?"

Everyone turned to Emily, whose eyes were now slanted in confusion. "Excuse me?"

The man held on to the table for support when the waiter walked by, nearly knocking him over. "It's me, Kevin," he slurred.

Emily shook her head. "I'm sorry, sir, but I've never seen you before in my life. You must be mistaking me for someone else."

He grabbed her arm. "Kevin Watson, remember?"

When Emily grimaced, Ray stood, knocking his chair backward. He darted around the table and grabbed the man's arm. "Look, mister, the lady said she isn't who you think she is. Now, move along. The bathroom's over there."

But the man stood his ground. "I can't believe it's really you. I thought I'd never see you again."

Ray nudged him in the right direction. "Okay, fella, you need to find someone to take you to a nice quiet spot to sleep it off."

Even as Ray pushed him away from the table, the guy was still trying to convince Emily that he knew her. All conversation at the table stopped as Emily reached for her margarita and drained half of it, visibly shaken.

Jordan imagined this wasn't the first time something like this had happened to her. When you look the way she did, a man would try anything to get your attention. "Don't I know you from somewhere?" was one of the oldest pickup lines in the book. Even she'd heard it a few times at bars.

When Emily finished her drink and set her empty glass on the table, Jordan quickly refilled it.

"A lot of women would give anything to have your problems," she said, hoping to lighten the mood. She touched the top of Emily's hand in a gesture of solidarity.

Emily blew out a loud breath and smiled her appreciation. "It gets old after a while, though," she said simply. "Times like this make me wish things were different."

"What a buffoon!" Rosie huffed. "Bet he's got a wife half sloshed back at his table while he's trying to pick up other women. Sheesh!"

"No doubt," Victor said, before turning back to Ray. "So, back to your story. You and Goose found a kink in the security tapes. Is that why you weren't able to party with us last night on the Lido Deck?"

Again a look crossed between Ray and Goose before the head of security responded. "No, I had to babysit Beau and his wife while they kissed and made up with a couple bottles of bubbly. But this morning something happened that demanded my attention."

"Mercy! I'm beginning to think this cruise is cursed," Rosie said. "What kind of problem this time?"

"One of the passengers was robbed," Goose said matter-of-factly.

"Criminy!" Victor exclaimed. "Shouldn't the thief be easy to identify with security cameras all over the ship?"

"You'd think so," Goose responded. "That's why Ray and I spent several hours looking at the tapes this morning."

"So who did it?" Jordan asked. "Another passenger?"

She glanced toward Rosie, remembering how the two of them had broken into Casey and Marsha's room the first night of the cruise. She hadn't even considered that there might be cameras in the hallways. Hearing there were made it even more critical to find a minute alone with Ray. She hoped no one had bothered to check the tapes that night. The panicked look in Rosie's eyes confirmed she was thinking the same thing.

Goose shook his head. "We think it was one of the stewards."

"I would think that would be a hard one to prove since they all have master keys, right?" Michael asked.

"Yes," Goose answered. "But there was one steward who stood out among all the other people entering the room—one who didn't belong on that floor."

"Stood out how?" Victor pressed.

Goose cleared his throat. "We were able to identify everyone else but him. He or she made it a point to keep his shirt collar up and his back to the camera, as if he knew exactly where they were. All we know is that he was about six feet tall and had dark hair."

"You could be describing half the crew. Tall, dark, and handsome, if I might add," Victor blurted before Michael shot him a look. "I'm just saying that finding someone to fit that description on a boat loaded with foreign men might be difficult." He patted his partner's hand, but Michael was still shooting daggers his way.

"That's true, Victor. That's why Ray and I are planning to question all the stewards, one by one, starting tomorrow, to try to get to the heart of the matter."

Lola turned to Ray. "Tomorrow?" When he nodded, she continued. "We only dock for ten hours at Philipsburg. You'll miss everything." She turned her attention to Goose. "Can't you and your men handle this on your own?"

Again, a silent conversation between Ray and Goose played out before Ray turned to her. "I'm directly involved, darling. I'm being paid to help on this one."

"What do you mean? Why would you have anything to do with it?"

Ray took a minute before responding. "Because it was Beau and his wife who were robbed last night."

CHAPTER 13

The mariachi band chose that precise moment to surround the table and play a lively rendition of a "Guantanamera," cutting off any further conversation.

When they finished, Goose held up his hand before they could begin another. "As much as we love listening to you, we need to settle up here and get back to the ship."

He reached for his wallet, took out a twenty, and passed it to the leader of the band. That brought a big smile to the man's face, and he nudged the others away from the table.

When they were gone, Lola questioned Ray again about why it was necessary for him to help Goose with the robbery investigation. "Did Beau or his wife get hurt?"

Ray shook his head. "No. Apparently, they slept through

the whole thing after those two bottles of make up champagne they drank."

"What all did the thieves get?" Michael asked.

"Thief. We think it was only one person. And he got that diamond and emerald necklace Charlese had on last night in the theater," Ray responded. "I tried to talk them into letting me put all their valuables in the ship's safe, but they wouldn't have anything to do with that. Beau said he felt safer with him and his wife wearing the stuff. He wouldn't even put it in the cabin safe."

"Guess he didn't figure on someone sneaking into his room and taking it right out from under his nose," Rosie said before grinning. "His semi-comatose drunken nose, that is."

Jordan shook her head, still too shocked to respond. She couldn't help wondering if Rosie had been onto something earlier when she suggested the cruise might be cursed.

Ray patted Lola's hand affectionately. "I'm sorry for bailing on tomorrow's fun in Philipsburg. I promise to make it up to you, honey. We'll do something special in Saint Kitts. But since I am getting paid to be Beau's personal security, any crime against him is my concern."

"I'll make sure we wrap it up quickly tomorrow," Goose said to no one in particular. "But don't worry. I've arranged for a driver to pick you up at the dock in the morning and take you to the marketplace for souvenirs. Afterward, he'll drive you wherever you want to go. I'd suggest you check out the excursions on tomorrow's activity sheet to see if any of them interest you. I've instructed him to work it out with the locals to give you a significant discount on any of the adventures."

"All I plan to do tomorrow is soak up some rays—after the shopping," Jordan said, finally pushing last night's robbery out of her mind. Chances were pretty good the jewelry was heavily insured, and Beau would get a nice chunk of change.

"Booze cruise for me," Victor exclaimed, slamming his hand on the table so hard he nearly knocked over the empty margarita pitcher. Leaning forward, he pointed a finger at his partner. "You promised, Michael. Remember?"

Michael laughed. "Oh, yeah, and you know what? After everything that's happened on the cruise so far, you won't get an argument out of me. I so need to relax and forget about things I have no control over. Let my boss get the ulcer instead of me." He looked around the table. "So, who's in?"

Only Victor raised his hand. Lola, Rosie, and Jordan all agreed that shopping and then hitting the beach sounded better to them. Jordan looked to see what Emily's response would be and was surprised to see the New Yorker deep in thought, totally oblivious to the conversation.

"Emily, will you be able to join us tomorrow for a girls' day out?"

Jarred from her thoughts, Emily looked up and shook her head. "Unfortunately, I have to spend the entire day on the phone taking care of company business back in New York." She tsked. "I swear I'm going to find someone competent enough to run the agency in my absence without calling me every hour on the hour. I'd pay a fortune for someone like that." She finally smiled. "You all have a great time, though. It's probably a good thing I'm not going. My back's still red from all that sun I got yesterday by the pool."

"We'll miss you," Jordan said, noticing Victor biting his lower lip to keep from snickering.

She didn't know why he felt threatened by her friendship with Emily. He had to know she wasn't the type to dump old friends when new ones came along. Although Jordan loved them all, she felt closest to Victor. That feeling went back to the very first day when she'd arrived at the apartment building he co-owned with Michael, carrying only a few suitcases and her goldfish, everything she'd owned at the time.

"I don't know about you, but I'm bushed. I'm going to head back to the ship and try to sneak in a nap before dinner," Rosie said, covering her mouth to hide a yawn.

"Me, too," Victor chimed in. "I'm thinking about going to the casino tonight and playing a little blackjack. Wanna come, Jordan?"

"Are you kidding me? I'm terrible at that game. Why would I want to throw away my hard-earned cash? When I spend my money, I want to have something to show for it. Besides, that woman I met at the distillery told me you can get a gorgeous shell purse in Saint Martin for about twenty-five bucks. That's where my money's going."

"What woman?" Lola asked.

"You know—that delightful British woman from the other cruise ship who gave us her drink coupons at the distillery."

"Seriously, Jordan, you're really not going on the booze cruise with us?" Michael asked. "That's all you and Victor have been talking about since he mentioned it in Miami."

"That was before I drank mojitos and margaritas all day long," she responded with a chuckle. "I have a feeling

I'm going to pay a price in the morning, and ibuprofen will become my best friend." She paused long enough to finish off her drink. "No sense wasting any since I've already done the damage," she said with a wink. "Anyway, I know I don't have to tell you this, but y'all have a great time tomorrow. We'll meet up later and compare stories."

The waiter appeared with the check, and everyone reached for their money to divide the bill like always.

Emily handed him her credit card. "This one is on me," she announced. "Trust me when I tell you it was worth every penny to spend time with you all and not have to think about my problems for a while. And don't even get me started on what's happened on the cruise ship."

For a moment Jordan thought she saw tears forming in the corners of Emily's eyes, but if there were any, she quickly blinked them away.

"I'm not looking forward to spending all day tomorrow listening to Beau go on and on about how he should be compensated. The man has more money than the state of Texas." Emily laughed, but it came off as fake. Something seemed to be bothering her.

"Anyway, I may never drink again, either," she added, lifting her empty glass for emphasis.

After the bill was paid, the gang made their way to the door. Jordan took one final look across the room, curious to see if the inebriated guy who had hit on Emily earlier was still there. She spotted him staring so intensely at Emily as she walked through the crowded room, he didn't even seem to care that his wife—at least, Jordan assumed it was his wife—was watching his every move with a look that could kill.

Unbelievable! Having witnessed all the grief Emily took because of her beauty, Jordan said a silent thank-you that she had more ordinary features and didn't have to put up with obnoxious jerks like that.

"Jerry Goosman! You said you'd call when you docked today. I waited all morning."

Jordan was still concentrating on the drunken guy across the room and nearly bumped into Rosie when everyone ahead of her stopped suddenly. A petite Hispanic woman dressed in a tight-fitting tank top and shorts that left nothing to the imagination sprang up from the table near the front door.

Before Goose could respond, she wrapped her arms around him, pressing her body into his in a move designed to get his attention. Goose's response left no doubt it had worked, before a slight reddish glow crept up his face. He looked as if he'd like to find a big hole and crawl in it.

Judging by the way the woman's hands were all over him, she was more than a casual friend. Jordan stole a glance Rosie's way, noticing the disapproval in her friend's eyes and hoping she didn't go off on Goose right then and there. Rosie could get very vocal with her opinion of men who cheated, and from the looks of it, that shoe probably fit Jerry Goosman.

The security officer used both hands to unlock himself from the woman's embrace. "Lara, I was tied up all day on board the ship with a security matter. We still need to talk about that business deal we discussed, but unfortunately, it will have to wait until next week or the week after."

Free of her hold, Goose bolted for the door, as if he couldn't get out of there fast enough, leaving the young woman with a surprised look on her face. She was probably wondering what business deal he'd been talking about.

The minute Jordan stepped outside the dimly lit bar, the bright Puerto Rican sun caused her to squint.

Before they crossed the street and headed toward the ship, Goose announced he was not going with them. "You all go ahead. I just remembered I was supposed to have a meeting with one of the business owners down the street. We're trying to set up an arrangement where he and several others will offer significant discounts on their inventory to the *Carnation Queen* passengers. If that works out, it will be another terrific benefit for the tourists."

He paused before adding, "I've already run the idea past the cruise director, and he agreed it would be a coup to get a deal like this worked out. I'll see you tonight at dinner or at the bar later on." He turned and walked off down the street before any of them could respond.

The rest of the gang started across the street, all chattering at once. Right before they went into the building that would lead them directly to the ship, Jordan turned for one last look at Puerto Rico. She knew that given her limited budget, this would likely be her only visit to the wonderful island.

That's when she saw Goose. He'd apparently doubled back and was walking toward the bar. She waved, thinking he'd changed his mind and would be returning to the ship with them. But he had his head down and didn't even see her. She opened her mouth to holler his name, then quickly slammed it shut when she saw him stop in front of Señor Frog's. Hesitating only briefly, he opened the door and disappeared inside.

*So much for Saint Jerry and his dedication to his wife
back in Miami at the Alzheimer's facility.*

It was nine thirty by the time Jordan and Rosie awakened from their so-called short nap. They had slept like
they'd been drugged—which, in fact, was exactly what
had happened. Inhaling deeply to clear her head, Jordan
decided margaritas doubled as a good sleeping pill. She
was pretty sure if someone had wanted to come into their
cabin and rob them like they had Beau, it would have
been like taking the proverbial candy from a baby. They
would have slept right through it, just as the confections
millionaire and his wife had.

Not that either she or Rosie had anything worth stealing. That is, unless you counted the Dallas Cowboys watch
her brother Danny had given her before he moved back to
Amarillo. Guess he thought that living rent free in her
apartment for over a month deserved some kind of compen-
sation, and he couldn't have made a better choice. Even
though Jordan knew the watch had been inexpensive—
Danny was as big a cheapskate as Victor—it was one of
her most prized possessions.

"Let's get a quick shower before we go up to the Lido
Deck," Rosie suggested, sitting up in bed and rubbing her
eyes. "Although I gotta tell you, if I wasn't so hungry, I
could sleep straight through the night."

"Me, too," Jordan agreed. "We need to find a minute to
corner Ray and tell him about breaking into Marsha and
Casey's room."

"And about Thomas," Rosie added. "In my opinion he
has the biggest motive for wanting to see Stefano dead."

"Right," Jordan said, before giggling. "Ray's going to kick our butts for breaking and entering."

"My butt's been kicked by way scarier people than Ray Varga," Rosie said, laughing out loud. "Besides, you're his pet. He'd never holler at you. I'm a different story, though. He loves bossing me around." She raised her fist in the air. "Bring it on, Ray."

"Hey, do you want to try out the Jacuzzi after we eat?" Jordan asked, still laughing because she knew Ray was smarter than to try to take on the hippie woman who was now hopping around the bed hollering about girl power—at least not without backup. Even then her money was on Rosie.

"Oh boy, does that sound terrific," Rosie said, finally settling down. "My back's still a little stiff from riding in the limo all day."

Both fully awakened now and in a good mood, they quickly showered, slipped on cover-ups over their bathing suits, and hurried to the upstairs grill. Before they left the cabin, Jordan tried to call Emily's room one last time to see if she wanted to join them. Her two other attempts had gone unanswered. She finally left a message telling her to join them later if she could.

The Lido Deck was crowded by the time they arrived. Jordan wondered if perhaps the other passengers had also partied too hard ashore and didn't want to dress up for dinner. As soon as she walked up to the grill, she discovered the reason everyone was eating there tonight. She'd forgotten it was burger and shakes night, and apparently there were a lot of people like her who preferred that fare over the fancy food downstairs.

With a large strawberry milkshake and a cheeseburger

piled high with grilled onions and jalapeños, Jordan found a table near the window. She and Rosie sat down to enjoy their food.

Looking out over the water, she made a mental note to change the patch behind her ear before she went to bed that night. The doctor who gave her the prescription told her to change it every three days even if she didn't feel queezy. The last thing she wanted was to miss out on the shopping tomorrow because she was seasick.

As the waves lapped against the side of the ship, she wondered how it would feel to be in the water right now. She drew in a sharp breath when an image of her treading water with hungry sharks and God only knew what circling popped into her mind.

"You okay?" Rosie asked, concerned.

Jordan smiled. "I was daydreaming," she replied, glad the interruption had made the vivid picture disappear.

"Do you think Goose is carrying on with that woman from Señor Frog's?" Rosie asked, changing the subject.

Making a quick decision not to tell her friend that she'd seen Goose go back into the bar after he'd obviously lied to them about a business meeting, Jordan shrugged. "Who knows? But I'd be willing to bet that he's not any different than a lot of other guys out there who can't say no when a pretty young thing throws herself at them. Even men who look like Thomas obviously get propositioned."

Rosie took a long drink of her chocolate shake. "Yeah, but Thomas at least has an understandable reason to check out other women. And we're not even sure he and Casey did the deed. Maybe it was just a lot of flirting. You know the old saying, 'Just because you're on a diet doesn't mean you can't check out the menu.'" She chuckled, obviously pleased with her cooking pun.

Jordan narrowed her eyes. "This from the lady who absolutely hates all cheaters?"

Rosie nodded. "I know. I must be going soft in my old age, but part of me feels sorry for the guy. It has to be tough on the old male ego wondering if your son is really your own flesh and blood."

"So what about Goose? His wife doesn't even know who he is anymore."

"I suppose you're right. I kind of liked thinking he was one of those really great guys I wish I'd met earlier in life, though. I hate that he slipped a notch off that pedestal I had him on."

"Yeah, me too," Jordan replied. "Speaking of Thomas, we really need to tell Ray what we know."

"Tomorrow, for sure," Rosie said, slurping the last of her milkshake. "Come on, there's a hot tub over there calling our names. Worry about that other stuff later."

Twenty minutes later, they were on their way back to the room, both agreeing the relaxing water, coupled with their full stomachs, had only made them sleepier. They decided to give in and get a good night's rest before tackling a full day of activities tomorrow.

Walking to the elevator, they passed by the Starlight Lounge where the gang had met the first night of the cruise—the night Jordan and Rosie had decided to play cops and see what Marsha and Casey were up to.

"Yowza! Is that who I think it is?" Rosie asked, pointing into the lounge.

Jordan jerked her head in the direction of Rosie's finger.

"Yep! Wonder how he managed to get away from his wife this time."

Just then Marsha looked up from the corner table where she was sitting so close to Beau Lincoln, you probably couldn't have slipped a finger between them. She waved.

"My guess is he used a couple of bottles of champagne," Rosie said, shaking her head. "That man ranks right at the top of my 'slimeballs I'd like to smack' list."

Jordan waved back at Marsha, deciding the woman was already trolling for game points, gearing up for the next stage of the competition in two days. She wondered what the probably-already-drunk-and-sleeping-it-off Mrs. Beau Lincoln would do if she could see her hubby right now, playing touchy-feely with a woman she'd nearly ripped off the stage in the theater the night before.

As Jordan stared at the two of them, she remembered the last words out of Charlese Lincoln's mouth after she'd slapped Marsha across the face: *Next time you decide to sleep with someone else's husband, you'd better make damn sure it's not mine, or I'll kill you myself with my bare hands.*

Jordan hoped for Marsha's sake that the scorned wife was indeed sleeping it off in her room.

CHAPTER 14

The next morning, Jordan, Lola, and Rosie were off the ship in Philipsburg by seven thirty. Victor and Michael had signed up for a cruise around the island and barely had time for breakfast. Ray and Goose were staying on the ship to finish up their investigation into the robbery. Today, they were planning to sit down with every crew member and question them, hoping to discover if any of them had walked away with Charlese Lincoln's diamond necklace. According to Lola, Goose and his security team had already conducted a surprise check of all employee quarters the night before but had come up empty-handed.

As Goose had promised, the driver, who identified himself as Ramón, was waiting when they'd disembarked. Quickly, they were loaded into a Lincoln Town Car and on their way for the day's adventure. Ramón

explained Saint Martin was split into two sides, one pop-
ulated by the French and the other by the Dutch. Jordan
was so caught up in the small island's history that she
totally forgot about shopping and lying in the sun on one
of the incredible beaches Saint Martin had to offer.

"Here we are," Ramón said when they pulled up to the
marketplace. He checked his watch. "It's nearly ten now.
How about we meet up back here around twelve thirty?
That'll give us plenty of time to grab a quick lunch before
I drop you off at Baie Orientale for an afternoon on the
beach."

"That's not one of those nude beaches I read about, is
it?" Lola asked. "Because I'm here to tell you, I can't
think of too many things worse than an 'oldie but goodie'
like me in my birthday suit."

Ramón laughed. "Orient Bay is Saint Martin's busiest
and most popular beach, but being on the French side of
the island, it is swimsuit optional. If you can handle seeing an occasional naked man wandering by, you'll do
fine. And believe me, some of those old French guys
should have looked in the mirror before letting it all hang
out. Still want to go?"

When they all nodded, he got out and held the door
open for them. "See you at twelve thirty."

One by one the three women piled out, excited about
the prospects of shopping and spending money and all
chatting at once.

Walking through the marketplace, Jordan had the distinct feeling someone was following them, although she
didn't see anyone or anything suspicious when she turned
around to check behind them. She chalked it up to all the

drama on the cruise, wishing again that she and Rosie had been able to talk to Ray at breakfast. But he hadn't shown up like he had every other day of the cruise so far. Which was totally out of character. Ray Varga was a health nut and thought breakfast was the most important meal of the day.

Lola had explained that Ray had gone down to the security office at six that morning, hoping to find out why Goose hadn't returned any of his calls. Since Ray was being paid to make sure Beau Lincoln and all his possessions stayed safe on this trip, he was more than a little concerned the head of ship security may have uncovered something crucial about the robbery and had decided to keep him out of the loop.

After strolling down every aisle in the marketplace, some more than once to compare prices, the three women stopped at a small snack stand for a soda just before noon. Jordan pulled out the purse she'd purchased and admired it once again. It was made completely of shells, exactly as the British woman had described. She was elated she'd been able to talk the saleswoman down to twenty-five bucks and even mentioned she felt like she should go to confession for stealing it before Rosie burst her bubble.

"Honey, trust me. These shop owners can sniff out an American tourist from a mile away and probably jacked up the price when they saw you coming."

It didn't matter that she still felt like a crook for haggling, she couldn't wait to show Victor. He was the only man she knew who appreciated a bargain like she did.

Reaching for her soda, she took a long drink before wiping the sweat from her brow with a napkin. Though the eighty-plus-degree weather didn't come close to rivaling the blistering Texas temperatures, the humidity on the island was stifling.

Feeling a sudden hunger pain, she pulled out a banana she'd snuck off the ship in her purse and was about to eat it when Rosie gasped. Still on edge about being followed, Jordan jumped, nearly falling off her chair.

"Hello, Rosie, Lola. You both look good," a voice said from behind.

Jordan twisted around, sure she would recognize that voice anywhere. Just as she turned, Alex Moreland scooped her out of the chair and twirled her in the air before giving her a kiss that curled her toes.

"Alex, what are you doing here?" she asked when he finally released her.

"I don't care how you got here, it's just so good to see you, Alex." Lola said, smiling at the newcomer.

"It's nice to know Ray can keep a secret." He pulled up a chair and sat down beside her. "You going to eat that banana?" he asked, eyeing up the fruit. "I spent all night getting here, and I haven't had a thing to eat since an airport vending machine cheeseburger right before midnight."

She handed him the banana, forgetting about how her stomach had growled minutes before. He smiled before he peeled it and then shoved a big hunk into his mouth.

"But how did you get here? You're supposed to be deep undercover in El Paso." She still couldn't believe her eyes as she watched him finish off the banana in two more bites.

He held up his hand while he finished chewing. "We nailed the drug lord, and when he crumbled, his entire operation came tumbling down like a stack of dominoes. His commanders couldn't cut a deal fast enough." He stopped to wipe his mouth and reached for her soda when she offered it. After draining the can, he grinned. "The man responsible for millions of dollars worth of heroin coming into Texas annually is now sitting in a federal prison, and if all goes well, that's where he'll stay until they carry him out in a coffin."

Jordan barely heard a word he said. She was too busy staring at the man she'd only talked to on the phone for the past few months. His dark blond hair was streaked with highlights, compliments of the hot El Paso sun. A little longer than she remembered, it now curled slightly at the ends.

When he caught her staring, he winked. "Are you glad to see me?"

Rosie laughed out loud. "Are you kidding? We've had to listen to her go on and on about you since the last time you were here. I, for one, am really glad to see you, if for no other reason than to get her talking about something else for a change. No offense, Alex, but I'm sick of hearing about you."

Jordan reached over and playfully punched Rosie's arm. "You are so in trouble, Rosie. Now Alex will get a big head, wondering if all I did these past two months was think about him."

Remembering the one and only night they'd spent together in Ranchero before he went back to El Paso, Jordan felt her cheeks heat up and hoped he hadn't noticed. The truth was, he had popped up in her mind many times in recent weeks, but she *had* thought about other stuff.

Sheesh!

"Good to know," Alex said, meeting her eyes with a teasing wink. "It might give me leverage when I wine and dine her this evening.

Jordan grunted. "Oh no! We have to be back on the ship by six."

Alex was staring at her, his eyes still playful. "That's not a problem," he said, shrugging. "I see you, me, and the rest of the gang at a nice dinner on board tonight. Then you, me, and—did I mention you and me alone while I show you how much I've missed you?"

When his words finally registered, Jordan narrowed her eyes in question. "And how do you propose to sneak on the ship?"

She was having a hard time concentrating under his intense gaze. The last time she'd seen him, he'd been so involved with helping her brother solve a murder that they'd only been able to spend a little time together before he flew back to El Paso and his undercover assignment. The idea of spending a night with him now seemed impossible.

He caught her staring and gave her a devilish grin. "Hold that thought, Jordan—at least until later."

"But how—"

"I told you, we wrapped up the undercover gig a few days ago. While Uncle Sam is deciding what to do with me next, they gave me a week off to chill."

"But how did you know I was here?" Jordan asked, still finding it hard to believe she was really staring into his those awesome blue eyes.

"I tried to get in touch with you but kept getting voice mail. You didn't even answer my emails." He looked around the table. "I tried everyone before I began to worry. I was so excited about seeing you, I'd completely forgotten this was the week you all were going on the cruise."

"Did you say earlier that Ray kept your secret?" Lola asked, before tightening her lips in a pout. "If he knew and didn't tell me, I'm going to kill him."

Alex patted her hand. "Don't blame Ray, Lola, and don't even think about doing any bodily harm. I made him swear not to tell anyone, especially you. I know how close you are to Jordan, and I was afraid you'd let it slip out. My surprise would've been ruined."

"I still can't figure out how you're going to wine and dine us tonight," Rosie said. "We don't eat until eight, and the ship sails at seven."

Alex leaned across the table and kissed her forehead. "As much as I love you, Rosie, you and the others will get dined, but only Jordan will get wined, if you get my drift."

"But how—"

"Okay. I can see I'd better explain everything before you wear me out with questions. When I found out you were on the ship, I pulled a few strings." A glint of humor crossed his face. "All these years with the FBI finally paid off. I called the Dallas field commander who got in touch with Wayne Francis, Michael's boss. He worked out the details so I could board the ship right here in Philipsburg and cruise the rest of the way with you."

Jordan sprang from her chair and showered his face with kisses. "You're going to be with me until we get to Miami?"

"Actually, I found out what flight you're taking back to Ranchero and booked it. I'm afraid you're stuck with me for an entire week."

"Fantastic!" Lola said. "Ray could use your help on the ship."

Alex narrowed his eyes. "Why would Ray need my help?"

All three women began talking at once, but then Rosie and Jordan gave in and allowed Lola to do the explaining.

"Did you know Ray hired on as private security for some rich businessman?"

"The pastry guy, right?"

"Yes, and I can tell you he's a class-A jerk. Anyway, a few nights ago, someone waltzed right into his cabin while he and his wife slept and made off with a pretty expensive piece of jewelry. Ray and Goose—he's the head of security on the ship—are working to catch the thief. That's why Ray's not with us right now."

"You know I care deeply for all of you, including Ray, and I'll be glad to help out any way I can, but I don't know what I could possibly do that they haven't already done. Ray's a damn good cop."

"Don't forget to tell him about Stefano's murder," Rosie blurted.

Alex cocked his head. "There was a murder on the ship?"

"We don't know that for sure," Jordan said. "But we think one of the chefs died from an allergic reaction to peanuts, and several of the other contestants had pretty good motives to kill him."

Alex threw back his head and laughed out loud. "So, how did you three jump straight from allergic reaction to murder?" He shook his head, still laughing. "I'm beginning to think your imaginations have all been working overtime. To be honest, Jordan, I can think of better ways to use your creative talents."

Jordan blushed at the innuendo, but she wasn't finished arguing her case. "When Rosie and I tell you about what we know, you won't be making jokes at our expense."

"What do you and Rosie know that I don't?" Lola asked, shooting Rosie a dirty look.

Rosie ignored Lola's question and looked at Jordan, who nodded. Turning back to Alex, she said, "We've been trying to get Ray alone for two days now, so we could talk to him. We think Thomas Collingsworth killed Stefano."

"What?" Lola exclaimed. "The guy who dresses like he just stepped out of a bad thrift store?" She frowned. "I don't buy it. I'd bet money that man couldn't even kill a tiny mouse, let alone a walking, talking human being."

"Whoa!" Alex said, holding up his hand. "Who is Stefano, and why would this Thomas guy want to kill him?"

"Because Stefano is probably the father of Thomas's only child," Jordan began.

"Criminy!" Lola exclaimed. "I can't believe you two kept that from me."

Jordan sent Lola a don't-be-mad-at-me look before she turned back to Alex.

"Keep going," he said, making a rolling motion with his hand to speed her up. Obviously, he was interested in more than just her creative mind now.

"And because somehow ground peanuts ended up in only Stefano's spice bottle that night."

When Jordan saw that she had Alex's undivided attention, she plunged ahead with what she thought was the smoking gun. "And finally, because Thomas was the only one who knew that Stefano was allergic to peanuts and didn't bother to say a word to the doctor until after Stefano was unable to be revived."

Alex studied her face. He was no longer smiling.

CHAPTER 15

Looking through her closet, Jordan mentally kicked herself for not bringing anything sexy to wear. It would be hard to show Alex how creative she was when all she had to offer was her usual dinner outfit of black slacks and a lightweight sweater.

Oh well. Maybe if I keep him so busy looking into my eyes, he won't even notice my outfit, she thought, reaching for the lowest cut blouse she could find.

She pulled out the green and black silk number she'd brought for the Captain's Gala at the end of the week. It was the same one she'd worn to the Cattleman's Ball several months before—the blouse her escort had said made her green eyes look like emeralds. A flashback of sitting in the emergency room that night in Fort Worth when her date was pronounced DOA popped into her head. She closed her eyes to make it disappear, and when it finally did, she shoved the top back into the closet.

No way she wanted to chance such a thing with Alex—just in case the blouse was cursed.

At the thought of the man who had wiggled his way into her heart with a pan of lasagna and homemade sangria, she giggled.

"Did you say something?" Rosie asked from the bathroom.

"No," Jordan hollered back. "I was just thinking about the night Alex cooked for me."

Rosie stepped out of the bathroom, her streaked blond hair hanging loosely down her back in a cascade of curls.

"Wow! You're getting all dolled up, aren't you?" Jordan commented. "I hope you'll remember that Alex is my boyfriend," she added playfully.

"Honey child, even if I did take a stab at that gorgeous hunk of manhood, I would be disappointed. He only has eyes for you."

"I hope you're right. There are some hot-looking crew members walking around the ship, and he is definitely appealing to females." She paused. "So, why are you wearing your hair down tonight instead of pulling it back in your usual French braid?"

"No reason."

"Oh no! You actually blushed," Jordan observed. "Tell me you aren't getting all sexy for Goose."

"Absolutely not!" Rosie exclaimed, much too vehemently to be believed. "The man's married, and you know how I feel about that."

Jordan studied her friend. "I believe you, but I see the way he looks at you. Before this goes any further, I need to tell . . ." But she stopped herself from blurting out that she'd seen Goose go back into the bar in San Juan where that sexy young woman waited.

"Tell me what?"

Jordan waved her off. "It's nothing."

Rosie's eyes twinkled. "Goose does flirt a little, and I wish I could say I hated it. Nothing will ever come of it, but it is nice that he finds me attractive." She moved around to the closet. "What are you wearing tonight on your first night alone with Alex?"

"Hopefully something to get his mind off robberies and murders." She frowned. "Did you see the way his eyes lit up when we told him everything that's going on around here?"

"Yeah. Like Ray—once a cop, always a cop. My guess is we won't be able to get a word in edgewise with Goose, Ray, and Alex all huddled together solving crimes. I probably curled my damn hair for nothing."

Jordan grinned. "Oh, I don't know. I'm sure we can scout out a good-looking guy for you to flirt with."

"Make him rich, and you're on." Rosie patted Jordan's behind. "Get dressed, sweet pea. I can't have Alex blaming me because you're late."

Ten minutes later, they were on their way to the restaurant, and Jordan could hardly contain her excitement. Finally settling on a rust-colored satin blouse and a simple black and rust sweater that toned down her unmanageable red hair, she could hardly wait to actually be with Alex. If they were lucky, they would get away by themselves as quickly as they could after dinner to catch up on each other's lives—among other things.

As soon as they approached the restaurant, Jordan

spotted Alex and gasped. If she thought the man looked good in jeans, the sight of him in navy blue slacks with a light blue button-down shirt that made his eyes resemble a cloudless sky nearly did her in.

She was tempted to ask if he wanted to skip dinner.

And those Paul Newman eyes told her he was thinking the exact same thing as they traveled down and back up the length of her. Ordinarily, she would have wised off with some remark like "I'm up here, Alex," but for some reason, tonight, she rather enjoyed the scrutiny.

He greeted them both with a kiss on the cheek, giving Jordan a whiff of his clean-smelling cologne and arming her with yet another argument for bypassing dinner and going straight for the *dessert*.

"I got here just as Victor and Michael were being escorted to the table. Since they didn't see me, I decided to wait for the two of you and surprise them, as well," Alex said.

"Did you get a chance to talk to Ray about what we told you earlier?" Rosie asked.

Alex shook his head. "I spent so much time filling out all the paperwork and then getting settled in my cabin, I barely had time for a quick shower before dinner. I'm hoping to get a chance to hear what Ray has to say while we eat."

"Hey there. Sorry we're late," Lola said, rushing up with Ray following close behind.

Ray shook Alex's hand. "Good to see you again."

"Okay then, it looks like we're all here except Goose," Rosie said, the disappointment in her voice probably apparent only to Jordan.

Ray scrunched his face and sighed. "I haven't been able to talk to him since last night."

"Wait. Didn't you and Goose question the crew members today?" Jordan asked.

"I did, but Goose didn't show up. His staff and I spent five hours questioning them. So far, we haven't found anyone who looks like the man on the security tape. And we still don't have a clue where Goose is. Right before I left the room, I talked to Orlando, who is next in command in the security department, and the only one on board with a background in criminal justice beside Goose, by the way. He was going to have someone go up to Goose's room and see if he left some indication as to where he could be. I told Orlando I'd be at dinner, and he promised to let me know as soon as he finds out anything."

Jordan debated whether to tell Ray about seeing Goose go back into the bar, and then decided to wait until Rosie wasn't standing right next to her. It was probably nothing, anyway, and Ray had mentioned that Goose had checked all the crew quarters *after* the ship had sailed from Puerto Rico. At least they could be certain he had reboarded and hadn't lost track of time while he "talked business" with the young woman at the bar.

"That's weird," Rosie said. "It's like the two of you were inseparable for the first few days of the cruise, and now you can't even get him to return your phone calls."

Ray shook his head. "It does seem strange. I wonder if Goose uncovered something about the robbery that he doesn't want me to know. That would explain why he's avoiding me like the plague."

"I'm sure that isn't the case, darling. Now, let's get in

there before Victor blows a gasket. You know how he is when he doesn't eat on time." Lola nudged Ray into the restaurant where the maître d' greeted them and led them to their table.

"What took you guys so long?" Victor asked, a little annoyed. "Well, I'll be! Is that who I think it is?"

Jordan nodded, laughing when her friend jumped up and embraced Alex in a bear hug. Michael followed suit.

"What in the world are you doing here, Alex?" Victor held him at arm's length before whistling. "Hmm. You do clean up well, my friend, if I have to say so myself."

While they feasted on appetizers and salad, Alex mesmerized them with stories about his latest undercover assignment. When he got to the parts about being in dangerous situations, Jordan had to restrain herself from freaking out. She knew his job was not without risks, but she hated actually hearing how quickly things could have gone bad, imagining all sorts of scenarios, none of them good. Snuggling closer to him, she reached for his hand under the table.

By the time the main course was served, it was like old times with everybody, including Alex, laughing and chatting as if it had been days instead of months since they'd all seen him.

Victor had him in stitches relating the story about Jordan and the sweetbread in the appetizer competition a few nights back.

"Honestly, Jordan, I'll eat just about anything, but even I don't think I could stomach that," Alex said, sympathizing with her while giving her hand another squeeze under the table.

She rewarded him with a promising smile, wondering

how much longer she could sit next to him without jumping into his arms. She kept glancing at her watch, praying the time would fly and she could finally be alone with him.

Just as dessert was served, a fortyish man with dark hair that grayed at the temples walked up to their table and tapped Ray's shoulder. Ray stood, then excused himself as he and the man he had introduced as Goose's next in command left the restaurant.

"Was it just me or did that guy look upset?" Rosie asked. "I hope everything is all right."

For the next few minutes, there was little conversation at the table. Everyone kept checking out the entrance, waiting for Ray to return and tell them what was going on. By the time they finished their dessert, he still hadn't made it back to the table, and although nobody verbalized their fears, they were all concerned.

"Here he comes," Jordan said, finally spying Ray walking back into the restaurant alone. "And he doesn't look real happy."

When he reached the table, Ray pulled out his chair and sat down, reaching for what was left of his beer and finishing it off.

Rosie, who was not known for her patience, looked past Alex and asked the question that was in everyone's mind. "Did they find Goose?"

Ray shook his head. "No, but we now have another problem on our hands."

"What kind of problem, Ray?" Alex asked.

"One I'd like to talk about with you for a few minutes after we finish, if that's okay."

Alex glanced toward Jordan, probably remembering—as she was—how their last time together was also interrupted by cop stuff. Knowing how much Ray valued Alex's investigative instincts, Jordan decided now was not the time to whine about it. She nodded.

Ray met her stare and smiled before turning to Alex. "We can go down to the security office where the others will be waiting. Hopefully, it won't take long to figure out what our next move should be." He made eye contact again with Jordan. "I'm sorry, sweetie. I promise to send him back to you as soon as we get this figured out."

"Get what figured out?" Victor asked.

Ray blew out a frustrated breath. "The security staff questioned the steward, and he told them Goose's room was unslept in as of this morning." He surveyed the gang around the table, almost if he were deciding how much to tell them. "As I said, they still don't know where Goose is, but they did find something in his room that was quite disturbing."

"Come on, Ray," Rosie begged. "Don't leave us with only our imaginations. You, of all people, know how scary that can be. What could they have possibly found in Goose's room tonight that has you this upset?

Ray lowered his voice. "Charlese Lincoln's diamond necklace."

CHAPTER 16

"So it's true? Goose found the necklace and kept you in the dark?" Lola patted Ray's hand, something she did to comfort him when he was upset.

He turned to face her. "I wish I could say that's the worst of it, but I can't." He stopped to cover her hand with his other one. "They also found a diamond ring and several thousand dollars hidden in his drawer."

"Did Beau even know he was also missing the ring and the cash?" Jordan asked. "I only remember you saying he lost the necklace."

Ray studied them for a minute as if trying to decide whether he should tell them the rest. Finally, he said, "They weren't Beau's. The ring was reported missing on the first day of the cruise, and the cash, the following day from two different rooms." He paused to allow his meaning to sink in.

"Holy smokes!" Victor exclaimed. "Are you saying what I think you're saying, Ray?"

"Unfortunately, I am, Vic. There's a strong possibility that Goose dressed up like a cabin attendant and robbed Beau and God only knows how many other passengers. Orlando said they didn't recover any of the stolen items when they searched the employees' cabins yesterday. There's only one way the stuff could have ended up in Goose's room."

Again, Lola patted his hand, probably thinking the same thing as Jordan: that Ray was blaming himself for not suspecting his newfound friend. But how could he have known? Goose's interaction with the woman in the bar in Puerto Rico had left the impression he might be a womanizer, but he'd not done anything to suggest he might be a thief as well.

"There's more," Ray said.

Immediately the chatter around the table ceased, and everyone moved closer.

"They also found a powerful sedative in his room. Orlando said the other robbery victims slept right through the whole ordeal, just like Beau and Charlese. And in all the cases, the victims complained of a headache the next day. The doctor said that's a common side effect for this particular sedative."

Jordan gasped. "Goose drugged them before robbing them?"

She made eye contact with Rosie from across the table. Rosie, who was the chatterbox of the group, especially when there was drama or gossip involved, hadn't said a word since Ray began speaking. She shook her head, making Jordan wonder if she was also blaming herself for being so wrong about Goose.

"Hold on," Alex interjected. "Even though it looks like that's the way this whole thing went down, don't forget we're Americans. A man is innocent until proven guilty—not the other way around." He turned to Ray. "How can I help?"

Ray's eyes lit up with gratitude. "I don't know yet. The first thing we have to do is find Goose and hear his version. There may be a perfectly logical explanation for all this, but I seriously doubt it. In my experience on the job, if it walks like a duck and talks like a duck . . ."

"Unfortunately, I agree," Alex said. "But every now and then there's an exception to that rule. I've never met Goose, but I'm willing to give him the benefit of the doubt until he has a chance to defend himself." He cocked his eyebrow. "What does his next in command think?"

"Orlando said it's all starting to make sense. He mentioned that theft has been on the increase lately. Not on every cruise, but at least one or two every six weeks or so over the past year."

"Do you think he's using the money to pay for his wife's care?" Lola asked.

Jordan's heart warmed as she stared at her friend. Lola always tried to see the good in people. Like the time a woman from Ranchero was accused of embezzling from the local bank. Lola immediately wondered if the woman had a sick child at home and felt she had no choice.

Until the *Ranchero Globe* posted a picture of the woman at a racetrack in Dallas.

"Ha!" Rosie said, finally. "If there even is a wife with Alzheimer's back in Miami."

After dinner, Alex and Ray left to meet up with Orlando at the security office. From the moment Alex had offered to help, it seemed like a weight had been lifted off Ray's shoulders. As much as Jordan wanted the FBI man all to herself, she couldn't help smiling, knowing this was one small way to give back to Ray for every nice thing he'd ever done for her.

And he'd done a lot of them. Ray Varga had assumed the role of her adoptive father the first day she'd walked into Empire Apartments, and God help anyone who messed with her.

Victor and the others were going to hit the sack after dinner to get ready for another early start the following morning when they docked at Saint Kitts. Without Goose setting them up with a driver and a tour, the plan was to hang out at the beach, do a little sightseeing and shopping, and then reboard the ship early.

They wanted to take advantage of the *Carnation Queen*'s awesome entertainment in the theater tomorrow night where a comedian named Donnie Steinman was performing. Lola had done a tarot card reading for Donnie earlier in the week and had taken a shine to him. Said he'd kept her in stitches the whole time she was trying to read his cards.

The gang was going to hit the seven o'clock family show in the theater, have dinner, and then go to an R-rated delivery in the Starlight Lounge at midnight. After that, Donnie was joining them in the bar for a few drinks.

Jordan decided to wait for Alex in the Jacuzzi. As soon as he and Ray finished consulting with the acting head of security, he would join her for a little relaxation before she showed him how glad she was to see him.

After walking back to the room with Rosie, she slipped on a bikini, wishing she looked half as good in it as Emily did in hers. That would all but guarantee Alex's undivided attention. But no amount of hoping would fill out her purple and pink swimsuit the way Emily filled out hers.

Thinking about Emily, Jordan made a mental note to call her new friend in the morning to see if she wanted to join them when they disembarked at Saint Kitts. She'd do whatever she could to convince her to take off her business hat at least for a few hours and just enjoy time with friends. The last several days had convinced Jordan more than ever that she'd rather be poor and surrounded by friends than rolling in money and alone.

Stepping off the elevator, she stopped for a quick ice cream cone on her way to the spa. If tonight went as she hoped, she'd need a lot of extra carbs for energy. And ice cream always had a way of cheering her up.

Because tomorrow was the last day ashore before heading back to Miami, most of the passengers were doing exactly as her friends were and calling it an early night. Consequently, the pool and Jacuzzi tubs were nearly deserted. She made her way toward the farthest one in the back, hoping for a little privacy for her and Alex.

Approaching the tub, she was relieved to see only one other passenger enjoying the hot bubbles; to her delight, it was George Christakis.

Perfect! It would give her another opportunity to tell him how much she appreciated his kindness earlier that week at the competition. He could have made a big fuss and exposed her for the fraud she was instead of slipping her a mint under the table.

"I was just thinking about how nice it was soaking in the water, and now my night has gotten even better," George said. "I've been waiting for a chance to get to know you better, Jordan. I'm guessing there is nothing dull and boring about you."

Jordan laughed, slipping off her cover-up and sliding in across from the famous chef. "Yes, if there's any drama for miles around, I can promise I'm in the middle of it somehow."

He smiled. "I have to admit, I had a lot of fun watching you eat the sweetbread the other night. I sensed immediately that you were not a connoisseur of that kind of dish, especially after seeing how the other gourmet appetizers ended up in your spare napkin."

Her own smile faded. "You saw me do that?"

He threw back his head and his laughter was loud enough to be heard at the other end of the deck where two middle-aged ladies were now staring at them.

"Oh yes! When I told Jeremy—he's my partner—about you, he laughed so hard he nearly cried. He made me promise to invite you to New York as our guest so he could meet you."

Jordan felt the tension in her shoulders ease up. "So, you're not going to tell anyone and make a big deal of it?"

"Why would I do that? Then I would have to sit next to that pretentious, arrogant ass for the rest of the competition."

Jordan chuckled. "I couldn't have described Beau Lincoln any better."

George shook his head. "I rather enjoy having you as a buffer between us to keep me from telling him exactly what I think about him." He paused and stared for a moment. "You remind me so much of Emily the first time I met her. She was young and timid, yet ambitious enough to take on the world. Although, I have to admit I'd be more than a little surprised to find one timid bone in your—"

"Emily was timid?" Jordan interrupted. "That's one adjective I would never use to describe her. The woman runs a multimillion-dollar talent agency, for God's sake."

"I said she was timid when I met her," he explained. "She walked into the restaurant about ten years ago when Chez Lui was just opening and trying to find its niche in the New York market. She'd recently moved to the city and was looking for a job while she finished her undergraduate degree at NYU." He laughed. "She was probably the worst waitress I've ever seen in my entire life and only lasted two days before I had to fire her."

"You fired her?"

He nodded. "She spilled a full carafe of my finest red wine on one of my best customers. It cost me several free meals to appease the old buffoon."

"So how did you become friends after that?"

George raised both eyebrows. "It was a challenge, but I pride myself on having a great eye for talent. I knew the minute I met her that she was going to make it big some day. In what, I didn't know, although I would have bet the farm it wasn't as a server. So, I invited her to have dinner with Jeremy and me at our brownstone in

Manhattan. I had no idea she would connect with our son Henri, who was eighteen months old at the time. There was instant chemistry between them. Immediately, we offered her a job as his nanny at a price that was way more than nannies were getting anywhere else. It was the best investment we ever made, and she eventually moved in with us. Even after she was accepted into law school at NYU, she stayed with us. Henri still lights up every time he sees her, though he's no longer a small child."

Jordan hung on his every word. It was hard to imagine Emily ever being poor and timid. "She was so lucky to have found you and Jeremy."

Just then a waiter walked up and handed George a drink.

"Do you want something, Jordan?" he asked while he signed the ticket.

She shook her head. "I don't think so, but thanks. I'm waiting on a friend."

"Oh, come on. Have one little cocktail with me," he insisted.

What would one tiny drink hurt?

"Okay, just one." She turned to the waiter. "I'll have a frozen margarita, please."

"Mexican or Italian?"

She scrunched her brow. "Mexican or Italian what?"

"Margaritas," the waiter answered. "One is made with amaretto and the other with tequila."

"I'll try the Italian one. It sounds yummy," she said, thinking about the Italian guy she hoped wouldn't spend too much more time fighting crime with Ray tonight.

When the waiter was gone, she turned back to George. "Tell me more about Emily. I want so badly to hate her because of the way she looks, but I can't. Although I think she works way too hard, I admire her for all she's accomplished."

"She's come a long way from that scared little girl who walked into my restaurant so many years ago," George said. "She was so beaten down, it took a long time to build her self-esteem back up."

Jordan shook her head. "I assumed, like I'm sure so many other people probably do, that when you look like Emily and have accomplished all that she has, you must have been born with all that confidence. It's hard to think of her any other way than as a successful businesswoman."

"Looks can be deceiving. And what about you? Were you born with all that confidence you exude?"

"Oh, please. If you only knew the half of it," she responded with a giggle, thinking about how terribly unqualified she was for her job as a culinary expert.

"I sense there's a story there, but it will have to wait," he said as the waiter appeared and handed Jordan her drink. He chugged the last of his cocktail and reached for the refill. Before he settled back against the hot tub, Jordan already had the margarita to her lips.

"I can't believe I've never had one of these before. This could be my new favorite drink. Thanks." She smiled up at the waiter.

"Lorenzo, pop your eyes back into their sockets and say good night to the lovely lady," George teased. "I have to agree, though, she is easy on the eyes."

The waiter flushed before grinning at George and then walking away.

"Easy on the eyes?" Jordan repeated, taking another big sip of her drink. "Pain in the behind, maybe, but that's the first time I've heard that one. . . ."

"Oh, pooh, you have to know you're beautiful, both inside and out." George reached across the hot tub to clink glasses with her. "Here's to getting to know each other better."

"I'll drink to that," Jordan said. "Especially if you promise to bring a pocketful of mints with you for the next leg of the competition."

"For you, my dear, always. And it will be our little secret."

Several drinks later, Jordan was feeling really relaxed with the hot bubbly water easing away the tension of the day. Sitting with the chef and sharing stories about growing up in West Texas made her forget she'd only just met him. It also helped to push the unpleasant events of the past week—like Stefano's death and possible murder and Goose's deception and thievery—out of her mind. And she'd almost forgotten Alex was taking his good old time getting to the Jacuzzi. If he didn't hurry, this would end as yet another wasted night. She'd never been a big drinker and usually fell asleep after two drinks.

She was on her third.

The Italian margaritas seemed to slide down her throat as easily as soda pop. And sitting in the hot tub with George was so enjoyable, she'd allowed him to keep the drinks coming. No sooner had she taken the last sip of one glass than the waiter would appear with a full one. And she was beginning to like the feeling that George thought she was "easy on the eyes." Thank God she didn't have to worry about him hitting on her.

"Where has Emily been hiding out?" he asked, interrupting her thoughts. "I haven't seen her in a few days."

"That girl needs to learn how to play," Jordan responded, sounding more like a mother hen than a concerned friend. "My guess is she's been holed up in the business center communicating with people back in New York." She sighed. "Sheesh! She's young and single, and she should be out partying all night instead of slaving away at the computer."

George's facial expression turned serious, and he studied Jordan for a few minutes before speaking. "How well do you know Emily?"

"I only met her on the ship," Jordan replied. "But we became instant friends. I know she was raised in Colombia by her aunt and uncle after her parents died."

George exhaled slowly. "Did she tell you her so-called missionary uncle treated her like hired help instead of part of his family—that she was never allowed to go anywhere or do anything because he made her work day and night at the orphanage?" His voice had elevated and was now angry. "For the life of me, I don't understand how anyone can do that to a child, especially one related to you. She had just lost her parents and needed love and affection. From the minute they picked her up at the Bogotá airport, they made her their personal slave. And they never missed an opportunity to tell her they'd send her away if she didn't do everything they asked of her. She said she was so exhausted by the time she crawled into bed every night that she didn't even have the energy to cry."

"How awful. Poor Emily," Jordan said when she was finally able to speak. "I had no idea. That could explain why she's so committed to her work and has no friends. It must be hard to trust anyone after such an ordeal."

"Who has no friends?"

Both George and Jordan turned as Alex slipped into the tub and promptly cupped Jordan's face in his hands before planting a wet kiss on her lips.

"So, this is your friend, eh, Jordan? You didn't tell me how handsome he was." The chef extended his hand. "George Christakis. I don't believe I've had the pleasure of meeting you yet."

Alex shook his hand. "Alex Moreland. I only came on board today in Saint Martin. It's nice to meet you." He turned back to Jordan. "Whoa! I recognize those glassy eyes. Have you been plying my girl here with drinks, Mr. Christakis?" he teased.

"Call me George. And yes, we have discovered she loves Italian margaritas."

"You have to taste this, Alex," Jordan said, shoving her glass his way before realizing it was empty. "Oops. Sorry. You'll have to order your own." She winked at George. "My turn to buy. Do you want the usual?"

George stood, reaching for his towel. "Unfortunately, I've had at least two over my limit, Jordan. And from the way this young man is staring at you, I'd say three's a crowd. If I don't see you tomorrow, we'll meet up the following night to taste desserts, for sure. I have a feeling none of those will end up in your napkin." He pulled on a shirt. "Do you want me to send the waiter over on my way out?"

"No thanks, George. I think it's time I get this pretty lady to bed. I appreciate you keeping her company. Maybe she won't be so mad at me for neglecting her tonight."

"It has definitely been my pleasure. But for the record, anyone who neglects this amazing woman needs to have their head examined." George made eye contact with

Jordan. "I hope our conversation tonight will remain between us. The drinks probably loosened my tongue more than I would have liked, but I sense you care for Emily as much as I do. She can certainly use a friend like you."

"What's said in the hot tub stays in the hot tub," Jordan said, laughing. "And thanks again for that mint, George."

"What was that all about?" Alex asked after George was out of site.

"Long story," she responded. "It will make for nice pillow talk later. For now, I want to know what you and Ray discovered tonight."

"Do you have any idea how much I've missed you?" he asked, ignoring her question. He touched her knee under the water and seductively massaged the tender area right above it, almost making her forget her morbid curiosity.

Almost.

"I guarantee I'm going to make sure you show me how much, but first, I'm dying to know what you found out about Goose."

Alex shook his head. "We skimmed through several hours of security tape and spotted him on the fifth deck around eleven o'clock two nights ago and then again on the Lido Deck that same night. After that, he simply vanished."

"And you're sure it was Goose?"

"Since I've never laid eyes on the guy, I have to trust Ray on that one. The man on the security tape wore a bright orange and blue checkered shirt that Ray said definitely belonged to Goose."

Jordan thought for a minute. "Goose told us a story about when his wife was in the early stages of her disease and bought him the shirt. He said he wore it so he wouldn't hurt her feelings, but then she forgot she'd already bought it and came home with another one."

"It is pretty ugly."

Jordan's mind had already moved on. "So how can someone just vanish from the ship?" she asked, before remembering her earlier vision of treading water and watching the ship move farther and farther away. "Could Goose have gotten drunk and fallen overboard?"

Alex nodded. "That's a big possibility, but for right now, we can only assume he's still somewhere on the ship. Another possibility is that maybe he suspected someone was close to discovering his extracurricular activities in the passengers' cabins. Knowing the ship the way he does, it makes perfect sense that he would be able to find a hiding spot and then slip off unnoticed in Saint Martin. Hell, he could be in Tahiti by now on a beach, sipping a drink with an umbrella."

Jordan stared at him. "You don't think that's what happened, though, do you?"

Alex blew out a breath. "Unfortunately, the cop in me goes right to a more cynical scenario."

"Like what?"

"Like Goose swimming with the sharks."

CHAPTER 17

Waking up in Alex's arms the next morning was like a dream come true for Jordan. Ever since he'd left Ranchero several months before and returned to El Paso and his job, she'd been counting the minutes until she could be held like this again.

She was startled from her daydreaming when he pulled her close and kissed her lightly on the lips.

"A penny for your thoughts."

She held her hand over her mouth. "Don't get too close. Morning breath will kill you," she deadpanned.

"What about morning lovemaking?" A hint of mischief flashed in his eyes.

"Hold that thought," she said, noticing it was already after seven. They'd have to hurry if they wanted to squeeze in breakfast before getting off the ship to explore the island.

They had nine hours ashore, and their day was already filled with activities.

Alex slid out of bed and walked to the restroom, giving her a good look at the muscles rippling down his back and narrowing at his slender waistline. Unable to help herself, she looked lower, and was glad she did.

The man had a great derrière.

After they showered and dressed, they headed off to the restaurant to hook up with the others. As soon as they walked through the door, Jordan spotted Emily sitting alone at a table near the center of the room. When they got closer, Jordan called her name, and Emily turned toward them and smiled.

Out of the corner of her eye Jordan watched Alex's reaction as he got his first look at the New Yorker. Dressed in a halter top with matching capris, the woman could have stepped right off the cover of *Vogue*. Alex seemed unimpressed.

"We missed you last night at dinner," Jordan said, then noticed the way Emily was staring at Alex. "Where are my manners? Emily Thorpe, meet Alex Moreland. He's an old friend from Ranchero and only boarded the ship yesterday."

Alex cocked an eyebrow. "An old friend?"

Jordan felt the color warm her cheeks. "Okay, a pretty close old friend."

He laughed and extended his hand to Emily. "So you're the famous lady entrepreneur from New York that Jordan has talked so much about. It's my pleasure to finally meet you."

Emily shifted her gaze from Alex to Jordan. "I hope she didn't say anything bad about me."

"On the contrary," Alex said. "She thinks a lot of you."

Emily smiled. "I'm glad. One of these days I'm going to convince your girlfriend to hang up her journalistic hat in Ranchero and come to New York to work with me."

Jordan opened her mouth in surprise. This was the first time she'd heard Emily say anything like this. She hoped she was teasing, because it would be a hard offer to turn down, if in fact, it was genuine.

"Yeah, right. This West Texas girl would get swallowed alive in the Big Apple."

"This North Texas girl didn't."

"You're from Texas?" Jordan asked, thinking she must've misunderstood her.

Emily took a deep breath and shook her head. "No, but I was raised in a small town in the South and know how overwhelming the big city can be, that's all." She patted the seat next to her. "Can you join me, or are you waiting for the others?"

"We're supposed to meet up with them," Jordan answered. "But if they show up, we can bring over more chairs."

For the first time, the little green monster threatened to make an appearance. Jordan sat down in the empty chair on Emily's right and motioned for Alex to sit beside her, as far away from Emily as she could get him. As much as she liked the woman, she wasn't ready to position Alex next to her—or worse, seated across from her where he would be able to stare into those sky blue eyes throughout breakfast.

"So, what have you been doing?" Jordan asked. "Did you visit Saint Martin at all yesterday?"

Emily shook her head in dismay. "I should have known

I wouldn't be able to have a real vacation this week. I spent all day in the business center, back and forth on the phone with the lawyers from a huge magazine. Apparently, one of my clients walked off the set in the middle of a really important shoot. Seems the photographer said something that didn't sit well with her." She stopped and inhaled a deep breath. "Thankfully, I was able to calm the diva down and get her back on the set. Although it cost me a case of Dom Pérignon for the editor, the crisis is finally over. I am so ready to forget about New York and pretty women with temper tantrums."

"Will you be able to join us on shore today?" Jordan asked.

Emily looked past her to Alex. "Unless you two want to be alone, I'd love to. Being with your friends makes me forget how lonely it is at the top of the corporate ladder—especially when you own the ladder."

"Well, lookee here. We were worried about you, Emily." Victor pulled over two chairs, and he and Michael sat down.

"I hated missing out on the fun yesterday," Emily replied.

Victor turned to Jordan. "Get any sleep last night, sweet pea?" he teased.

"Leave her alone," Lola said, suddenly appearing with Ray and Rosie. "Our girl deserves a few sleepless nights." She winked at Alex.

"Did you hear any news about Goose?" Alex asked when Ray was finally seated.

"Nothing," Ray replied. "But we did get the results of Stefano's autopsy this morning."

"And?"

"Just as we expected. Stefano died of anaphylactic shock brought on by an allergic reaction to peanuts. Case closed."

Jordan caught Rosie's eye, suddenly realizing they hadn't yet told Ray their theory about Thomas being in cahoots with the two lady chefs.

"Why case closed, Ray? Don't you think it's strange that Stefano was allergic to nuts, yet his was the only spice bottle that had ground nuts in it?" Rosie asked.

"And that the security tapes from the kitchen somehow were magically disrupted for a few minutes?" Jordan added.

Alex's head shot up. "Ray?"

The retired cop shook his head. "I know that all sounds a bit fishy, pardon the pun, but Goose and his team pretty much ruled out anything other than a careless accident."

"Yeah, but we now know that Goose is a thief. Is it possible he's a murderer, too?" Victor asked, always ready for drama.

"Victor, you shouldn't jump to conclusions like that," Michael admonished. "And we don't even know for sure that Goose is a thief. Remember what Alex said about innocent until proven guilty."

"Oh, so now you're trying to tell me he just happened to have those jewels in his room for safekeeping?" Victor rolled his eyes. "Seriously, Michael."

"Enough about Goose. I'm sick of hearing about him," Rosie said. "Let's talk about how much fun we'll have on our last day to play before we begin our final two days at sea."

"I agree," Jordan said, reaching for Alex's hand under the table. "Like Alex said, Goose is probably somewhere in the South Pacific lying on a beach. That's exactly what

I want to do today right here in beautiful Basseterre, Saint Kitts. I watched a video of the island last night, and a lot of the sites are must-sees. The white sandy beaches with their beautiful clear blue water are definitely on that list for me."

Ray cleared his throat. "Actually, Alex and I have a surprise for all of you. Last night Orlando told us about a great snorkeling package that takes you cruising around the island. It ends up at a wonderful spot where he said you can see just about every kind of fish native to these waters."

"I love snorkeling," Victor said, before his face fell. "But that kind of adventure package is usually pretty pricey. Michael and I spent most of our mad money on the booze cruise in Saint Martin."

"You didn't let me finish, Victor," Ray said, shooting him a disapproving look. "Orlando knows the owner of the tour boat line. Before we left the room this morning, he called to say he's worked out a deal for everyone connected to the cook-off. Even the contestants are coming along. And the really good news is, we're getting the VIP treatment for half price."

"Well, what are we waiting on?" Victor said, shoving the last of his blueberry muffin into his mouth.

Ray shot him another one of his looks that normally would have made a grown man cringe. Victor totally ignored it.

"The boat leaves in two hours, so we'd better hurry if we want to see a few of those sites Jordan talked about before we board. Lunch is complementary, and we'll be back with enough time to spend a few hours on one of those magnificent beaches," Ray said.

In record time, they were lined up single file ready to

exit the *Carnation Queen*. Jordan couldn't help noticing that although Emily had agreed to join them, her friend wasn't her usual gregarious self. She wondered if there was something more going on back in New York than a simple high-maintenance client. She vowed to keep Emily close to her and Alex and to try to figure out what was really the matter.

Well—maybe not too close to Alex, she thought as she squeezed in between the two of them on the walkway leading to the capital city of Saint Kitts.

After they boarded the small boat and were on their way around the Caribbean coastline, Jordan finally decided to get Emily off to the side. She spotted her alone near the back against the railing, apparently taking in the gorgeous landscape passing by.

"Are you all right?" Jordan asked, sliding in beside her. When she didn't respond, Jordan tapped her shoulder. "Emily?"

She turned with a start. "What? Oh, sorry. I was deep in thought and didn't hear you." She shrugged. "As much as I try, I just can't get my mind entirely off work."

Jordan shook her head. "You have to quit doing that, Emily. That stuff will still be there waiting for you when we dock in Miami, and you can take care of it then." She stared a moment before continuing. "Are you sure that's the only thing bothering you?"

Emily sighed. For a moment Jordan thought she was about to confide in her, but then she seemed to change her mind and simply smiled.

"Of course. What else could it be? It's just hard to

forget my work—even for a day. I'm so looking forward to snorkeling with you all.

Jordan debated whether to let her know that George Christakis had shared her story, but then she remembered he'd asked her to keep it to herself. Instead, she concentrated on the scenery. They were passing what looked like a deserted beach when something caught her eye.

"Oh my! Are those monkeys over there?"

Emily pulled the binoculars from around her neck and looked in the direction Jordan was pointing. "They are. They're chasing each other up and down the beach, and they're adorable. Here, take a look." She passed the binoculars to Jordan.

"I wish I had a good camera to get a shot of that," Jordan said.

"Get a shot of what?" Alex asked, sneaking up and snaking his arms around her, effectively holding her captive against the railing.

Not that she was complaining.

She held the binoculars out to him, noticing the way Emily's body stiffened with Alex so close. What was up with that?

"They're cute," Alex said. He released Jordan from his stronghold. "Hey, you two, the captain sent me to get you. We've got a little over an hour before he's going to put down the anchor, and he wanted everyone to grab a sandwich and a drink before then."

"You go, Jordan. I'm not very hungry. I'll just stay here and take in the awesome scenery."

Jordan grabbed her hand. "Oh no you don't. It's time to have fun. We'll see more of this later." She tugged on Emily's sleeve until the other woman finally gave in and allowed Jordan to lead her to the opposite side of the boat where the others were gathered.

An hour later, they were all in snorkeling gear, and one by one, they jumped into the water. Over the next sixty minutes, Jordan saw some of the most gorgeous fish she'd ever seen, including a baby shark. When she began to follow it, Alex came up behind her and pulled her back, explaining when they surfaced that where there was a baby, there was probably a mother nearby watching every move.

Although she knew nothing about sharks, she was pretty sure every mother turned into an aggressor if she thought her baby was being threatened. No way Jordan wanted to tangle with a ticked-off mama shark.

Alex had managed to draw Jordan away from the others for a few minutes underwater as they explored a distant coral reef. Being with him made the trip more fun, but having his body pressed into hers as they watched a school of yellow fish dodging all around them was something she wouldn't soon forget.

On the cruise back to the pier, Jordan introduced Alex to all the contestants, who up to this point had stayed pretty much to themselves. As expected, Marsha, who made sure Alex got a closer look at her black-and-white striped bikini—or rather, strips of cloth masquerading as a bikini— even managed to rub against him on at least two occasions. Jordan was ready to join forces with Beau's wife and do some serious bodily harm to the "skank," as Charlese Lincoln had dubbed her.

But Alex seemed immune to the attention, making Jordan vow to show her appreciation that night.

"Are you coming to the competition tomorrow night,

Alex?" Marsha asked, bending down to pick up her napkin—a maneuver designed to give Alex a look at her cleavage.

"I wouldn't miss it for the world," Alex said, smiling at Marsha before turning back to Jordan. "Any chance to see my girl on stage doing what she does best, and I'm there." He bent down and kissed Jordan's cheek.

Marsha pursed her lips in a pout, obviously not used to being ignored. After another overt though unsuccessful attempt to focus Alex's eyes on her chest, she walked away, obviously upset Alex was not as easily entertained as Beau—or Stefano. In that split second, Alex rose to the top of Jordan's seriously-going-to-be-rewarded-later list.

"I think that deserves a drink," Emily said, handing a wine cooler to Jordan and a beer to Alex.

"What does, Emily?"

"Seeing the look on Marsha's face when Alex ignored her and kissed you. I'd watch my back if I were you," she joked as she sipped her drink.

"So, Marsha," Rosie hollered from a few feet away as she made her way toward the chef, "what were you and Casey doing in the kitchen before the Greased Lightning Elimination Round?"

It didn't take a rocket scientist to figure out Rosie had had a little too much to drink. The older woman's slurred words were the first clue. As her friend got right up in Marsha's face, Jordan cringed, knowing Rosie wasn't finished with the sexy chef yet.

Casey rushed over like a knight in shining armor and stood beside Marsha, whose mouth still hung open. Jordan stifled a giggle, knowing the two chefs had no idea how powerful the woman with the long, blond braid could be. Even working as a tag team, Marsha and Casey didn't stand a chance.

"Where would you get a silly idea like that?" Casey asked, squeezing between Rosie and Marsha.

By this time both Ray and Alex had walked over to see what was going on. It occurred to Jordan that neither had heard the story about the two women in the ship's kitchen, since she and Rosie were still waiting for an opportunity to talk to Ray alone.

"I heard you talking in the bathroom," Rosie lied. "One of you killed Stefano, and I want to know which one." She turned to Thomas, who was now standing close by. "Or did you kill him?"

Alex gently took hold of Rosie's arm and guided her away from Marsha, who had now recovered from the initial shock and looked ready to go to war.

"We were nowhere near the kitchen that day. You must've heard wrong," Marsha said, eyes narrowed and now daring Rosie to say something else. "Or you had a little too much to drink—like now."

Rosie jerked forward, nearly breaking Alex's hold on her.

"Hold on, Rosie." Ray moved in between Casey and Marsha before addressing the two women. "There's a steward on the ship who begs to disagree with you. He admitted cutting out a few minutes of the kitchen security tape for the two of you."

"That little jerk," Casey said, throwing her arms in the air. She turned to Marsha. "I told you he couldn't be trusted. But no, you were so sure that a little make-out session would keep him quiet."

Jordan glanced at Ray, wondering why he hadn't told

them about this new information when he and Goose joined them at lunch the other day. When the corners of his mouth curled in an obvious gotcha smile, it dawned on her that he'd been bluffing.

He took one step closer to Marsha. "Did you put ground nuts into Stefano's spice bottle?"

Marsha gasped. "What? Of course not."

"Then what were you doing in the kitchen?"

Her eyes begged Casey for help, but the other chef only shrugged. By now everyone on the ship had formed a circle around the two women and was waiting to hear their explanation.

"We only wanted to mess with him," Marsha finally admitted. "We were going to dilute the spice bottle with salt to ruin his halibut."

"Did you know he was allergic to peanuts?" Alex asked, moving up next to Ray as if he anticipated trouble.

"We had no idea the little shit had a problem with that," Casey chimed in. "We didn't want to kill him. We only wanted to embarrass him in front of Christakis. God knows Stefano has taken great pleasure humiliating me on several occasions."

"So you're admitting you tampered with his spice bottle before the competition?" Ray asked.

"Hell no," Casey said. "The baskets were already sealed when we got there."

CHAPTER 18

By the time the captain glided the boat into the slip, Ray had calmed everyone down. He'd put Lola in charge of keeping Rosie port side while Marsha and Casey were starboard. Once they docked, the gang caught a cab to Turtle Beach, a lovely strip of white sand rimmed by beautiful turquoise water. After the snorkeling trip, none of them wanted to stay in the sun for long, and they returned to the ship after only an hour.

Walking down the concrete pier to the boat, they were uncharacteristically quiet. Jordan was already mentally planning a little alone time with Alex followed by a nice power nap cuddled in his arms before tonight's comedy show. They could all use a few drinks and a lot of laughs after Rosie's confrontation with Casey and Marsha on the excursion boat.

Okay, maybe more laughter but less liquor for Rosie.

As they started up the ramp into the ship, something caught Jordan's eye, and she stopped to stare at the orange emergency boats mounted on the side of the *Carnation Queen*. Six of them were attached at each end with three smaller brown ones in the middle.

Seeing them hanging from the ship reminded Jordan of the Titanic, and she began to do the math to calculate if the boats would accommodate all the passengers in case of an emergency. Once again, she caught a movement on the middle brown boat. Thinking her eyes might be playing a trick on her, she pressed against the rail for a better look.

This time she was able to make out a strip of orange and blue plaid material flapping in the wind—a piece so small it would have been easily missed unless you were looking directly at the rescue boat.

She closed her eyes, picturing Goose wearing the identical plaid shirt that had been a gift from his wife, and she caught her breath. "Oh no!"

Alex was at her side immediately. "What?"

She pointed. "That's Goose's shirt," she said as the others circled her, then followed her gaze in the direction of the life boat.

"Holy crap! What does that mean?" Victor asked, moving closer to the railing.

"Jesus, Mary, and Joseph!" Ray said to no one in particular. "I have to get security down here right away." He turned and ran up the ramp, showed his ID to the security officer, and was on the phone to Orlando within minutes.

"I need access to the rescue boats," he commanded after hanging up the phone.

The security officer nodded to one of the stewards,

who motioned for Ray to follow him. With the rest of the gang right behind them, the steward led Ray to the third deck. There they met Orlando, who was obviously out of breath from running, and they walked to the side where the boats were attached to the ship.

"I'll check it out," the acting head of security said, reaching for the gloves his assistant handed him from what looked like a large tackle box.

Cautiously, he made his way onto the small boat and pulled the fabric off. He held it up for everyone to see. "I'm pretty sure this is Goose's shirt." After slipping it into a small plastic bag that he pulled from his pocket, he turned back to take a better look.

As they waited patiently to hear if it was just a bad coincidence, their hopes for a happy ending were dashed with Orlando's next words.

"It looks like there's blood on the edge of the boat. Hand me the box, Ray."

After Ray handed it to him, Orlando knelt down to get a sample. Jordan held her breath while he tested it.

"It's definitely blood," Orlando confirmed, a defeated look on his face.

Jordan patted Rosie's shoulder when she heard her gasp. Although they couldn't be a hundred percent sure, it was looking pretty good that something terrible had happened to Goose here. But with no other evidence, all they could do was contact the Saint Kitts Coast Guard and notify the American authorities in Miami of a possible man overboard.

Jordan's gut told her that Goose was dead, but even though both Ray and Alex agreed with her, there was no way to prove it. She couldn't help wondering who would

pay for Mary Alice Goosman's care now—if there even
was a Mrs. Gooseman.

Jordan walked into the theater with Alex and strode
toward the front row where the others were waiting. With
all that had happened, there had been no time to sneak in
either a few minutes alone with Alex or a nap. Alex had
gone with Ray and Orlando to the security office to notify
the authorities, and he'd barely made it back in time for
the competition. Apparently, they'd met with both Wayne
Francis and Emily to discuss the fate of the cook-off.
Uncertain if Goose had fallen overboard or simply
walked off the ship in Saint Martin and disappeared,
they'd decided the show must go on since twenty-five
hundred people had paid good money to see it.

Unable to think about anything else except Goose and
his wife since she'd first spotted the torn shirt on the rescue boat, Jordan welcomed the distraction of tonight's
competition. With a heavy heart, she gave Alex a peck on
the cheek, then walked onto the stage. All of the contestants were already there except Marsha Davenport.

Since the chefs were cooking desserts, Jordan felt sure
a trip to the Lido Deck afterward for fast food wouldn't
be necessary, particularly if the entries were made of
chocolate.

She could only hope.

She surveyed the judges' table, not surprised to see that
Beau was missing, too. She suspected the two were off
somewhere doing something inappropriate. As an image
of the two of them rolling around in bed popped into her
mind, she squeezed her eyes shut to erase it.

"Are you okay?"

She opened them to see George Christakis at her side, his face showing his concern.

She nodded, linked arms with him, and then allowed him to lead her to the judges' table where he pulled out the chair for her.

"You'll do fine tonight, Jordan," he said, sitting down next to her. "It's desserts. Even I'm looking forward to it. Did I ever tell you I have a mean sweet tooth?" He patted his slightly pudgy belly and winked.

"Hope you're right about that," she said, returning his smile. "Otherwise I'll be looking for—"

She stopped talking when Marsha sauntered onto the stage and meandered over to her station. Her hair was slightly disheveled, and once again Jordan fought to get that rolling-in-the-hay image out of her head.

As if on cue, Beau walked up the steps a minute later grinning like the proverbial cat that had just swallowed the canary. After he smiled seductively at Marsha, Jordan was positive she was right about what the two had been doing. Thoroughly disgusted, she stared as the *canary* patted her bed head before giving *the cat* another half smile.

"Make you want to vomit?" George whispered into her ear.

"Oh yeah," Jordan replied, wondering where Charlese Lincoln was hiding while all this hanky-panky was playing out. The woman definitely loved the bottle, but surely she could see what was going on. Was Beau's money so enticing that she put up with his antics?

Sheesh! Nothing is worth that, Jordan thought as she made eye contact with Alex, who was sitting between Rosie and Victor in the front row. He winked.

Okay, maybe Alex is.

The crowd noise died down when Emily appeared on
the stage in a bright pink sundress that showed off her
slightly sunburned shoulders. Jordan was glad she had
insisted her friend forget about work for at least a few
hours earlier that day. From the way Emily was smiling,
it appeared that even the short time playing had done
wonders for whatever had been bothering her.

"Good evening, ladies and gentlemen," the hostess
began. "Welcome to the semifinalist round of the Caribbean Cook-Off. After tonight's competition, two contestants will be eliminated, and tomorrow's event will
feature the lucky remaining two going head-to-head with
their presentation of main entrées. The winner of tomorrow's competition will walk away with the grand prize of
an advertising contract worth over half a million dollars."
She waited for the applause to die down. "Keeping that in
mind, it is especially important that each contestant give
us their best effort here tonight. So, chefs, are you ready?"

After they all nodded, she walked over to Casey's station and opened the basket. "Tonight each of you will have
sixty-minutes to prepare your favorite dessert. As you can
see, the table in the back is loaded with fresh fruits of all
kinds and plenty of other delicious items to make a great
dessert. The only requirement is that you find a way to
incorporate these four ingredients." She reached into the
basket and pulled out the items. "We have triple sec, tapioca, ground cinnamon, and blueberries." She placed the
items back into the basket and returned to center stage.
"And one other thing. Since Marsha won the appetizer
round, she chose chocolate as the one ingredient that no
other contestant can use tonight."

After introducing the contestants and the judges once again, she raised her arm. "Okay, chefs. Your hour begins now."

The digital timer overhead began counting down as the chefs took off for the table at the back of the stage. Before long, wonderful aromas began to fill the air, and Jordan eased back into her chair and allowed her shoulder muscles to relax. Tonight would be her reward for making it through the competition so far. Tomorrow's main entrées might be a whole different ball game, though. She might as well enjoy it while she could.

She peered out into the audience and wondered if Thomas Collingsworth was out there somewhere. Now that he'd been eliminated, would he support Casey? Thinking about those two, Jordan spotted Rosie, glad they had found a few minutes to tell Ray everything they knew about the lady chefs and Thomas. As expected, Ray had gone ballistic when they'd confessed to entering Marsha's room illegally, and he'd lectured them nonstop for fifteen minutes.

But at least he hadn't brushed them off and had promised to check it out. Acting on that and the information he'd tricked Casey into revealing on the snorkeling trip, he and Orlando questioned the *Carnation Queen* kitchen employees again, but this time they took Alex with them. It hadn't taken long to find the man responsible for cutting out those ten minutes of the security tape before splicing it back together. After Alex threatened to have him arrested in Miami for tampering with evidence, the man confessed, saying he'd agreed to do it in return for a night with Marsha—a payback he had yet to collect on.

Orlando had promptly fired him and had him escorted

to his room where he would remain until the ship docked
in Miami in two days. Then they'd kick him off the ship.
As both Ray and Alex had pointed out, with no solid evidence that any crime had been committed, that was all
they could do. The good news was he'd been able to ver-
ify Casey and Marsha's story that the baskets had already
been sealed when they'd snuck into the kitchen.

The buzzer sounded, jarring Jordan from her thoughts,
and she glanced up in time to see the contestants throw
up their hands and step away from their stations. The hour
had flown by, and Jordan was looking forward to tasting
the heavenly smelling desserts.

Once again Emily went to center stage to address the
crowd. "Okay, folks, it looks like we're ready to start the
judging. The contestants have their entries plated and
ready to go. Shall we start with Luis?"

Luis walked over and stood in front of the judges'
table. "I call this Jumbleberry Delight," he said as the
stewards carried the plates to the judges and the twenty-
five tasters.

Jordan had no idea what a jumbleberry was, but the
dessert looked yummy, overflowing with three different
berries. She lifted her fork to her mouth and took the first
bite. She didn't recognize the flavor, but whatever it was,
it tasted wonderful. In a flash she had finished hers, wishing she had more.

As if he had read her mind, George stood. "Emily, is it
possible for Jordan and I to have another sample? We
want to be sure and get a good taste before we give you
our opinion." He sat back down and patted Jordan's knee.

Jordan decided she loved this man.

The second helping went down as easily as the first,

and she swiped at her mouth with the napkin. Luis's entry reminded her of back home in Ranchero where Myrtle Malone served the best desserts in the county at her little diner. After tasting Luis's jumbleberries, Jordan was confident the man could give Myrtle a run for her money. She scribbled a 5 on her card, reminding herself to find out later from George what a jumbleberry really was.

"Okay, judges. Let's start with Beau Lincoln." Emily took her place beside Luis. "Tell us what you thought about this dessert, Beau."

Beau sniffed and wiped his mouth with his napkin before looking directly into Luis's eyes. "I thought it was dry. I didn't taste much of the orange liqueur, and the cinnamon overpowered the rest of the dessert. For that reason I gave it a 2.5."

The audience groaned as Luis glared at Beau, convincing Jordan there really was animosity between the two men. Did Luis have a thing going on with Marsha, too? Could this be the result of a little jealousy, or was Beau merely attempting to secure Marsha's repeat win tonight by giving the other contestants a low score?

"Jordan?"

She jerked her head up. "Oh, sorry. I thought it was delicious, Luis. Unlike Beau, I found the cinnamon a delightful addition, and the drizzle completed the flavor." She picked up the card from her lap. "I gave it a 5."

The crowd erupted in applause, and she heard Beau grunt beside her.

After the crowd noise died down, Emily said, "With two votes in, Luis, you have a 7.5. Let's see what George has to say."

George stared at Luis for a moment as if trying to

decide which way to go. Finally, he exhaled and began. "I was a little nervous when you explained that the drizzle was made from the triple sec, since I normally wouldn't think of mixing the berries with the strong orange flavor, but I have to admit I was pleasantly surprised."

The corners of Luis's lips tipped in a half smile as he waited for the rest of the critique.

"Like Jordan, I loved the way the cinnamon and the berries seemed to compliment the tapioca perfectly. Sometimes tapioca can be overcooked, but you did a nice job with yours. Because of that, I also gave your dessert a 5 and hope you'll allow me to try out this recipe in my restaurant."

The smile on Luis's face widened before he shot Beau a go-to-hell look.

The crowd was on their feet as Luis walked back to his station. Jordan found herself smiling, not because the dessert had been so good—though it had been—but because she and George had thwarted Beau's obvious attempt to sabotage Luis's chances.

Score one for the good guys.

"Seems Luis has set the bar pretty high tonight," Emily said, taking center stage again. "Let's find out what Casey whipped up for us." She waited while the stewards passed out the plated dessert.

Casey walked around her station to stand in front of the judges. "I call this Baked Pineapple a l'Orange," she explained as the dishes were set in front of the judges. "I crushed the blueberries and heated the triple sec to make a nice citrusy glaze."

Jordan took one look at hers and inhaled deeply. This one wouldn't be as easy as the first one. She'd never been much of a pineapple eater, but it didn't look too bad. At least it wasn't a baked gland. She took a second peek to make sure of that before she took the first bite. Although it wasn't something she would order in a restaurant or choose from a buffet table, it was edible. The blueberry drizzle might have had a little too much cinnamon, but the overall flavor was good.

She giggled to herself, thinking she was beginning to think like a real judge.

"Beau, tell us what you thought of Casey's Baked Pineapple a l'Orange," Emily said.

"I thought it was almost perfect. I say almost because I think it could have used more cinnamon and a little less tapioca. Still, I thought it was good enough to give it a 4." He held up his card.

Jordan watched Casey's reaction, expecting her to be a little miffed at not getting a 5, but the chef was smiling, making Jordan wonder if the three of them—Casey, Marsha, and Beau—had worked out an arrangement that would allow Marsha to win and share the money with Casey. Marsha would certainly make a better candidate for the ad campaign in a world where sex was key to selling products.

"Jordan, what did you think about Casey's dessert?" Emily asked, moving to her left to stand in front of Jordan.

"Again, I have to disagree with Beau. I thought it had a little too much cinnamon for my taste. Still, it was evenly cooked with just the right amount of orange flavor." Mentally, she high-fived herself. Maybe George was starting to rub off on her.

She reached for the card and held it up. "But I gave Casey a 3.5 only because—"

"Beau Lincoln, I'm going to kill your cheating ass."

A collective gasp went up in the audience about the same time Jordan heard Beau swear under his breath. She turned in time to see Charlese Lincoln running down the aisle toward the stage with a half full glass in her hand, shouting obscenities at both her husband and Marsha.

She was on the steps to the stage now, her face beet red with anger. When she got to the last step, she fell, sending the glass sailing through the air, its contents spilling out, before it hit the stage floor and shattered into pieces.

"Dear God!" Emily said, rushing over to the fallen woman with George right behind her.

George bent down to examine her as the crowd settled into an eerie silence, waiting to see if Charlese was hurt.

"Get the doctor," George hollered. "This woman's not breathing."

CHAPTER 19

As Armando Ferrari, the ship's doctor, fired up the defibrillator one more time, Jordan had the sinking feeling that there was nothing the physician could do to help Charlese Lincoln. Along with the rest of the people in the packed theater, she couldn't believe the scene playing out in front of her. Beau's wife was only in her late twenties, and other than drinking too much, she hadn't given any indication of an underlying medical problem. So how could a fall cause enough damage to stop her heart?

The sound of the doctor's voice shouting "Clear" and the thud that followed as he shocked Charlese's heart one more time echoed across the theater. Eerie silence. An occasional murmur from the front row.

Beau stood up but remained behind the judge's table with a stunned look on his face, watching as if the

emergency resuscitation was happening to a stranger rather
than to his own wife.

After listening to the woman's chest with a stethoscope, the doctor turned to Emily and shook his head.
"She's gone," he said simply, then bent down and sniffed
her mouth before straightening back up. "But we have a
much bigger problem here, I'm afraid. Can someone get
the head of security down here immediately?"

The ship's executive chef, who had stayed in the background until now, was leaning over Charlese and already
dialing his cell phone. One of the stewards bent down and
reached for the defibrillator to repack it.

"Be careful not to touch the body," Ferrari warned.
"This is now a crime scene."

"A crime scene?" Ray asked after he and Alex had made
their way up on stage. "What makes you say that, Doc?"

Ferrari gave Ray the onceover. "And you are?"

"Ray Varga. I'm working private security for the Lin-
colns." Ray pulled Alex forward. "This is Alex Moreland.
He's FBI. We've been working closely with the *Carnation
Queen*'s acting head of security on another matter."

"What's going on, Ray?" Orlando said, out of breath
from jogging down the aisle and up the steps.

Ferrari moved closer to Orlando. "I believe this woman
has been poisoned," he whispered loud enough for everyone on stage to hear.

A collective gasp was followed by an instant murmur-
ing that quickly escalated into the din of everyone talking
at once.

"Quiet, please," Orlando ordered before bending down
to examine the body. "And why do you think she was
poisoned?"

"Lean over her face, and you'll smell bitter almonds." When Orlando did as he was told and then nodded, the doctor continued. "See how her skin is so red? That and the almond odor are classic symptoms of cyanide poisoning."

"Dear God!" Jordan whispered. "How could she have been poisoned?"

Alex stepped forward, switching from casual observer to cop in a flash. "Orlando, did you bring the box with you? Someone needs to glove up and bag what's left of the cocktail glass. You might even be able to get a sample of the whiskey if you hurry before it evaporates." He pointed to the liquid that had rapidly spread over a large portion of the stage floor.

Orlando nodded to one of his assistants, who ran from the stage to get the equipment. "Get the rest of the guys and start evacuating the theater," he instructed another one. "We may have a murder on our hands."

Jordan and the others waited poolside for Ray and Alex to come up and fill them in on the details. It had been three hours since Charlese's death, and they were going crazy wondering what had happened. Left to their own imaginations, they'd come up with all kinds of wild scenarios that ran the gamut from suicide to accidental poisoning. Each theory, however, ended with Beau Lincoln as the bad guy.

Finally, right before midnight, Ray and Alex showed up. Any idiot could tell from their expressions they brought bad news. After Alex kissed her forehead, he flopped down in the chair next to her.

"It's almost certain it was cyanide," he said, stroking the inside of Jordan's arm. "But without an autopsy and toxicology results we can't be sure."

"Do you have any idea how she got the cyanide?" Victor asked.

"No," Ray answered. "We suspect it was in the liquor since she was obviously drunk, but Orlando's checking to see if any food was delivered to their suite tonight. Cyanide works quickly, taking anywhere from one to fifteen minutes to kill a person. That means we have a small window, and since she was carrying a glass of Scotch, more than likely that's how she ingested it."

"Fortunately, they were able to salvage a tiny amount of the liquor, and Orlando will get that off to the lab in Miami as soon as we dock the day after tomorrow," Alex said.

"It's hard to believe we only have one more day at sea before the cruise is over," Lola said, shaking her head. "I declare, I've seen more dead bodies on the *Carnation Queen* than I see on *CSI* every week." She lowered her head and sighed. "I can't quit thinking about what happened to that poor woman tonight."

"How's Beau doing?" Jordan asked, reaching around Victor to pat Lola's hand.

"Not too good," Ray replied. "We're looking at him as a person of interest, and he's not real happy about that."

"He was on stage the entire time," Jordan said before adding, "and I can't prove it, but I'd bet money he was with Marsha Davenport before the competition. I don't see how he could have poisoned his wife."

"Why's that, sweetie? It wouldn't be the first time a

killer lied about where he'd been during the time a crime was being committed," Ray said.

"They were both late and came in within a few minutes of each other. She had that look—you know, messy hair, flushed cheeks. And they kept making goo-goo eyes at each other."

"Ooh, goo-goo eyes," Victor repeated. "That's it. Lock the bastard up."

Jordan shot him a look that shut him up immediately.

"I'll have Orlando check into that tomorrow," Ray said, pausing to rub his forehead as if he had a migraine. "There is one other thing. About six tonight Beau called room service for a bottle of Scotch for him and a bottle of champagne for Charlese. When the purser delivered the booze, Beau asked for a bucket of ice even though he has never asked for ice with his Scotch before and the champagne was already chilled. The purser was gone about fifteen minutes, and when he returned with the ice, he offered to pour both Beau and Charlese a drink like he'd done every other time he'd brought their liquor. He remembers thinking it odd that Beau refused a drink after specifically ordering a bottle and insisting that they deliver it immediately."

"You think he slipped the cyanide into the liquor when the purser left the room?" Rosie asked, scooting her chair closer to better hear the details.

"I don't know. Orlando's man found the empty champagne bottle, along with the opened bottle of Scotch on the table in the room. Either Beau changed his mind and poured himself a drink, or Charlese helped herself to his whiskey after polishing off the champagne. We do know she was carrying a tumbler with Scotch and ice, not the champagne glass, when she collapsed on stage."

"The preliminary check for cyanide in the Scotch from the bottle was negative," Alex piped in. "But that only means no one was able to detect the classic almond odor at first blush in either the liquor or her drinking water. However, that's not unusual and doesn't mean the booze wasn't the cyanide source. The rule of thumb is that if you can smell the almonds, the levels are too dangerous to drink. My guess is that Charlese would have been too drunk, after the champagne, to notice even if there had been an odor, and since liquid cyanide is pale blue or colorless, she wouldn't have seen a color change in her drink."

"Wait a minute. Are you saying the cyanide could have been in the water she drank?" Victor asked, his eyes widening. "Isn't that the same water we all drink?"

"Yes to both questions. Cyanide can be found in some water supplies, both public and private, but the levels are usually not high enough to cause problems," Alex explained.

"Sheesh! So it could have been her water?" Jordan said while shaking her head. "Not that she was drinking a whole lot of H-two-O tonight."

"Cyanide can be delivered as both a gas and a liquid. Of course, the gas kills the fastest," Alex commented.

"The gas method is a little far-fetched, don't you think?" Rosie asked.

"It's not as far out there as you might believe," Alex explained. "Cyanide gas can be produced several ways, including the burning of certain plastics. Then there's cigarette smoke that can release it, and even the stuff you girls use to take off acrylic nails."

"Charlese definitely had fake nails," Lola said. "Do you think that's what did it?"

Alex shook his head. "Gas poisoning is a long shot, plus she still had all her nails intact. I'm leaning toward the booze. And let's not forget, the cyanide could have been in the champagne bottle, too, even though that's less likely since the poison works quickly."

"So, you think she finished off the champagne, then reached for the Scotch?" Michael asked. "She did seem really snookered when she walked up the steps."

Alex nodded. "There was only a small amount of Scotch gone, so we think that's exactly what she did. Since she would've had to have consumed the entire bottle of champagne in fifteen or twenty minutes—the time it takes the poison to kill—that's our theory. If it had been in the champagne, she would have been dead before she got to the Scotch. Of course, there is the possibility the cyanide was in the glass already and the Scotch just got poured on top of it." He paused to look up when Rosie gasped. "Just to be on the safe side, though, I had the captain make an announcement warning people not to drink the water from the tap or use ice cubes until we can sort this out. He's agreed to furnish bottled water free of charge until we dock."

"We heard him about an hour ago but didn't know what to make of that. I can't believe he took an order from you," Victor said. "No offense, Alex, but aren't you just a passenger like the rest of us?"

Alex looked at Ray, who nodded. "Not anymore. This might very well be a murder of a United States citizen, and the FBI has jurisdiction in international waters. When they found out I was on board, they put me in charge of the investigation."

"And not a minute too soon," Ray added. "The ship has only six men designated as security, and Orlando is the only one with any police training. He was an MP in the army, and he knew he was way out of his league. I thought he would cry with relief when he was told to hand over the reins to Alex."

"I'll bet," Rosie said.

"Frankly, I am, too. It's been a long time since I actually investigated a murder, and back in Ranchero, it was usually a domestic violence thing. I'm relieved Alex has agreed to take charge."

"So, Alex, what happens next?" Michael asked.

"Nothing, really. I've advised your boss and Emily to cancel the rest of the competition, only because the stage is now part of a crime scene. They'll go forward with the Captain's Gala tomorrow night, but the stage will be off-limits. They're working on building an elevated area in the front of the first row that will function like a stage for the introduction of the ship's officers before the party gets underway."

"So we won't know how Charlese was poisoned until after the cruise is over?" Michael asked.

"That's right. It will take up to a week after we dock in Miami to get the test results back, and even then we may never know how the poison was introduced. Ray and I will take another stab at questioning the kitchen employees, but I don't expect any big news flashes there. According to the purser, both the Scotch and the champagne were sealed when he delivered them to Beau's room. Even Emily confirms that story."

"Emily? How did she see the bottle?" Jordan asked, wishing the night would end so she could get Alex alone. The smell of his aftershave was working overtime on her senses.

"She was in the kitchen conferring with the head chef about tonight's competition baskets. She remembered the purser calling Beau an American jerk after the call, which is when she noticed the sealed bottle of liquor."

"Where is Emily?" Lola asked. "She seemed really upset earlier, and I thought for sure she'd come up with you two after you'd finished with Orlando down there."

"She was upset," Alex replied. "Especially when the decision was made to cancel the rest of the competition. She got really angry at first, saying Charlese's death had nothing to do with the contest, but then she calmed down. She left shortly after that for her room and told us she'd confer with Wayne in the morning to try to find a way to salvage the contest somehow."

At the mention of her friend, Jordan felt a pang of sympathy. She was the only one besides George Christakis who knew about the life of servitude Emily had been subjected to with her aunt and uncle. She and Michael's boss had worked so hard planning the cook-off. Now it was ending in the worst possible way—with the death of the wife of one of the judges.

Earlier, during the doctor's frantic attempt to revive Charlese, Emily had retreated to the back of the stage. Jordan had followed in an attempt to comfort her. Noticing Emily's hands shaking badly, she'd covered them both with her own. Emily had responded by jerking her hands away and shouting, "Leave me alone." That reaction had caught Jordan off guard, but within seconds, tears had welled up in Emily's eyes, and she'd apologized profusely, blaming her unexpected outburst on crazy nerves.

Still, Jordan wished her friend had come up to the upper deck with the rest of the gang tonight. If there was another group of folks more qualified to comfort someone during a crisis situation, Jordan hadn't met them yet. She made a mental note to find some alone time with Emily after breakfast in the morning and let her know her friends were there for her if she needed them.

"So what happens now, Alex?" Victor asked.

Alex shrugged. "I'll do what I can from here and then turn the case over to the Miami field office. My guess is they'll want to have a detailed conversation with Beau and the kitchen staff. As for me, I'll be on a plane back to Ranchero." He gave Jordan a smile that nearly melted her heart.

"What about Beau?" Rosie asked. "Is he taking Charlese's death pretty hard?"

Ray grunted. "If by taking it hard you mean he's spouting off like a jerk, then yes, he's taking it hard. When they declared his room a crime scene and moved him to another suite, he pitched a fit. His old room was the biggest one on the ship, and he's not real pleased with his new one. Can you believe it? The man just lost his wife, and he's upset because the room is a few feet smaller. What an ass!"

"Now that's an understatement," Jordan said, remembering the way Beau had acted with Marsha. "What if Beau and Marsha were in this together?"

Alex ruffled her hair. "There goes that overactive imagination that I adore." He stood and helped Jordan to her feet. "There's really nothing more to be done tonight, and since I have a busy day tomorrow, I'm heading to bed." He reached for Jordan's hand. "Come on, love. I want to go make goo-goo eyes at you and mess up your hair."

CHAPTER 20

The next day Jordan waited around nearly thirty minutes after breakfast for Emily to show before finally giving up and heading to her friend's room. Although the purser told Jordan he hadn't seen Emily leave that morning, there was no response when Jordan knocked. Assuming Emily had slipped out for an early meeting with Wayne to discuss how to proceed with the competition, she made a mental note to hook up with her later.

For now she had the entire morning to herself. Alex and Ray had a full day ahead with the investigation, and although she hated losing the time with Alex, they didn't have a choice. He was on the job now. Victor and Lola were earning their keep by running a trivia tournament and teaching tarot reading classes respectively, and Rosie was caught up in preparations to serve her last lunch at the small café. Jordan had no idea where Michael was, but since he no longer had to worry about the cook-off, he was probably with Victor having fun playing games with the passengers.

Victor had begged her to join him, but she'd never been good at trivia with the exception of sports questions. Besides, she had only one day left to work on her tan, and she intended to make the best of it.

After she left Emily's, she went up to her room and slipped on a swimsuit. Since she rarely had time to indulge in her love of mystery novels, she was really looking forward to a little peace and quiet to start the book she'd purchased in the gift shop. Before she left the room, she tried Emily one more time, but as with the previous three other attempts, she was forced to leave a message.

Being the last day of the cruise, the pool was jam-packed, with everyone trying to soak up as much sun and as many alcoholic concoctions as possible. Jordan made a quick sweep of the area and was disappointed to see that all the lounge chairs were either occupied or had a towel draped over them. Vowing not to let a little thing like that ruin her day, she made her way to the shallow end of the pool. If she had to sit on the edge with her feet dangling in the water to start her novel, so be it. She was determined to have a nice leisurely day reading.

Halfway there she was surprised to see Marsha Davenport by herself in the middle of the deck, looking gorgeous in her purple bikini. She was even more surprised when Marsha smiled.

Jordan smiled back.

"Looking for a chair?"

Jordan nodded. "Not likely to find one today. Looks like the entire ship is out here."

Marsha picked up the towel lying on the chaise lounge next to her and gave it a pat. "You can have this one. I don't think Casey's going to make it back." She grinned. "She's tied up with one of the other chefs going over her résumé for a new job search."

Yeah right! We all know which chef she's with. "Tied up" might be the perfect choice of words.

Jordan sat down. "Thanks. I've been trying all week to get to this book."

"I wanted to thank you for the great score you gave my sweetbread appetizer the other night. Because of you I won."

"Sorry things haven't worked out the way you'd expected," Jordan said, putting her book down.

Why read a mystery novel when she had a puzzle right in front of her. All she had to do was figure out the clues. She hoped that old saying "Loose lips sink ships" wasn't true, because she fully intended to get the lady chef talking.

"That's for sure," Marsha responded. "I was really counting on that advertising contract in New York. Guess I'll have to go back to that dump they call a steak house in Fort Worth."

"It's too bad, because I personally thought you had the best chance to win," Jordan said, laying it on thick to loosen her up.

Marsha beamed. "I appreciate your saying that."

"Beau Lincoln really seems to think you're the best chef out there." Jordan waited for Marsha's response, expecting the woman to lash out.

Instead Marsha shrugged. "Yeah, he's kind of a jerk, though."

Now that certainly wasn't the response Jordan had anticipated.

"Really? I thought you two were good friends." She paused before adding a zinger. "At least his wife thought so."

This time anger *did* flare in Marsha's eyes before she shook her head. "She was wrong. There was never anything between Beau and me other than a friendship."

And now your nose is going to grow, Jordan thought, nearly blurting out that she'd been hiding in the closet the night Marsha tried to seduce Beau.

Better to keep that information to herself for the time being.

"Did you know that Emily Thorpe and Wayne Francis are trying to figure out a way to continue the competition?"

Marsha's eyes lit up. "That's fantastic news. Will Beau still be judging, or will it just be you and Mr. Christakis?"

"I don't know," Jordan answered honestly, noticing the hope fade from Marsha's face.

The woman knew that without Beau Lincoln and the perfect scores he gave her, she probably didn't stand a chance against Luis. Since the dessert round, Luis had easily become George's favorite with his delicious Jumbleberry Delight.

Jordan still had no idea what a jumbleberry actually was but decided it was probably best to remain ignorant. Look what had happened with Marsha's sweetbread.

"I've been really impressed with you, Jordan," Marsha said. "I think you and I could be friends."

What a suck-up!

Jordan decided to let that one slide. She'd ruin her plan to lure Marsha into talking if she confessed that hell would have to freeze over before the two of them ever became friends.

"So, Marsha, I heard Beau was on the short list of suspects in his wife's killing. What do you think about that?"

"There's no way he could have done it."

"How can you be so sure?" Jordan asked, even though she knew the reason Marsha was so positive about it: Marsha thought she was Beau's alibi. The sexy chef figured it was impossible for Beau to have killed his wife because he'd been busy getting it on with her yesterday at the time the real killer would have been preparing Charlese's poisoned cocktail.

Of course, Marsha hadn't been privy to the latest information about Charlese's death. She couldn't possibly know that the man she'd called a jerk moments ago might very well have slipped the cyanide into his own bottle of Scotch. He must have known his alcoholic wife wouldn't be able to resist sneaking a drink or two while he played house with another woman.

"I was having a drink with him before the competition that night."

Yeah, right! A drink!

Marsha narrowed her eyes. "So it wasn't him even though he wanted to leave her."

"He wanted out of the marriage?" Jordan held her breath for a second, waiting for the answer.

Marsha nodded. "But he told me that leaving her was out of the question."

Jordan's brain went on high alert. This conversation had taken an unexpected turn, and her inner amateur sleuth catapulted into overdrive. "Why?"

Marsha lowered her voice. "I probably shouldn't be

telling you this, but it doesn't matter anymore." She
looked from side to side before continuing. "Beau said
Charlese tricked him into not signing the prenup his lawyers had drawn up before the wedding. Without it, the
bitch stood to get half of everything he owned, including
his Sinfully Sweet empire, if he divorced her. He wasn't
about to give all that up."

Jordan bit her lower lip to keep from screaming. Marsha Davenport had just given her the ultimate motive for
Beau to kill his own wife: money.

It was all Jordan could do to stay in the chair and finish the conversation. She wanted to jump up and run to
Alex with what she'd just heard. Let him make fun of her
overactive imagination now.

"I've had more than enough sun for today. I'm going to
head back to my room," Marsha said, standing up and
gathering her towel and suntan lotion. "I hope to see you
later at the competition if they can work that out. If not, I
guess we'll meet up at the Captain's Gala tonight. Enjoy
the rest of the day."

Jordan's mind raced as she watched Marsha walk
away. The woman had just betrayed her own lover, who in
all likelihood had killed his wife to avoid giving up half
of his confections empire.

Now all Jordan had to do was prove it.

"You and I have a lot to talk about," Alex said, nibbling
on Jordan's neck as she brushed her teeth.

"Don't stop doing that or I'll have to kill you," she
said, spitting out the toothpaste and wiping her mouth
before turning to plant a sloppy wet kiss on his lips.

"Minty. I like that," he said, licking his lips before moving her to the side and sliding in front of her.

She faked a scowl. "And here I thought my soft neck was irresistible to you, but all you really wanted was access to the mirror."

He gave her a sheepish grin. "Your soft neck *is* irresistible, love, but a guy has to have a backup plan for bathroom time. I didn't grow up with all that abuse from my three sisters without learning something useful."

"Are you telling me that you kissed your sisters' necks, you perv?"

"Hell, no! They were a pain in my butt growing up, always bossing me around and getting their laughs by making fun of me with their friends. I had to be inventive to get any bathroom time in our house." He stopped to chuckle. "I remember once when one of my tricks scarred my sister Kate for life."

Jordan inched her way in front again and ran a brush through her unruly red curls. "Tell me you didn't do something juvenile like throwing cold water over the shower curtain."

"Worse. One night I placed a rubber mouse inside the bathroom door and attached a string that I pulled underneath the door to the other side. Kate was usually the one who camped out in the bathroom in the mornings, and she was also the one who was the most squeamish about rodents and spiders of any kind. Right after she went into the bathroom, I made a squeaking noise hoping she'd turn around. Then I pulled the string. Needless to say I had the bathroom all to myself that morning. Kate still rags on me about it."

Jordan moved out of his way again. "Okay, you win.

You can have the mirror if you promise never to mention rats to me again."

He patted her bottom before she got completely away from him. "Deal. Now let me get ready. I have a big evening ahead."

The shaving cream on his face made him look really hot in some crazy kind of way, and Jordan had to resist going in for another kiss. Instead she walked over to the small closet where the outfit she'd picked for tonight's party hung beside his clothes. She'd thought long and hard about wearing the "cursed" green blouse but then decided she was being superstitious. How could the blouse have anything to do with her date ending up dead that night? Besides, the emerald green of the blouse and her black flowing pants would contrast nicely with the dark gray suit he was wearing.

"I'm sorry this trip has turned out to be such a bummer for you. I know how much you were looking forward to the competition. And now I can't even spend the kind of time with you that I'd planned," he said wistfully.

"I know." She pulled the blouse from the closet and slipped it on. "But having you in charge of the investigation makes me feel more secure, not that I think Ray couldn't have handled it."

"Technically, the only thing I'm in charge of is Charlese's poisoning. Ray is working with Orlando on both the robbery and Goose's disappearance, and Stefano's death is officially labeled as accidental. I'm sure the *Carnation Queen* will end up paying through the nose to Stefano's family, but the authorities have closed the book on it."

"I still have my doubts about his death being accidental," Jordan said, stepping into the pants and tucking her blouse in at the waist. "But I can't prove anything. Casey and Marsha—" She inhaled sharply, reaching for the wide black belt she'd brought. "I almost forgot to tell you what Marsha told me by the pool earlier today."

"What were you doing talking to Marsha? I thought you said the two of you weren't friends."

"We aren't—or least I didn't think we were until she started brownnosing me. She's setting me up to give her a good score in case the competition is back on."

"That's pretty much a dead horse. No way they can work it out now."

"You're right. I'm sure Emily and Wayne did their best. Anyway, Marsha said Beau told her that his wife had tricked him into tearing up their prenuptial agreement. Said he would have had to hand over half of his hefty assets if he divorced her."

Alex cocked his head around the bathroom door, his face now clean shaven and looking even hotter than before. "Is that right? I have the guys in Miami checking to see if there are any high-dollar life insurance policies on Charlese. I'll put a bug in their ear about this, too. It does make for one helluva motive, especially since he was fooling around with Marsha."

"Oh, so now you believe me about that?"

He whistled when he saw her in the outfit. "Who can argue with messy hair?" He winked and then shut the door just as she shot him a look.

CHAPTER 21

The huge theater was already buzzing with activity when Jordan and Alex walked in. Looking up, Jordan was intrigued by the way the overhead lights cast a soft glow over the crowd. Dressed in everything from long flowing gowns to casual cocktail dresses, the women complimented the men in their suits and tuxedoes. Usually on a seven-day cruise, there was a Captain's Gala the first few days at sea and then again on the last day. Because of the cook-off, tonight's party was the only one, and the passengers had come out in droves.

Jordan scanned the dimly lit room for the rest of the gang and finally spied Rosie waving from a large circular table behind the theater seats. She waved back just as a handsome young waiter approached with a tray of appetizers.

She eyed the hors d'oeuvres suspiciously. They looked tame enough, but she'd thought the exact same thing about Marsha's sweetbread. She could hear her mother saying, "Fool me once, shame on you; fool me twice, shame on me." She wasn't about to go down that road again.

"What are these?"

"Tomato bruschetta."

"What's in them?"

"Roasted red tomatoes with mozzarella and a touch of garlic and basil." He pushed the half-empty tray toward her. "Try one. They're excellent."

When she hesitated, Alex reached in for one, making a big production of popping it into his mouth. "It's delicious, Jordan. Really." He took another one and held it up to her lips. "If you absolutely hate it, I'll finish it for you, I promise."

She decided there was no use arguing since the man could talk her into anything. She took a small bite and slowly chewed it while both Alex and the waiter patiently watched.

"You're lucky that was good," she teased, reaching for another one and rewarding the waiter with a huge smile before locking her free arm with Alex's. "Now, come on. Rosie's about to kill someone the way she's waving her arms for us to get over there."

They weaved their way through the crowd to the table. After giving Rosie a quick kiss, Jordan blew one to Victor, Michael, and Ray, and whistled. "Wow! You guys clean up nicely. I had no idea you all were this handsome."

"Right back atcha, sweet pea," Ray said, bending over to kiss her forehead. "Alex, you look good, too."

"Thanks. I'm glad I don't have to do this more than

once or twice a year, though," Alex said, stepping aside so Jordan could sit down. "I'll take a pair of faded jeans and a cowboy shirt any day."

"I heard that," Ray said, scooting over so Jordan could be next to Lola, who was decked out in a gorgeous turquoise blue caftan.

"You're one hot mama," Jordan said, squeezing the older woman's hand. "Have we missed anything?"

"Just a whole bunch of appetizers," Rosie answered. "For lunch I made that stir-fry recipe that I got from the Thai couple who just moved in above my apartment. You know, the one you posted in your column a few weeks back and called Pollo Fino Revuelto? Best chicken stir-fry I've ever tasted. I made a complete pig of myself before we ran out of it. I'm still so stuffed, I couldn't possibly eat another bite." She held up her cocktail glass. "Chocolate martinis are a whole different story, though."

"Jordan, what would you like to drink?" Alex asked when the waiter stopped to take their order.

She was so busy noticing how his dark gray suit brought out the deep blue of his eyes, she didn't even hear him. The man was definitely a gorgeous specimen, and tonight he was all hers. She planned on making the best of their last night on the ship, and God help anyone who interfered. She was imagining something incredibly romantic like a late-night stroll on deck followed by just the two of them in a hot tub.

"Jordan? Your drink?"

"Oh, sorry. I'll have a frozen margarita."

Alex studied her with a cool, appraising look. "What was going on in that pretty little head of yours? You were a million miles away just then."

She pinched his cheek playfully. "Wouldn't you like to know?"

His eyes flickered with mischief. "Did it involve me?"

"You'll just have to wait and see. Now go find me a couple of those bruschetta things. Unlike Rosie, I'm starving."

Jordan looked around the table at her friends while she waited for Alex to return with the appetizers. Seeing everyone all dressed up brought back memories of her childhood in Amarillo and playing dress-up with her mother's old gowns. Having only brothers, she'd often wished for a sister, and now she had two of the best ever in Rosie and Lola. She loved these people like family.

Just as Alex returned, the captain walked onto the makeshift stage and the crowd noise died down. Caught up in the gala atmosphere, it was easy to forget about the tragedy the night before. But seeing the head of the ship standing on the makeshift stage with the beautiful red curtain shimmering in the background brought it all back. It was a stark reminder that although they were all celebrating the last day of the cruise with cocktails and great food, there was a crime scene behind that curtain.

Ever since this afternoon when Michael had relayed the news that the cooking competition was definitely called off, Jordan had been especially anxious to talk to Emily. But she was nowhere to be found and hadn't returned the many messages Jordan had left on her phone. Although the contestants were bound to be disappointed because there would be no winner now, Luis and Phillip had gotten the good news that George Christakis was offering them each an entry-level job at his restaurant in New York. Jordan wondered if Casey and Marsha had heard that announcement yet—and if they had, was glad not to have been there when they got the news.

"Has anyone talked to Emily today?" Rosie asked, looking stunning in a black cocktail dress, her blond hair pulled back into a French twist.

When no one spoke up, Michael shook his head. "She was with Wayne earlier, but I haven't seen her since. Are you worried about her?"

"I am," Jordan said, turning back to the makeshift stage. She was trying to get her mind off Emily and concentrate on the ship's various department heads, who were currently being introduced.

But it was a losing battle.

When she couldn't stand it any longer, she whispered to Alex, "Would you mind if I left you here with the gang for a few minutes? I want to check on Emily."

"Of course not. I know how worried you are about her. Frankly, I am, too." He checked his watch. "I'm waiting on a report from Miami. If it comes in, Orlando is going to call to let me know. I may have to run down to the security office for a few minutes, anyhow. Go take care of your friend. If either of us gets tied up, we'll meet at dinner in an hour. Okay?"

She kissed the top of his nose before explaining to the others where she was going. Walking out of the theater, she couldn't shake an overwhelming sense of doom and gloom. Something was definitely wrong with Emily, and tonight she might need a friend more than ever. Jordan intended to be there for her, even if it meant giving up precious moments with Alex.

Standing outside Emily's cabin, she debated telling her she knew about her horrible teenage years. Sometimes, walls could be broken only when a person shared a horrible experience like that. Jordan prayed that would be the case with Emily, if she decided to reveal what George had confided in her.

After knocking several times, Jordan was about to walk away when Emily opened the door.

"Hey, Jordan. Did you need something?"

Jordan's mouth dropped open when she saw her friend. She'd imagined Emily holed up in her room in pajamas, isolating herself from the world because of whatever had been bothering her for the past few days. That's not the impression she got as she stared at the woman. Dressed in an off-the-shoulder, pale pink cocktail dress with matching stilettos, Emily was definitely not planning to isolate herself anytime soon.

Jordan put her arms around her, noticing the way Emily stiffened at the contact. "I'm so glad you're feeling better. I was concerned about you."

Emily pushed a strand of blond hair out of her eyes. "No need to worry. I'm fine."

When she didn't invite her in, Jordan asked, "Are you on your way to the party? If so, I'll walk with you."

Emily looked surprised by the question. "I'm not going."

Determined to help her friend, Jordan waltzed past her, uninvited. The first thing she noticed was the difference between Emily's cabin and her own. Nearly double the size, it had a sliding glass door that opened onto a private patio.

"Holy cannoli! Guess it pays to know someone. This room is gorgeous."

Emily glanced down at her watch. "If the only reason

you came by was to check on me, you can see that I'm fine. I'll try to meet up with all of you at dinner." Again, she peeked at her watch.

"Are you waiting on someone?"

"No," she answered quickly, but her tone said differently. "There seems to be another problem in New York that my incompetent assistant can't work out. I swear I'm going to fire her the minute I get back home. Anyway, I need to finish up here."

"Dressed like that?" Jordan was getting weird vibes from her friend. Emily was definitely a little nervous about something, judging by the way she shifted her weight from one foot to the other, her eyes darting to the door at the slightest sound.

Convinced the last thing her friend needed was to be alone right now, Jordan decided to delay her exit in the hope that maybe Emily would open up to her. "Would you mind if I take a quick look off your balcony? I'll probably never have an opportunity like this again."

Emily nodded. "A quick one, though. I hate to rush you, but I really do need to get back to my paperwork."

Jordan slid the door back and walked out onto the deck. The balcony alone was almost as big as her room, and the view was spectacular. She walked up to the railing and sniffed the salty ocean air, thinking this was how the ocean should be viewed. She leaned over to get a better look at the rippling waves as the ship glided through the water, and she noticed they were right over the middle rescue boats.

"You really need to go now, Jordan," Emily snapped before Jordan could comment on it.

Confused, she met Emily's gaze, noticing her friend

was breathing rapidly now. Jordan walked back into the room and shut the door. "Are you sure you're okay?" She was more than a little worried about her friend's strange behavior.

"I'm fine." Emily spat out the words and glared at Jordan. "I just need you to go."

Warning bells sounded in Jordan's head. Something was terribly wrong here, but she didn't know what it was or how to fix it. If Emily wasn't ready to talk about whatever was bothering her, there was nothing more she could do to help her. Frustrated, she walked past Emily to the door. Halfway there, someone knocked, and she jumped.

"Dammit!" Emily swore. "I told you I had business." She rushed past Jordan and opened the door.

If Jordan had thought her visit up to this point had been a bit strange, she now realized things were about to cross over into bizarre. Beau Lincoln, dressed in a tuxedo and holding a bottle of champagne chilling in a bucket in one hand and two glasses in the other, stood outside Emily's door with a cocky grin on his face that almost made her want to throw up.

His eyes lit up when he saw Jordan. "Hot damn! Ever since I got your call to come down here for some fun, I haven't been able to think about anything else. Now, I find out there will be two beautiful women instead of just one, and I'm ecstatic." He walked into the room and placed the champagne and glasses on the table. "Who wants a drink to get the good times started?"

Jordan shot Emily a look, finding it hard to believe what she'd just heard. In that moment, everything became crystal clear as to why Emily had been in such a hellfire hurry to get her out of the room: she'd been awaiting a private "party" with the sleaziest man on the ship.

Eew!

Disgusted, Jordan reached for the door. The faster she got out of there, the better. She chastised herself for being such a poor judge of character and for feeling sorry for Emily. The woman was as bad as Marsha—worse, since Beau's wife was probably not even cold yet.

"I wouldn't do that if I were you, Jordan," Emily said.

"I think I've seen about as—" Jordan's hand shot up to her mouth when she turned around but not fast enough to stifle a gasp.

Emily Thorpe, the woman she thought of as her friend, was pointing a gun directly at her head.

"Emily, what are you doing?" she shouted, trying to figure out what was going on.

"What the hell is this?" Beau asked. "You called me down here promising all kinds of great things, and now you pull a gun on me? Give it to me." When he took a step closer to her, she slammed the side of his head with the revolver.

Moaning, he slumped to the carpet, blood oozing from a three-inch gash near his temple.

"Emily, I don't know what you're thinking, but you need to give me the gun before you really do hurt one of us."

"Shut up, Jordan. I told you I had business to take care of. You should have listened to me." She kicked Beau in the side, causing him to yelp. "I'm going to make you wish you'd never met me."

Jordan repeated the earlier request. "I don't know where you got that gun, but you need to put it down."

The New Yorker threw back her head and laughed, except it came out as more of a cackle. "Compliments of our friend Goose."

"Goose? How did you get his gun?" No sooner had the words left Jordan's mouth than a horrible vision ran through her head. It was the image of Goose's orange and blue plaid shirt and the scrap of that material that had caught on one of the rescue boats—the one that was right below Emily's balcony. "Goose fell from out there?"

"You could say that," Emily said, her hands now shaking so badly Jordan was afraid the gun might go off accidentally.

"And what would *you* say?" She had to keep Emily talking until she could figure out a way to get the weapon out of her hand.

"I'd say the man signed his own death warrant when he walked in here demanding a million dollars." She huffed. "He had no idea who he was messing with. For a security professional, he wasn't all that smart, if you ask me. He should've never accepted that whiskey on the rocks when he got here. He thought he was so smart because he insisted that I pour myself a drink from the same bottle." She snickered. "The fool had no idea the inside of his glass was coated with a fast-acting sedative. In ten minutes time, he was so groggy he offered no resistance when I led him outside. Getting him over the railing proved to be a little more difficult, but I did it. And now, he's shark bait."

Jordan was horrified, and for the first time she realized that the woman standing in front of her now was probably mentally ill. How could she have missed seeing the signs before?

"Emily," Jordan pleaded one more time. "No one has to know about this. We can say that Goose got drunk and fell into the water by himself. But you have to let me and Beau go. We'll get help for you, I promise." She took a deep breath and moved closer to Emily, hoping she didn't end up on the floor like Beau.

"I know how much you hated your life in Colombia with your aunt and uncle. They robbed you of your teenage years. Let Beau leave, and you and I can talk about it. If you talk about it, it will no longer have power over you."

Emily's head snapped up. "How do you know about that?"

"George told me. He's as worried about you as I am."

A lone tear ran down Emily's cheek, and for one promising minute, Jordan thought she had gotten through to her. That tiny hope was dashed when the woman raised the gun again.

"Get back, Jordan. I don't want to hurt you, only Beau, but I will if you force me to."

"Why me? What in the hell did I ever do to you?" Beau asked, now holding his hand over the wound above his eye in an attempt to stop the bleeding.

The noise that came out of Emily's mouth sounded more animal than human. She got down on her knees and placed the muzzle of the gun against his forehead.

"You, my friend, are responsible for everything in my life that caused me pain, and tonight, you're going to pay for it."

CHAPTER 22

"Get up, Beau," Emily ordered before turning to face Jordan. "Grab a couple of scarves out of the top drawer behind you."

"You've got the wrong guy, lady. I don't know you from Adam," Beau said indignantly.

For a man with a gun so close to his head, Beau Lincoln was being awfully confrontational, dangerously so, in fact. Whatever had made Emily think he'd caused all the grief in her life was at the core of her anger right now. Coming across with attitude wasn't the best way for him to defend himself and diffuse the raging volcano building inside the woman.

"You just met Beau a few days ago, Emily. And although I'd have to agree he's a slimeball, how could he possibly be responsible for all your pain?"

"Shut up about that, Jordan," Emily screamed. "Just get the scarves."

Jordan did as she was told and handed a red and a blue scarf to Emily, thinking the expensive silk accessories probably cost more than her own entire outfit.

Emily threw the red one back at her. "Tie up his legs."

"Emily, do you really—"

"Just do it, Jordan, or I'll shoot him right now."

Jordan bent down and wrapped the scarf around Beau's legs. He didn't even try to resist, making Jordan think he'd finally realized Emily was not fooling around and that she was close to going off the deep end.

"Now tie his hands behind his back," Emily growled. "Tight enough so he can't feel his fingers."

"Honestly, Emily, you have mistaken me for someone else. Please don't do this to me," Beau whimpered, fear in his voice now.

Emily stepped in front of him and did a slow 360-degree turn in front of him, giving him an up-close look. "Brianna Sloan. Recognize the name, moron?"

He shook his head. "Trust me. I would never forget a woman like you."

"Then how about my grandmother's brownie recipes?" She spit at him. "Does that ring a bell?"

"What are you talking about? I never—" He stopped, his mouth open, his eyes filling with terror as recognition washed over his face. He lowered his head. "I thought you were dead."

She slapped him across the face so hard a red handprint appeared on his cheek. The wound over his eye began to bleed again, but with his hands tied behind his back, all he could do was blink when a drop of blood slid down his face.

"I may as well have died. You never even bothered to come to the hospital to find out about me or your baby." Emily's voice broke, and she paused. "You told me you loved me on more than one occasion, and I believed you, but all you wanted were the recipes. I heard you were bragging about how you duped me into giving them up right before you dumped me." She turned away to swipe at a tear sliding down her cheek. "You called me a two-bagger—said the only way you could even touch me was with two bags over my head." She swiped a plastic bag off the table and in a second had it over his head.

Beau tried to protest but only succeeded in falling across the bed.

"Guess you're just a one-bagger," she said, curling her lips in a sarcastic smile. "How does it feel now?"

"Emily," Jordan shouted. "He'll suffocate. I know you're not that cruel."

"Do you think he gave a flying flip about how cruel he was to me? I've waited a long time for this."

She allowed Beau to fight for several more minutes before yanking the bag from his head. As he gasped for air, coughing uncontrollably, she jerked him to his feet once again.

Standing directly in front of her, he finally managed to catch his breath and begin breathing normally.

He stared defiantly at her. "There's no way you could be Brianna Sloan. I have no idea why, but you're lying through your teeth. Even the most expensive plastic surgeon in the world couldn't take that fat, pimply faced mouse of girl and turn her into you. So, what's your angle? Are you looking to get some easy money out of me?"

Emily's arm swung back so quickly, he was unprepared when she delivered a solid left hook to his chin. Screaming in pain, he fell backward, hitting his head on the edge of the table, which elicited a slew of obscenities from his lips.

Emily didn't even flinch. She was beside him in a flash and shoved her foot hard into his chest, the stiletto heel digging into his skin while he screamed in agony.

"All these years I've been thinking about what it would be like when I finally got my revenge. I wondered what you'd say when I confronted you. I have to admit I thought you might be at least a little remorseful. Never in a million years did I expect to see you act like that same cocky jerk who ruined my life back in Ranchero." She took her foot off his chest and glared at him. "For God's sake, Beau, I was only fifteen years old. You could've been arrested. Lucky for you I lost the baby when I ran from you and ended up wrapping my dad's car around the bridge abutment and refused to tell the authorities who the father was." Her voice caught. "I prayed you'd come to see me once you found out how injured I was. When that didn't happen, I wanted to die right along with your bastard child."

Jordan hadn't said a word throughout this entire confrontation, thinking maybe if she let Emily release all the pent-up anger that must've been smoldering all these years, she could talk some sense into her. The most important thing now was to get the gun out of her hand.

At first Jordan believed, as Beau had, that this was just a case of mistaken identity, but after hearing Emily's story, she remembered Wayne Francis telling a similar one earlier in the week. He, too, thought the girl who had been so humiliated by Beau had ended up in a terrible accident and died that night.

"Emily," she began, wanting to comfort her friend, despite the fact she still had Goose's loaded gun in her hand. "I can't even imagine how much pain you were in back then. Young love can be devastating, but hurting Beau now won't take that pain away. I promise if you give me the gun, I'll go with you to talk to anyone you want once we're back on shore."

"Oh, I'm not going to hurt him, Jordan." She laughed. "I'm going to kill him just like he did to that innocent girl so long ago. My father couldn't even look at me after he'd discovered I'd been pregnant. Said I had disgraced him with his congregation and he could no longer look any church members in the eye."

Jordan inched a little closer to Emily. "Is that why he sent you to Columbia to live with your aunt and uncle?"

Emily lowered her head but not before Jordan saw the pain in her eyes. "He couldn't get rid of me fast enough. Since I had no friends and had been airlifted to Children's Hospital in Dallas the day of the accident, no one bothered to visit me. He conveniently told everyone I had died of complications. When I was discharged, he drove me straight to the Dallas airport and put me on a plane—not that anyone in Ranchero would have recognized me, anyway. My face was so badly mangled I didn't look anything like I used to."

Her voice dropped to a whisper. "He preached fire and brimstone all my life, so I don't know why I expected him to do anything other than condemn me for my sins. When he sent me to live with his sister and her husband who ran a missionary school in Colombia, he said he hoped God would forgive me because he never would. How ironic that he died hating me. He never did see me as the victim in all this."

"What about your mother? Didn't she have a say in your going to Colombia?"

"He ran her off long before I ever really got to know her. Then he blamed me for all her cheating. Said I was just as bad as her."

Jordan took a chance and moved another step closer. Keeping Emily talking seemed her best strategy. At least then, she wouldn't be making good on her threat to kill Beau.

"Look at what you've made of your life. Something good did come out of all that pain, Emily."

"It's Anna," she corrected. "And if you call being treated as a slave from the minute my plane touched down in Bogotá, then yes, my life did change. My uncle, who was at least a hundred pounds overweight himself and had breath that could have stopped a train, used to tell me how ugly I was and that I was fortunate he could see past my looks to the beautiful girl I was inside." She sniffed back her tears. "Yeah, I was lucky, all right. Lucky enough to work like a dog and never allowed to have any friends. He even farmed me out to some of the families around the school to babysit, but I never saw any of the money," she said sarcastically.

"Why didn't your aunt try to stop him?" Jordan asked.

Emily huffed. "She was more afraid of him than I was. But I got my revenge on him just like I'm going to do with Beau. One night when he was all liquored up, I slipped a little drain cleaner into his beer. It was just enough to make him violently ill, and while he was in the hospital I took a bag of emerald stones that he'd stolen from one of his church members. I boarded the next plane back to Dallas." She snickered. "I would have loved to have seen his face when he pulled up that plank of wood on the floor and discovered his precious gems were gone. Even my aunt didn't know they were there. He had no clue he'd spilled the beans to me one night while he was drunk."

Jordan turned when Beau moaned, and she saw him grimace in pain. She had to find a way to get the gun from Emily, then get out of there and bring back help.

But Emily wasn't through talking.

"In Dallas, I used some of the emeralds to hire a world-renowned plastic surgeon. He literally had to wire my jaw shut and remake my entire face. Because of it, I lost eighty pounds. When I looked into the mirror for the first time after surgery, an entirely different person stared back at me. That's when I decided to go to New York. I thought if I changed everything about my life, maybe the resentment wouldn't eat at me every minute of the day. I couldn't remember the last time I had slept through the entire night. Still can't."

"Emily, look at you. You have so much more than Beau does. And you don't have to get revenge. He'll probably go to prison for the rest of his life for killing his wife." Jordan knew that was reaching, but right now she didn't have anything else up her sleeve.

"I didn't kill her," Beau protested, before Emily kicked him in the back.

"Shut up. Even hearing your voice makes me angry." She shook her head. "You were the one who was supposed to die, you jackass. Not your wife. She was just another innocent victim of yours, like me. Stefano wasn't supposed to die, either."

Jordan was confused at the reference to Stefano. How did the Italian chef who'd died of an allergic reaction play into this story? She couldn't resist asking about it. "You killed Stefano?"

Emily's eyes darkened. "He was a casualty of war, so to speak, although I don't think there were too many tears shed over his death." She got right up in Beau's face. "I remembered you telling me how your mother had died of an allergic reaction to nuts. You said that's why you never ate any of my grandmother's brownies with nuts in them. You even mentioned that right after you started college, you'd been rushed to the hospital with breathing problems because you'd accidently eaten pecan-crusted fish. The doctor warned you never to eat nuts again if you wanted to stay alive."

"Then how did Stefano end up with them?" Jordan asked.

"I specifically asked everyone involved with the competition if they had any food allergies. The idiot kept his a secret. When I found out Beau hadn't even bothered to return the questionnaire, I decided it was the perfect way to kill him without casting any suspicion on myself."

"So you just randomly put the ground nuts in Stefano's basket?"

"I had no idea whose basket they ended up in that day, but it didn't matter. I knew Beau would taste all the food, and my mission would be accomplished." She smirked. "You have to admit, Jordan, it would've been the perfect murder."

The loud knock at the door startled all of them, and Jordan screamed.

"Emily, open up. It's Alex Moreland. I need to talk to you."

"She's got a gun, Alex," Jordan yelled before Emily turned it on her.

"I didn't want to involve you in all this, Jordan. You're the only person besides George who has ever been kind to me without wanting something in return."

Alex's voice screaming outside the door for the purser was enough to throw Emily over the edge. Her eyes widened, and she used her free hand to jerk Beau to his feet.

"Move," she commanded, prodding him in the back with the weapon. "Jordan, get over here. I need your help."

Emily opened the door and shoved Beau out to the patio. When his body was pressed against the railing, she pointed to his feet.

"Grab on and help me lift him over the side."

When Jordan was slow to react, she screamed, "Hurry before your boyfriend breaks in and I have to kill him, too."

Without thinking of the consequences, Jordan lunged for the gun, but she had grossly underestimated Emily's strength, which, as it turned out, was considerable.

The crazed woman pushed Jordan into Beau's back and pressed her own body against both of them, rocking so that their combined weight would push Beau over the edge.

"It's not too late, Emily. I promise Alex will see to it that Beau is punished," Jordan said, trying to get her hand on the railing for leverage.

Just as Alex entered the room shouting her name,

Emily gave one final push, and all three of them tumbled over the side of the ship. There was a sickening thud as Beau's body slammed into the side of the same rescue boat that Goose had hit the night he died. For a split second Jordan thought they would be safe, but then his body bounced off the boat into the murky water, taking her and Emily with him.

CHAPTER 23

The chilly water enveloped Jordan as she plunged deeper. In that instant when she realized she was going to die, her life flashed before her, along with all the things she hadn't yet accomplished. Then her body began to rise. She kicked her arms and legs, propelling herself upward. As soon as she broke the surface, she sucked in a huge breath and began to tread water to keep afloat.

Seconds later, Emily's head surfaced close to Jordan, and she, too, struggled to keep from going back under.

From where they were, Jordan could see the ship in the distance. Knowing the large cruise ship wouldn't be able to reverse directions quickly, she prayed Alex already had a rescue operation underway. She tried to swim toward the ship, but she'd depleted her energy trying to keep her head above water, and it was a losing battle.

There was nothing else to do but wait and hope help wasn't too late.

Several yards away, Beau's head popped out of the water, but because his extremities were still tied, he disappeared again within seconds. Without hesitating, Jordan took a deep breath and paddled to the spot where she'd last seen him. Once there she sucked in another gulp of air, then dove under the water. Even with her eyes open, she couldn't see a thing. Hoping to touch something that might help her pinpoint Beau's location, she made wide sweeping motions with her arms.

With her lungs about to explode, she finally gave up and began to push herself topside. Halfway there, her hand brushed against something, and she grabbed on. Realizing it was part of Beau's tuxedo, she tugged, using every ounce of strength she had left. But Beau was a big man, and he wasn't helping. With only enough air left for one more attempt, she swung her legs rapidly and jerked his body.

Finally, she and Beau began to ascend.

When her head broke the surface a second time, she was so out of breath, she thought both she and Beau would die, despite her best effort. He was above water now, but he was unconscious—maybe even dead. Glancing up, she saw one of the rescue boats being lowered into the water. Realizing there was a man overboard, or in this case a man and two women, the *Carnation Queen*'s passengers were lined up along the railing and shouting to them. Although from that distance it was faint, it was still music to her ears, and for the first time since her body hit the cold water, she had hope.

With her breathing now coming in short fast bursts,

she knew she wouldn't be able to tread water and hang on to Beau much longer, and she prayed for the strength to last until the rescue boat reached them.

She was surprised when Emily suddenly appeared beside her. Because she worked out daily, Emily was having a much easier time staying alive than either Jordan or Beau and wasn't even breathing heavily. She smiled before reaching and tearing Beau out of Jordan's grip. With one good shove, she pushed him farther out to sea, still smiling when he went underwater for the last time.

Horrified, Jordan braced herself for the same fate. Emily had proven she was the stronger of the two earlier on the balcony. Already exhausted from trying to rescue Beau, Jordan didn't stand a chance but prepared to do battle just the same when the woman moved closer.

With tears streaming down her face, Emily reached over and gently touched Jordan's cheek. "Thank you for being my friend. You'll never know how much that meant to me."

Then she closed her eyes and dove beneath the water.

"No!" Jordan screamed, frantically searching with both her hands and legs to feel for Emily.

But it was not to be. The troubled woman was gone, and no rescue operation would be able to save her.

Totally exhausted now, Jordan remembered the survival training her dad had insisted on before he'd allow her or her brothers on a boat. Bending her back, she lay atop the water with her legs floating halfway to the surface. No longer struggling, she stared at the stars and prayed Alex would reach her.

Just when she was certain the boat would not get to her before her strength gave out, she heard his voice and looked up to see him a few yards away in the rescue boat. Strong arms lifted her out of the water. Now as limp as an overcooked noodle, she was unable to help them. When she was almost in the boat, she gazed into the most beautiful blue eyes she'd ever seen.

In that moment she knew this man would never let anything happen to her. The pent-up tears she'd been holding back poured down her face as Alex covered her with a blanket and pressed her shivering body close to his. His own tears were making trails down his cheeks, and he didn't seem to care if anyone saw them.

She sobbed and held on tightly. "They're both gone."

He pulled her closer, rocking her back and forth as if she were a child. "I know."

Even cocooned in the arms of the man who had won over her heart, Jordan could sleep only fitfully. Alex had been so gentle with her after the rescue, purposely not asking about the events that had led to her ending up in the water. He'd simply stroked her hair and told her things would be okay.

But she knew they would never be the same. The few times she'd managed to nod off, she'd awoken with the image in her head of Emily smiling at her in the moment just before she dove to her death. Alex was always there to take her in his arms again without a word. Emotionally and physically drained, she was grateful he hadn't insisted she tell the story yet. He'd recognized she was incapable of rehashing it without a complete breakdown.

Alex Moreland was a keeper. And that thrilled her as well as scared the heck out of her.

Around six, Alex suggested they get up and get some breakfast since both of them were having a hard time getting back to sleep. Somewhere in the middle of the night the ship had docked in Miami, and preparations were already underway for disembarkation. Neither she nor Alex had eaten dinner the night before, and she was starving.

They were joined by Rosie, Ray, and Lola at the restaurant. Victor and Michael were sleeping in and had sent word they would meet up with them in an hour to do the required Customs paperwork before they left the ship.

Jordan was unusually quiet at breakfast, unable to stop thinking that if she'd picked up even one clue from Emily, maybe she could have prevented the woman from killing Beau and then herself.

"Jordan, are you able to tell us what happened yet?" Alex asked while they killed time sipping coffee after breakfast.

She met his gaze. "I'll try. I know how important it is to your investigation."

"You don't have to do it right now if you're not ready, love." He reached for her hand under the table.

"I need to tell you the details while they're fresh in my mind. That way you can pass them on to the authorities in Miami. Maybe I'll feel less guilty if I can get Emily's story out in the open." She sighed. "I don't even want to think about what would've happened if you hadn't showed up when you did, Alex. She was like a crazy woman."

He squeezed her hand. "I was getting worried about you, and I wanted to talk to Emily. Remember when I told you I was waiting on a report from Miami?" When she nodded, he continued. "It came in around twenty minutes after you left the theater. It was the results of my request for background checks on all the ship's employees and everyone connected to the cook-off."

"And?" Ray put his cup down and leaned closer.

"There was no Emily Thorpe until fourteen years ago. A further check on the Social Security number she'd listed showed that it had belonged to an eighty-five year-old woman from New York who had died fifteen years before. Apparently, Emily stole her identity."

"Her name is—was—Brianna Sloan," Jordan said, wishing she could forget it all but knowing she had to go on. "She grew up in Ranchero."

"What?" Lola nearly jumped out of her chair.

"And no one recognized her? Didn't Wayne Francis say he'd lived there all his life?" Ray asked.

Jordan nodded. "So did Beau, but apparently Emily—Anna, as she called herself—looked nothing like she did back then. At only fifteen she left town after a horrible car accident in which she ran her car into a bridge abutment. Her father was a preacher and disowned her when he found out she'd been pregnant. Told everyone she'd died in a Dallas hospital."

"For the love of God, I won't ever be able to understand how people can preach Christianity and then treat their own kin that way." Lola commented.

"You haven't heard the worst of it," Jordan said, lowering her head before she recounted Emily's story. "Apparently, the reason she wrecked that night was because she was speeding after being dumped unceremoniously by the one and only Beau Lincoln."

"Holy crap! Are you saying she'd been planning revenge on Beau all these years?" Ray asked.

"Yes. She wasn't a popular teenager, and when he showered her with attention she fell hard for him. After he got her to hand over her grandmother's recipe for brownies with her secret ingredient—alcohol—he dumped her and then publicly humiliated her. She's been carrying that rage around all this time, keeping up with Beau and Ranchero for years. When she heard KTLK talking about the cook-off, she jumped on the bandwagon, planning to find a way to kill Beau before the ship docked back in Miami."

"Was she going to throw him overboard?" Lola asked.

"Years ago, Beau had mentioned to her that he was allergic to nuts, to explain why he couldn't eat any of her grandmother's brownies that contained them. When she found out he hadn't even bothered to send in the cook-off questionnaire that would've listed his allergy, she masterminded an ingenious plan. It would have been the perfect crime."

"Until Stefano dropped dead before Beau had a chance to taste the nut-laced fish the Italian chef had prepared," Ray said, nodding. "It was clever, if I have to say so myself."

"I just can't help feeling I let Emily down," Jordan said. "If I had only—"

"Stop right there, young lady," Ray interrupted. "You're sitting here with two men trained to look for clues who were also around Emily—three, if you count Goose. We all missed the signs, so quit beating yourself up."

"Speaking of Goose, I forgot to mention that Emily killed him, too," Jordan said, grateful for the love she felt from the people around the table.

"Wow! I didn't see that one coming. All this time we thought Goose had skipped the country." Ray crinkled his eyes in deep thought. "I wonder if that had anything to do with what we discovered in his room."

All three of them turned to him.

When he reached for his coffee and took a long sip, Lola slapped his shoulder playfully. "You know how I hate to wait, darling. You can't just drop a bomb like that on us, then sit back and pretend like it was nothing. Tell us, please, or I'll be forced to beat it out of you."

Ray grinned, obviously enjoying the attention. "Okay, the other day when we searched Goose's room, we found a tablet with a bunch of notes about a man named Kevin Watson from Dallas. Seems he's a nurse who works in a private hospital run by a plastic surgeon. This doctor is world renowned for his work with children with cleft palate and facial deformities so extensive no one else would touch them."

Jordan's eyes lit up. "Emily's face was really messed up in the accident. She had plastic surgery in Dallas."

"What did the note say about this Watson guy, Ray?" Alex asked.

"Very little. Goose only listed the man's name and telephone number. When we were able to reach Watson on his cell phone, he was vacationing in Puerto Rico with his wife. All he would tell us was that he thought he'd recognized a former patient of his in a bar in Puerto Rico this week. Although the woman denied she'd ever seen him before, Goose came back later and questioned him about it. He told him he'd mistaken her for Anna Sloan, a former patient of his at the hospital." He paused. "Oh good God, he probably was talking about Emily."

"And five bucks says this Watson dude was the one at Señor Frog's in Puerto Rico. You know, the drunk who insisted he knew Emily?" Lola paused to allow that to sink in. "You walked him back to his table. Remember, Ray?"

Before Ray could respond, Jordan gasped. "Now I get it. That's why Emily killed him. She said Goose came to her room demanding a million dollars. He must've used the info he got from this nurse to research Anna. Somehow he made the connection between Anna and Emily, then threatened to expose her if she didn't pay up."

"Good Lord! What that man wouldn't do for money," Lola exclaimed before adding, "I guess he felt like he was drowning in debt trying to keep his wife in that nice facility."

"That and keeping the thugs from roughing him up or worse when he got back to Miami," Alex said.

Ray's eyebrow arched. "What do you mean?"

"The report from Miami mentioned Jerry Goosman took quite a beating before this trip."

"We know," Lola interrupted. "He intervened when some kid was getting the snot kicked out of him. Goose ended up taking a few hits himself."

"That's what he told the police in the emergency room that night, but they didn't buy it. Number one, there were no reports of a banged-up kid in any of the local hospitals, and two, word on the street was that Goose was into a vicious loan shark for a lot of money. The cops think the beating was a reminder not to be late on the payment."

"It's all starting to make sense now," Ray said.

Alex narrowed his eyes in deep thought. "I'm wondering how Goose knew to contact Watson at all."

"I saw him go back into the bar after we all left that day," Jordan said. "At the time I thought he was just going to hook up with that woman who stopped him on the way out and seemed to know him more intimately than just as a business partner."

"You've probably just solved the mystery of how and why Goose was killed," Alex said. "Since Beau is dead, I guess we can close the books on Charlese Lincoln's death, too. He was the only one who stood to gain anything with her out of the picture."

"Emily killed her," Jordan blurted. "Not deliberately, though. It was another failed attempt to get to Beau."

"How in the hell did she manage to do that?" Ray asked before shaking his head. "I'm beginning to think either Emily Thorpe was the smartest woman alive, or I need to bone up on my criminal investigation skills."

"You and me both, Ray." Alex laughed before turning back to Jordan. "This is getting good. Tell us how she pulled that one off."

"I'm not a hundred percent sure exactly how she did it, but she mentioned she'd coated a cocktail glass with a sedative before she handed Goose a drink that night. When he got suspicious, she poured herself a glass from the same bottle, making him think there wasn't anything harmful in the whiskey. A fatal mistake on his part since she was able to lead him to her balcony before he totally passed out."

"But how could she have done that with Beau's drink? The waiter said he personally delivered it to Beau and Charlese that night," Lola asked.

"I don't know," Jordan said, hitching one shoulder. "Didn't the waiter say Emily was in the kitchen when Beau ordered the drinks? My guess is she found an opportunity to lace the inside of the cocktail glass with cyanide, thinking Charlese would be safe because she'd drink from the champagne glass."

"Sounds plausible," Ray said. "What Emily had no way of knowing is that Beau would refuse the drink—"

"Probably," Jordan interrupted, "because he was hot to trot to get to Marsha's room for a quickie."

Ray nodded. "And once Charlese finished the champagne, she poured herself a glass of Beau's Scotch in the tainted glass, then headed for the theater to confront her cheating husband."

"I can't help but admire Emily a little," Lola said. "Two big powerful men—Beau and her uncle, and three, if you count Goose—came at her intending to hurt her in some way, and she managed to take them out."

Jordan smiled at her friend and mouthed, *Thank you for that*. It was just the right amount of humor to whittle away some of the guilt she felt for not being able to help Emily. After all she'd endured—the horrible living conditions in Colombia and the humiliation she'd suffered because of Beau—she'd figured out a way to survive. At least until the pain had become so overwhelming, she couldn't deal with it anymore.

But the reality was that in Emily's quest for revenge on Beau, two innocent people had also died. And even if Goose wasn't totally without blame, he still didn't deserve to die the way he did, either.

Jordan decided she wasn't there to judge—Someone way more powerful than her had that job. For now, it was enough to know that Emily was finally at peace.

CHAPTER 24

The gang was subdued while they waited in port to go through Immigrations and Customs, the final step of their Caribbean cruise. Given everything that had happened aboard the *Carnation Queen*, this vacation was one Jordan would never forget.

They collected their bags, cleared Customs, and hailed a taxi back to the hotel in Miami. Since the flight to Dallas was scheduled for early the next morning, they planned to have a quiet dinner in the hotel restaurant and then hang out for a few hours in the piano bar. But first, the women were going to take a trip to the facility where Mary Alice Goosman lived. As it turned out, that part of Goose's story was not a lie.

The plan was to tell Mary Alice in person why Goose would no longer be coming to see her. Not that she'd understand, but they'd talked it over and decided it was the least they could do. Ray had received information from Orlando about the nursing home where Goose's wife resided and had even managed to get his hands on Goose's other orange and blue plaid shirt before the cops came on board and went through his stuff. They intended to leave the shirt with the woman in the hope it might bring her comfort in some small way.

After everyone was settled in the hotel, the three women set out to find the nursing home twenty miles from their hotel, according to the concierge. In the taxi on the ride over, they decided Jordan would do the talking, and Rosie and Lola would act as backup.

The taxi pulled up to a large building, the front yard of which bloomed with more flowers than Jordan had ever seen in one place other than a botanical garden. She took it as a good sign since she'd imagined an Alzheimer's facility as being dark and ominous-looking, with screaming patients and foul odors.

They hopped out of the car and instructed the driver to wait. Silently, they strode up the walkway just as George Christakis sauntered out of the building. His face lit up when he saw them.

"What are you doing here?" Jordan asked, confused. George didn't even know Goose.

"One of the security cops from the ship told me about Goose's wife. I had a few hours to kill before my flight leaves for New York, and I thought I would run by and give her my condolences." He lowered his eyes but not before Jordan saw a tear threaten to spill over.

Jordan turned to the others. "Can you guys give us a few minutes? There's something I want to say to George."

Rosie nodded and led Lola to the bench in front of a gorgeous display of yellow and blue flowers.

Jordan grabbed George's elbow and walked with him to a waiting cab. "I haven't had a chance to tell you how sorry I am for your loss, George. I know how much Emily meant to you."

He sniffed before the beginning of a smile crossed his face. "I loved her like a daughter, and I'll miss her terribly. I had no idea her pain was that deep. I'm grateful that you offered her friendship, because she didn't make friends easily."

"It was hard not to like her."

"I know. Well, I guess this is good-bye. I can't tell you how glad I am to have met you, Jordan McAllister. Just thinking about you makes me smile." He reached out and took her in his arms. "My offer is open for you to come to New York and visit any time you want. You can stay with Jeremy and me just like Emily did."

"I'd like that," she said, knowing it would probably never happen. "It was a pleasure to meet you."

"The pleasure was all mine, my dear." He slid into the backseat of the cab and shut the door.

Jordan watched the cab drive away before heading over to where Rosie and Lola waited.

"He is such a nice man," Rosie said. "Too bad he's already spoken for."

"Most of the good ones are," Lola said, shaking her head. "Come on. We'd better get in there and get this over with."

Jordan opened the door slowly, wishing there was some way they could get out of this but knowing it was something they had to do.

Once inside, they were greeted by a nice-looking older woman at the front desk who directed them to the administrator's office. There they were met by a tall, slender middle-aged woman who introduced herself as Nancy Lockhart.

"We're friends of Mary Alice Goosman's husband," Jordan explained. "Unfortunately, we've come with bad news for her. Goose was killed on the cruise ship this week."

Expecting the woman to be surprised, maybe even a little upset, Jordan was confused when she didn't even react.

"We already know. George Christakis was just here." She smiled. "What a lovely man. He explained what had happened and assured us that he would be taking care of Mary Alice's room and board as long as she's alive."

Jordan stared, unable to speak. Why would George get involved with a woman he didn't even know? She was about to ask that question when Rosie beat her to it.

"Why would the famous celebrity chef do that? He doesn't even know her." Rosie had the same unbelieving look on her face as Jordan knew she must have on hers.

"He said he was friends with the woman responsible for Goose's death and explained she had also been killed on the ship," the administrator said. "Apparently, he and his son will inherit this woman's money. Mr. Christakis felt since Goose could no longer take care of his wife, it was the least he could do in the other woman's name. He said there were extenuating circumstances involved, and despite the fact that his friend had taken Goose's life, she had been a fair and decent person. He felt sure she would be pleased with the way he was spending some of her money."

Jordan choked up. She'd been dreading coming to see Goose's wife because she'd have to tell her Goose was never coming to visit her again. But she also hated knowing without Goose's financial support, Mary Alice would have to be transferred to one of those facilities that her husband had lied, cheated, and stole to keep her out of.

"Can we see her?" She was still fighting to hold back tears.

"I don't think that's a good idea. Her moments of lucidity have almost completely disappeared. I sat with her a little while ago and explained that her husband won't be coming to see her anymore. How much of it she comprehended, we'll never know." The administrator stood. "She seems to have gone into a shell and won't talk to any of us. A visit from all of you might confuse her more. I hope you understand."

Jordan blew out a relieved sigh. "Of course. Thank you so much for telling us about her." She handed the women Goose's blue and orange plaid shirt. "Give this to her when you think it's best. She may remember that she gave it to him. Maybe it'll bring her some comfort."

"Thank you. I know she'll be glad to have it one day— just not today."

With nothing further to say, the three of them walked out the door and climbed into the cab.

The mood was very somber that night at the hotel. During dinner Jordan brought the men up to speed on their visit to the nursing home. Ray admitted to having had a conversation with George Christakis that morning, after hearing Emily's story. He'd planned on giving him only the basics, but when the New York chef heard about Goose's wife, he'd taken a special interest.

What Christakis had ended up doing for Mary Alice—and for Goose—went above and beyond, but it didn't surprise Jordan. She'd known from the moment George had sneaked the mint under the table after the horrible sweetbread incident that he was an extraordinary man. Emily had been lucky to have him in her life. And just as he'd taken Emily under his wing, the man had made sure that Mary Alice Goosman would live out the rest of her life in comfort.

The next morning they boarded the plane to Dallas. Rosie switched seats with Alex so he could sit next to Jordan. Since he would have to go back to playing FBI in another day or two, Jordan intended to make the most of what little time they had left.

Snuggling closer, she asked, "How long will you be able to stay in Ranchero this time?"

He pushed back the hair that had fallen over her eye. "Oh, I don't know. Two or three years maybe."

She straightened up and faced him. "You didn't quit your job, did you?"

He laughed. "Not hardly. I got promoted."

"Oh my God! You definitely deserve it, but how will that keep you in Ranchero for a few years?" She almost hated to ask, worried his next words would burst her little bubble of hope.

"You're now looking at the assistant head of field operations for Texas."

She twisted around to hug him. "Congratulations, Alex. What exactly does that mean as far as where you'll live?"

"That's the good part. I asked for and received permission to stay in Ranchero in that little house I rented earlier this year. I love it because it has so many great memories."

He winked and Jordan felt her face flush. The small house on the other side of town did hold fond memories, especially the bedroom.

"Since I will be traveling most of the time anyway, they decided the hour's drive to Dallas wouldn't be so bad. Starting tomorrow I will officially be a Ranchero resident—and not a minute too soon, I might add."

"What do you mean?"

"I forgot to tell you the best part. I belong to the Italian American Foundation, and every year they have a huge weekend-long festival where members from all over the world get together to party. This year they chose Plano as the locale."

"When is it?" Jordan was getting excited now.

"At the end of August when the Texas heat hopefully won't kill those old guys from Italy. I've attended the festival only once before since most of them take place in Europe, and I'm more than a little excited about it. One of my great-uncles from Palermo is coming."

"It's wonderful that you'll have your own place then, but you could have stayed with me, you know."

He smiled. "I do know, but I'm not sure you have enough room for three houseguests."

She looked confused. "Three? What are you talking about?"

He squeezed her shoulder. "My sister Kate works for a group of lawyers who represent the organization. She's been given the assignment of overseeing the entire festival, from preparation to final cleanup."

The thought of finally meeting Alex's sister both excited and scared Jordan. What if Kate hated her? Knowing how close Alex was with all his sisters, Jordan feared Kate's disapproval would be the kiss of death for her and Alex's relationship.

"Wait a minute. You said *three* houseguests. You and Kate make two. Who else?"

"Oh, did I forget to mention that my mother is coming with Kate and that she's dying to meet you?"

RECITES

ANNIE ROTH'S PIGS IN THE BLANKET

(My mother's famous recipe: Not for beginning cooks)

Yields 12–15 stuffed cabbage rolls

1 tablespoon butter
½ cup finely chopped onion
1 pound ground beef
¼ pound ground pork
2 large eggs
2 teaspoons salt
¼ teaspoon black pepper
1 can (8 ounces) tomato sauce
½ cup cooked rice
1 large head of cabbage

6 cups tomato juice
*2 cans (10 ¾ ounces each) tom*ato soup

Preheat the oven to 350° F.

In a medium skillet over medium-low heat, melt the butter and sauté the onions until translucent, about 5 minutes. Set aside.

In a large mixing bowl, combine the ground beef, ground pork, eggs, salt, pepper, and tomato sauce. Add the rice and the onions and mix well. Set aside.

In a large pot, bring 1 gallon of water to a boil. Meanwhile, remove the core from the cabbage: cut around it with a paring knife and then use the tip of the knife to gently dislodge the loosened core and pull it out. Place the entire head into the pot of boiling water, cored side up. Boil for 3 minutes or until the outer leaves are slightly translucent and pliable. Remove the cabbage from the water and peel off the outermost leaves. If necessary, use the paring knife to cut the leaves away from the head. Then, put the head back into the water and boil for 2 minutes more or until the next layer of cabbage leaves is translucent and pliable. Once again, remove the cabbage from the water and peel off the outer leaves. Repeat this process until you have all the leaves you need.

On a flat work surface, lay out one cabbage leaf lengthwise and spoon about a ¼ cup of the meat mixture onto its center, adjusting the amount according to the size of the leaf. With the hard-stem end of the leaf facing you, flip first one long side of the leaf and then the other toward the middle to partially cover the meat mixture. Starting from the hard-stem end, roll the leaf away from you to create a compact bundle. Use toothpicks to keep the leaf closed, if necessary. Repeat the process with the remaining leaves until all the filling is used. Place the "pigs" in layers, seam side down, in a Dutch oven or a large greased casserole dish and, if desired, top them with some of the leftover cabbage leaves, coarsely chopped.

In a medium bowl, mix together the tomato juice and the tomato soup and pour over the pigs. The mixture should almost cover them. Cover the dish and bake for 2½ hours or until the cabbage is tender and the meat is cooked. Serve with mashed potatoes using the red sauce as the gravy. Cabbage rolls freeze well before and after cooking.

• • •

TROPICAL MANGO VINAIGRETTE

Yields 2 cups

1 mango, peeled and sliced (For strawberry vinaigrette,
*   substitute 6–8 strawberries.)*
2 packages (0.7 ounce each) dry Italian dressing mix
¾ cup extra-virgin olive oil
¾ cup balsamic vinegar
2 large ice cubes

Place the first four ingredients in a blender and pulse until the mixture is smooth. Add the two ice cubes, one at a time, pulsing after each addition until the ice is mostly pulverized, about 1 minute total. Refrigerate in an airtight container.

• • •

SINFULLY SWEET CHOCOLATE
KAHLÚA BROWNIES

Yield: Approximately 20 brownies

¾ cup unsweetened cocoa
½ teaspoon baking soda
⅔ cup melted butter, divided
¼ cup boiling water
¼ cup Kahlúa
2 cups granulated sugar
2 eggs, lightly beaten
1 teaspoon vanilla extract
1 ⅓ cups all-purpose flour
¼ teaspoon salt
½ cup coarsely chopped walnuts or pecans
1 bag (12 ounces) semisweet chocolate chips

Preheat the oven to 350° F. In a large bowl, combine the cocoa and baking soda. Stir in ⅓ cup of the melted butter. Add the boiling water and Kahlúa, stirring until well blended. Stir in the sugar, beaten eggs, vanilla, and the remaining ⅓ cup of butter, then the flour and salt. Fold in the nuts and chocolate chips, and pour the batter into a greased 13-by-9-by-2-inch baking pan. Bake for 35–40 minutes or until the brownies are firm and begin to pull away from sides of pan. Cool completely before cutting into squares.

. . .

ROSIE'S CHICKEN STIR-FRY

Pollo Fino Revuelto

Serves 6

1 cup baby carrots
10 tablespoons butter, divided
1 package (16 ounces) sliced mushrooms
½ cup extra-virgin olive oil, divided
1 cup orange pepper, cut into bite-size pieces
1 cup yellow pepper, cut into bite-size pieces
1 cup onion, cut into bite-size pieces
1 cup celery, cut into bite-size pieces
1 cup fresh sugar snap peas
1 bottle (11.5 ounces) Thai peanut sauce, divided (I use Bangkok Padang Peanut Sauce)
3 boneless, skinless chicken breasts, cut into bite-size pieces
2 tablespoons flour
2 tablespoons cornstarch
1 teaspoon salt
1 teaspoon black pepper
6 cups hot cooked rice

In a medium saucepan, bring 1 quart of water to a boil. Add the carrots and cook for 5 minutes or until the carrots are tender crisp. Drain and allow to cool. Cut the carrots into bite-size pieces and set aside.

In a medium skillet over medium heat, melt 6 tablespoons of the butter and sauté the mushrooms for 7 minutes or until golden brown. Set aside.

In a large skillet, heat 2 tablespoons of the olive oil and add the orange and yellow peppers, onion, celery, and sugar snap peas. Drizzle 2 tablespoons of the peanut sauce over the vegetables and cook for 7–8 minutes, stirring frequently, until the vegetables are tender but still crunchy. During the last minute of cooking, add in the carrots and mushrooms. Remove the vegetable mixture to a bowl and keep warm. Wipe out the skillet with a paper towel.

In a large bowl, combine the chicken, flour, cornstarch, salt, pepper, and 2 tablespoons of the peanut sauce. Toss to coat.

In the large skillet, heat ¼ cup of the olive oil. Add the coated chicken, breaking up any pieces that stick together. Stir-fry for 4 minutes or until chicken is brown on all sides and cooked through.

Pour the remaining peanut sauce into a microwave-safe bowl and microwave on high for 20 seconds. For each serving, place approximately 1 cup of the cooked rice on a plate and drizzle 2 tablespoons of the warm peanut sauce over it. Place approximately 1 cup of the mixed vegetables over the rice and top with approximately ½ cup of the cooked chicken. Drizzle 2 additional tablespoons of peanut sauce over top.

Note: The peanut sauce has a bite, so use according to your taste. This is a recipe I made up after one of my favorite restaurants took it off the menu. I think mine is better than theirs!

• • •

JUMBLEBERRY DELIGHT

Serves 6–8

3 cups halved fresh strawberries
1½ cups fresh blueberries
1½ cups fresh raspberries
⅔ cup sugar
3 tablespoons quick-cooking tapioca
½ cup all-purpose flour
½ cup quick-cooking oats
½ cup packed brown sugar
1 teaspoon ground cinnamon
⅓ cup melted butter
Nonfat cooking spray
Ice cream or whipped topping for serving (optional)

Preheat the oven to 350°F. In a large bowl, combine the strawberries, blueberries, and raspberries. In a small bowl, combine the sugar and the tapioca and mix well. Sprinkle the sugar mixture over the berries and toss well. Let stand for 10 minutes.

Meanwhile, in another small bowl, combine the flour, oats, brown sugar, and cinnamon, making sure to break up any lumps in the brown sugar. Stir in the melted butter to coat.

Pour the berry mixture into a greased 11-by-7-inch baking pan and spoon the flour mixture evenly over the top.

Bake for 45–50 minutes or until the filling is bubbly and the topping is golden brown. Serve warm with ice cream or whipped topping. Refrigerate any leftovers and microwave to reheat.

. . .

KING RANCH CHICKEN

Pollo de la Hacienda del Rey

1 can (14.5 ounces) chicken broth
12–13 soft corn tortillas
4 tablespoons butter
1 cup chopped onion
½ teaspoon minced garlic
1 package (16 ounces) sliced mushrooms
1 medium green pepper, chopped
1 container (16 ounces) fat-free sour cream
1 tablespoon flour
1 tablespoon cornstarch
1 can (10 ounces) diced tomatoes and green chilies
1 package (1 ounce) dry taco seasoning
3 cups diced, cooked chicken breast (approximately 3 large breasts)

Nonfat cooking spray
1 package (24 ounces) shredded Colby and Monterey
   Jack cheese

Preheat the oven to 350° F. Pour the chicken broth into the bottom of a Dutch oven or other large pot and soak the tortillas in the broth for 10 minutes (do not cook). Meanwhile, in a large skillet over medium heat, melt the butter and sauté the onion, garlic, mushrooms, and green pepper. Stir in the sour cream, flour, and cornstarch, heating until smooth and bubbly. Add the tomatoes, taco seasoning, and chicken, and mix well.

Spray a 9-by-11-inch casserole dish with nonfat cooking spray. Remove the tortillas from the broth and cut each one into 6 strips. Layer half of the tortilla strips in the bottom of the casserole. Cover with half of the chicken mixture, followed by half of the cheese. Sprinkle with salt and pepper. Repeat the process, ending with the cheese layer. Bake the casserole for 30 minutes or until cheese is bubbly.

• • •

SINFULLY SWEET'S BAILEYS IRISH CREAM TRUFFLES

FOR THE TRUFFLES:
   3 cups semisweet chocolate chips
   1 cup vanilla chips
   ¼ cup butter

3 cups powdered sugar
1 cup Baileys Irish Cream
½ cup chopped walnuts
Nonfat cooking spray

FOR THE TOPPING:
1 cup semisweet chocolate chips
½ cup vanilla chips
2 tablespoons butter, in pieces
4 tablespoons Baileys Irish Cream

TO MAKE THE TRUFFLES:

In a small pan over low heat, melt the chocolate and vanilla chips with the butter until they are soft enough to stir, being careful not to overcook. Gradually add the powdered sugar and the liquor, stirring until smooth. Stir in the nuts and mix well.

Spray an 8-inch square pan with the nonfat cooking spray and spoon the fudge into the pan. Using a sheet of plastic wrap, gently press to smooth out the fudge.

TO MAKE THE TOPPING:

In a small pan over low heat, melt the chocolate and vanilla chips until smooth enough to stir. With a fork, beat in the butter and liquor until smooth. Spread the topping over the fudge with a knife. For a smoother surface, use a piece of plastic wrap on top, as above.

Refrigerate 1–2 hours or until firm.

GRILLED HALIBUT CARIBBEAN STYLE WITH PINEAPPLE AND MANGO SALSA

Chef Maciek Kucharewic's Personal Recipe Using the Killer Ingredient

Serves 4

4 halibut filets
Salt and pepper to taste
2 tablespoons butter, melted

FOR THE SAUCE:
2 tablespoons minced shallots
1 tablespoon crushed peppercorns
½ cup white wine
1 tablespoon freshly squeezed lemon juice
1 teaspoon white wine vinegar
1 cup heavy cream
2 tablespoons butter, cubed

FOR THE SALSA:
2 cups diced mango
2 cups diced pineapple
2 tablespoons diced red onion
3 tablespoon diced red pepper
1 teaspoon finely chopped mint
2 tablespoons seasoned red wine vinegar
1 teaspoon sugar

FOR THE GARNISH:
   1 medium tomato, finely chopped
   ½ cup sweet corn
   1 teaspoon blackening spice
   1 teaspoon ground nuts

Season the halibut filets with the salt and pepper to taste and sear in a very hot pan until golden brown. Glaze with the melted butter. Remove from heat and set aside.

For the sauce, combine the shallots, peppercorns, white wine, lemon juice, and white wine vinegar in a skillet. Bring to a boil over medium heat, then lower the heat and continue cooking until the liquid evaporates. Add the whipping cream and simmer until the sauce has reduced by half. Slowly add in the butter, one piece at a time, swirling the pan gently until melted.

For the salsa, combine all the ingredients in a small bowl and set aside.

For the garnish, combine all the ingredients in a small bowl and set aside.

For each serving, place one filet on a plate, spoon over a quarter of the sauce, and garnish with 1 tablespoon of the garnish mixture. Spoon a quarter of the salsa next to the filet right before serving.

SINFULLY SWEET'S CRÈME DE CACAO PEANUT BUTTER FUDGE

1¼ cups plus 1 tablespoon unsalted butter
1¼ cups creamy peanut butter
½ cup semisweet chocolate chips
1½ teaspoons vanilla extract
3 cups confectioners' sugar, sifted
3 tablespoons crème de cacao

In a medium saucepan on low heat, melt together 1¼ cups of the butter, the peanut butter, and the chocolate chips, stirring until smooth. Remove from the heat.

Stir in the vanilla extract, confectioners' sugar, and crème de cacao, mixing well to ensure that no lumps remain.

Using the remaining tablespoon of butter, grease a 9-inch baking pan. Pour the fudge mixture into the prepared pan. Refrigerate for at least 1 hour, preferably overnight. Cut into squares and enjoy.

CARNATION QUEEN'S TOMATO MOZZARELLA BRUSCHETTA

Yields approximately 36 pieces

*1 can (10.5 ounces) diced fire-roasted tomatoes,
    drained*
½ cup fresh basil leaves, washed and spun dry
2 tablespoons extra-virgin olive oil
3 cloves garlic, peeled
Kosher salt and freshly ground black pepper
1 large loaf French bread, cut into 1-inch slices
¾ pound fresh mozzarella cheese, cut into ¼-inch slices

Preheat the oven to 375° F. In a food processor, pulse the tomatoes, basil, olive oil, and 2 cloves of the garlic until slightly chunky. Season with salt and pepper to taste.

On a baking sheet, line up the French bread slices and toast in the oven for approximately 3 minutes or until golden brown. Remove the pan from the oven and, working quickly, rub the remaining clove of garlic on the toasted side of each bread slice. Place a slice of mozzarella cheese on top of each bread slice and return the pan to the oven for about 45 seconds or until the cheese is slightly melted. Remove from the oven and spread 1 tablespoon of the tomato mixture on each slice. Serve warm.

*Aspiring sportswriter Jordan McAllister never imagined
she'd be a food critic. And while she may not know
a flank steak from a filet mignon, she certainly knows
how to rustle up trouble . . .*

FROM

Liz Lipperman

BEEF STOLEN-OFF

A CLUELESS COOK MYSTERY

As the food columnist for the *Ranchero Globe*, Jordan McAllister catches the eye of cattle baron Lucas Santana, who invites her to the Cattlemen's Ball, hoping a positive review from the ball might boost the county's sagging beef sales.

To ensure Jordan enjoys herself, Santana sets her up with a prime cowboy companion for the event—Rusty Morales. Jordan's delighted to go with him and two-step the night away. But instead, she winds up in the emergency room where her date is DOA.

When Rusty's mother begs her for help, Jordan knows she needs to grab the bull by the horns and get to the bottom of this mystery before she corrals herself into trouble . . .

Includes recipes from Jordan's food column!

"A sparkling new cozy star!"
—Cleo Coyle, national bestselling author

facebook.com/TheCrimeSceneBooks
penguin.com

M1161T0812

FROM
Liz Lipperman

A CLUELESS COOK MYSTERY

LIVER LET DIE
BEEF STOLEN-OFF
MURDER FOR THE HALIBUT

Includes recipes from Jordan's food column!

"Jordan McAllister heads up an appealing cast of characters in the fun new Clueless Cook series from Liz Lipperman . . . Plot twists, action, and lots of scrumptious food make this a mystery not to be missed!"
—Misa Ramirez

"A culinary critic mystery with good taste, charming characters, and plenty of delicious twists. It's a recipe for a truly enjoyable story."
—Linda O. Johnston

M7G0610

31192020335269